I0618806

SCEPTER OF SALVATION

THE MAGIC OF INHERIAN: SCEPTER OF
SALVATION, BOOK 1

TERRY SPEAR

TERRY SPEAR

Terry Spear

PUBLISHED BY:
Terry Spear

Scepter of Salvation
Copyright © 2010 by Terry Spear

Print ISBN: 978-1-63311-058-8
Ebook ISBN: 978-1-63311-060-1

Discover more about Terry Spear at:
http://www.terryspear.com/

❀ Created with Vellum

SYNOPSIS FOR SCEPTER OF SALVATION

Scepter of Salvation

Princess Talamaya turned 18 in the human kingdom of Damar, just like her twin brother. Only when she comes of age, she must wed the king's choice. When her brother comes of age, he's allowed to sit on the council. But everything changes when a wizard pits beast and man against each other in Inherian–all because of the loss of the Scepter of Salvation and she must return it to their kingdom.

Princess Talamaya and her friends, Lady Kersta and Lady Mexia, must retrieve the Scepter of Salvation when her brother is poisoned.Visions plague Talamaya of a world beyond her own, of a destiny she has to fulfill.But the barbarian king is also after the scepter, and the black-hearted wizard who is trying to gain control will do anything to keep them from retrieving it.

She must free a knight from his madness.

Help a female dwarf escape from the dwarven mines.

Aid an Amazon fighting the Dark Elves.

Rescue even the barbarian king.

Save a crusty old dwarf from the wolves of Elan Pass.

And outwit the dark wizard once more.

Above all else, she must always take the path of righteousness.

Which is much easier said than done.

ALSO AVAILABLE BY TERRY SPEAR:

Heart of the Cougar Series:

Cougar's Mate, Book 1

Call of the Cougar, Book 2

Taming the Wild Cougar, Book 3

Covert Cougar Christmas (Novella)

Double Cougar Trouble, Book 4

Cougar Undercover, Book 5

Cougar Magic, Book 6

Cougar Halloween Mischief (Novella)

Falling for the Cougar, Book 7

Heart of the Bear Series

Loving the White Bear, Book 1

Claiming the White Bear, Book 2

The Highlanders Series: Winning the Highlander's Heart, The Accidental Highland Hero, Highland Rake, Taming the Wild Highlander, The Highlander, Her Highland Hero, The Viking's Highland Lass, His Wild Highland Lass (novella), Vexing the Highlander (novella), My Highlander

Other historical romances: Lady Caroline & the Egotistical Earl, A Ghost of a Chance at Love

~

Heart of the Wolf Series: Heart of the Wolf, Destiny of the Wolf, To Tempt the Wolf, Legend of the White Wolf, Seduced by the Wolf, Wolf Fever, Heart of the Highland Wolf, Dreaming of the Wolf, A SEAL in Wolf's Clothing, A Howl for a Highlander, A Highland Werewolf Wedding, A SEAL Wolf Christmas, Silence of the Wolf, Hero of a Highland Wolf, A Highland Wolf Christmas, A SEAL Wolf Hunting; A Silver Wolf Christmas, A SEAL Wolf in Too Deep, Alpha Wolf Need Not Apply, Billionaire in Wolf's Clothing, Between a Rock and a Hard Place, SEAL Wolf Undercover, Dreaming of a White Wolf Christmas, Flight of the White Wolf, All's Fair in Love and Wolf, A Billionaire Wolf for Christmas, SEAL Wolf Surrender (2019), Silver Town Wolf: Home for the Holidays (2019), Wolff Brothers: You Had Me at Wolf, Night of the Billionaire Wolf, Joy to the Wolves, Wolf Wore Plaid

SEAL Wolves: To Tempt the Wolf, A SEAL in Wolf's Clothing, A SEAL Wolf Christmas, A SEAL Wolf Hunting, A SEAL Wolf in Too Deep, SEAL Wolf Undercover, SEAL Wolf Surrender (2019)

Silver Bros Wolves: Destiny of the Wolf, Wolf Fever, Dreaming of the Wolf, Silence of the Wolf, A Silver Wolf Christmas, Alpha Wolf Need Not Apply, Between a Rock and a Hard Place, All's Fair in Love and Wolf, Silver Town Wolf: Home for the Holidays (2019)

Wolff Brothers of Silver Town

Billionaire Wolves: Billionaire in Wolf's Clothing, A Billionaire Wolf for Christmas, Night of the Billionaire Wolf

Highland Wolves: Heart of the Highland Wolf, A Howl for a Highlander, A Highland Werewolf Wedding, Hero of a Highland Wolf, A Highland Wolf Christmas, Wolf Wore Plaid

Red Wolf Series: Seduced by the Wolf, Joy to the Wolves

~

Heart of the Jaguar Series: Savage Hunger, Jaguar Fever, Jaguar Hunt, Jaguar Pride, A Very Jaguar Christmas, You Had Me at Jaguar (2019)

Novella: The Witch and the Jaguar (2018)

～

Romantic Suspense: Deadly Fortunes, In the Dead of the Night, Relative Danger, Bound by Danger

～

Vampire romances: Killing the Bloodlust, Deadly Liaisons, Huntress for Hire, Forbidden Love

Vampire Novellas: Vampiric Calling, The Siren's Lure, Seducing the Huntress

～

Other Romance: Exchanging Grooms, Marriage, Las Vegas Style

～

Science Fiction Romance: Galaxy Warrior

Teen/Young Adult/Fantasy Books

The World of Fae:

The Dark Fae, Book 1

The Deadly Fae, Book 2

The Winged Fae, Book 3

The Ancient Fae, Book 4

Dragon Fae, Book 5

Hawk Fae, Book 6

1

Talamaya sat fuming behind the men seated in a circle at her father's high council session in the human kingdom of Damar. Having no say in anything being discussed, she gave her father an irritated look for making her attend. Blocking out the words of the financial advisor, Pelan, who stroked his gray beard while his rusty voice droned on about the cost of managing the kingdom, she turned her attention to her twin brother, Grisom. No matter how hard she tried, she couldn't settle the grudge she'd harbored toward him since early that morn. Sitting beside their father, Grisom—newly appointed to the position of executive officer of the council—held his head high.

When *she* turned eighteen a few minutes after her brother, her father elevated *her* to the position of a marriageable royal maid, insisting she wed within the month. Wishing she'd been born a man for the millionth time, she growled at her lot in life.

Midmorning rays of sunlight streamed into the chambers from twenty feet above, warming the chilly room. The warmth of the golden rays on her skin, the wine she had consumed with her morning meal, and Pelan's dry discourse on money matters, soon lulled her into another unfamiliar world.

Blinding cold, wet, heavy snow, and something dangerous in the chilly blanket of white eluded her. A goddess? A demon? The beautiful creature called to her, caressed Talamaya's skin with icy tenderness, chilling her to the bone.

A shadow moved across the skylight briefly, shattering Talamaya's strange vision, which only compounded the worry she had that she was losing her mind. Staring up at the skylight she imagined only a gryphon the size of a shire horse, half eagle, half lion, could block the sun that much. She shook her head. Gryphons never flew that close to the castle while the archers manned their guard posts.

Whispered secrets, hints of something ominous to come, and the images that plagued her mind since early that morn unsettled her. Even her mother, who normally had a smile for every waking moment, had seemed on edge, casting a wary glance at her more than once during the morning meal.

Talamaya ran her fingers over the jeweled dagger at her waist, ignoring one of the council member's questions concerning the finances. But when her mind drifted, she again envisioned a redheaded creature, resting on a rocky crag, slapping a silver-scaled tail into the sea. In none of the books she'd read on real or mythical creatures had she ever come across something like that. To wipe the disturbing image from her mind, Talamaya tapped her foot on the white marble floor. Two of the council members turned their stony, gray-bearded faces toward her and glared.

She silenced her foot and ran her hands over her gown. The ice blue silk felt cool to her touch as she attempted to ignore the men—who without a doubt disliked her being here—aggravating her further. After all, she didn't like being here, either.

Certain her mother had never attended such a boring affair

to impress Talamaya's father when *she'd* turned eighteen, Talamaya harrumphed out loud.

Her father quirked a brow at her, then frowned. The look meant she'd get a lecture following the meeting for certain. Then to her mortification, her stomach growled. One of the men sitting closest to her shook his head. Her heated skin prickled with annoyance.

Glancing out the western window, she wished instead she practiced with her new bow and arrows, or...she considered the elevation of the sun in the sky and sighed. She hadn't missed her quarterstaff sparring practice with her friends, thank the heavens. Her stomach tensed as she considered the nighttime activities scheduled.

Rumors had it, her mother planned a feast that evening, and most likely a dance would follow. If her parents thought they'd announce her betrothal to Og...

She had no intention of marrying her father's Vice Counselor.

Her brother spoke, sounding like he'd been sitting on the council for years, but she ignored his words. Only slightly taller than their father at six-foot-three, Grisom epitomized the male qualities of the Damar humans. Stately, more rugged than the elf kind who lived on their western border, stalwart, and dark-haired with eyes as brown as freshly plowed Damarian soil... that's how he and most of the men looked to her. All the same, and totally boring.

Talamaya twisted a brown curl that had slipped from the collection of hair braided against her head and examined it. Same color as the men's, only slightly lighter in part, streaked by the rays of the sun.

She turned her attention back to her brother. If she were queen, she would certainly change a few notions concerning the woman's role in their society.

The elf queen of Mesa had as many powers as her husband did. The elven women, too, were seen as equal members of their society. That's what Talamaya believed the Damarian women also deserved. But Grisom would follow their father as king, and all Talamaya could hope for was a good husband. The wine she drank that morning curdled in her stomach.

A bloodied feather suddenly drifted to the table from the skylight above, and Talamaya looked skyward. Nothing. She looked back at her table. Nothing there, and when she glanced at the council members, no one seemed to have seen it either. Too many sleepless nights must be affecting her mind.

Catching her eye, Og gave her a small smile. She quickly shifted her gaze. The man, twice her age, wore too many extra pounds of flesh and gray hairs to suit her. Overbearing and opinionated described his personality perfectly. Definitely, not her idea of a suitable husband. There was no way she would marry him, ever.

Her father stroked his chest-length brown beard sprinkled with silver. "Now that we've discussed financial matters, we must turn our attention to a topic of grave concern. For two moons, I've sought counsel with the soothsayer and our prophets. The news is always the same. By the new moon, we will battle with the barbarians."

War? Talamaya straightened her back. Her father had never mentioned that war threatened Damar. Maybe a hushed word or two to her mother in their chambers had leaked to Talamaya, but she'd always thought they were discussing her reluctance to marry, nothing more.

A whisper of voices ensued as the men spoke under their breaths with one another.

King Sal raised his hand, signaling silence and a need to address the council. The men ceased their chatter. "Though our soldiers are highly trained, the barbarian hordes could easily outnumber us, the way they breed like dogs."

Talamaya's cheeks warmed. A shuffling of seats followed. No man *ever* made crude comments like that in front of a woman.

Her father's gaze switched to her, and this time *his* cheeks grew flushed. He'd forgotten she was there.

She shifted nervously in her seat. Just when things got interesting, too. Now what? Would he send her from the room?

He cleared his throat and addressed the council again. "The soothsayer warned me our only hope in succeeding against the barbarians is retrieving the Scepter of Lanai."

Muffled voices spoke with concern. The vice counselor raised his hand. King Sal nodded.

"My lord, and fellow council members, for years our people have risked their lives to obtain the scepter. No one has ever returned alive. No one but Malachon."

Words were spoken in haste. Talamaya never knew what had made the knight go mad. Was it the quest for the scepter that had driven his mind into a frenzy of disjointed, often incoherent thoughts?

"Yes," King Sal said. "But it is our only hope. The scepter will protect us from man or beast. A select group of the bravest and strongest of our men will go."

"And their reward?"

King Sal stroked his beard and furrowed his brow. Talamaya knew then, whatever he said next, he did with the gravest concern. "Should one of them reach the scepter and hold it within his grasp, and successfully return it to our kingdom, he will..." Everyone waited with breaths reserved as he hesitated. He ran his hands over the arms of his gold gilt throne, then rose. The council members stood as if honoring the knight who could accomplish such a quest. Talamaya followed suit.

"He will hold the crown to the realm."

The crown to the realm? Talamaya's head reeled with the notion. Did her father mean to give up his throne, his rule to the worthy knight? Her family had ruled for a thousand years. And now they would give it all up for some scepter?

She waited for someone to object, but no one did. Not even her brother.

Her father patted Grisom's shoulder. "Our fate rests in young Prince Grisom's hands and those of the men he chooses to accompany him."

Og smiled at Talamaya. "I will ride with Grisom."

Grisom clasped his hand. "With honor, we shall ride together."

Talamaya gripped the arm of her chair. There wasn't any way that she wanted to lose her brother to whatever evil lay in wait for him on his journey.

Her father said to her brother, "I will meet in private with you, Grisom, to discuss your journey." Then to her surprise, her father tapped his staff on the floor and ended the session. "Our men will ride at dawn."

Suddenly, a gryphon screeched, the width of its gray wings cutting out the sunlight briefly. It screamed again as arrows sought its heart. The sharp-barbed weapons entered its tough hide. Blood dripped from the wounds. Talamaya looked down at the droplets puddled on her chair.

"The archers will finish it off." Og motioned for everyone to leave the council chambers at once.

An ear-piercing scream from the creature made the members move quickly to vacate the room.

But it was too late.

The monstrous beast dove through the open skylight. With wings outstretched, it attempted to land, his back feet readied to connect with the floor. Instead, it slammed into chairs, sending them flying. Talamaya and the others close to her, scrambled out of its path.

He lunged toward her with his sharp beak, and she yanked her jeweled dagger from her belt. Before she could use her weapon, her brother jerked her away from the writhing creature. The wicked talons on its forelegs scratched at the floor while its lion tail twitched. With a fatal shriek reverberating off the thick stone walls of the chamber, the gryphon let out its last breath and collapsed, bloodied feathers floating to the floor and table.

"Must have been deranged to fly this close to the castle," one of the council members said, his hand clutching his blue robes.

"*Or* under someone's influence," the financial counselor retorted.

Talamaya turned to him. "Who could control a wild gryphon?" His look of rebuke as if to remind her to mind her own business, made her wrinkle her brow at him when he brushed on past her. Then she caught sight of Og headed straight for her like a ravenous cat-like cheetaur lunged after its next meal.

Quickly, she slipped between the men, bumping into two, excused her ineptness, then headed back to her bedchambers. She had no intention of speaking to the man who wished to marry her for the increased power it would give him with the royal family.

Certain he was up to no good with all the excursions he'd conducted to the barbarian borders, she truly didn't trust the man. He said he'd done so to spy on the barbarian troop movements, but she didn't believe him. The way his gray eyes leered at her whenever he caught her eye concerned her, and the way he hushed his words whenever she caught him speaking with one of his men, made her even more suspicious.

When her brother came into view, her thoughts switched to

concerns about the war looming before them and her brother being sent on the impossible journey.

"Grisom!" she hollered and raced to meet him.

He crossed his arms and scowled at her. "*You* are supposed to be spending some time with the Vice Counselor, Talamaya. That's the only reason Father permitted you to attend the meeting in the first place!"

"Permitted?" Talamaya copied her brother's stance and folded her arms. Her brows knitted together in irritation. "Father *forced* me to go!"

"He shouldn't *have* to force you. You should be an obedient daughter and do as he asks." He whirled around. His regal ice blue robes trimmed in gold, slapped at her legs as he headed for his chambers.

Although they were twins, they'd never been really close. How could they be? He was being groomed for the role of Damar's future king. And she? Marriage to the despicable Og was to be her glorious fate.

But even so, she couldn't quiet her alarm concerning her brother's perilous journey. She hurried after Grisom. "I don't want you to go find the scepter. Grisom, you cannot go."

"I must. If anyone else retrieves it, we'll lose our position as the ruling family."

"You'll claim it for Father then?"

When he didn't slow his pace, she grabbed his arm to stop him.

Turning to face her, Grisom glared at her. His dark eyes focused on hers with a fury she'd never known while his lips drawn straight across, remained silent.

Something foul was afoot. Something she didn't understand. She'd lived in his shadow for years, knowing he was to be her ruler someday, but she and her brother rarely quarreled.

"Grisom, you'll get the scepter so Father can remain in

power, right?" Talamaya prompted her brother, hoping to hear that he would do so, despite his icy manner.

"You heard him. Whoever gets the scepter will rule Damar."

Talamaya released her brother's arm. Her words dropped to a whisper. "You intend to rule in Father's place?" She knew her brother would, someday. But not like this. When her father could no longer pound his staff, when he no longer had the strength...

Tears pooled in her eyes, but she held them back. Turning eighteen was to be the best time of her life, the time when she came of age, married, and had a family of her own. But not if she had to wed Og. And now even the future for Damar was uncertain.

"Vice Counselor Og wishes a word with you." Grisom strode into his chambers and shut her out.

The delicate tie that bound them together suddenly snapped, and she felt as though she were adrift at sea. Her thoughts swirling with confusion, she turned and found Og waiting for her a few feet away, undoubtedly hearing some of the conversation she'd had with her brother and not wanting to interrupt.

The smile returned to his lips and he bowed to her.

She bowed her head slightly in greeting. Her lips remained emotionless; her gaze focused on the lack of warmth his gray eyes held. He closed the gap between them while she stood steadfast.

"Princess Talamaya, I hope you'll be as concerned for me as you are for your brother when we journey tomorrow to Lanai."

"My prayers go for all the young men who accompany my brother on his quest."

She hadn't intended to say young, but the word slipped out just the same. Would he think she mocked him for believing him too old? He *was* too old, as far as she was concerned. She desired to wed a man closer to her age...well, someday. In reality, there wasn't anyone she'd considered interesting enough to marry. Well, maybe an elf or two. But her father would shove a dagger into his heart if he knew how she felt.

Still the elves' blond hair and light-colored eyes intrigued her. And, too, the way they gave their women an equal role in their society endeared them to her.

"May I have your word that you'll consider your father's advice while I'm away?"

Talamaya smiled. "My father oft gives me advice. Which words of wisdom do you wish to know about?"

Og's cheeks colored considerably and the muscles in his neck tightened.

To her disappointment, the smile quickly returned to his lips. "Should I return with the scepter, *I* will choose my bride."

No way would this overbearing lout obtain the scepter if her brother couldn't. "Then you would become king and have any choice of maiden you desire."

"Yes, and she would still be you, my dear princess." He straightened his posture. "I wish to wear something of yours, a favor to help me earn my quest."

"My brother will wear my favor, my lord."

"He wears Lady Saqualian's amulet when we ride tomorrow."

Lady Saqualian? Talamaya pursed her lips in frustration. So *that's* who her brother wished to marry? The only woman in the crown region of Damar Talamaya didn't get along with? Great. To think if her brother was successful, he'd have the dragon lady ruling beside him.

"Let me think on it. I have never given my favor to anyone for any reason."

Og bowed. "I understand how solemn my request is and the

value that's attached to such an appeal. Tomorrow before I leave will be sufficient time to learn of your answer."

He would allow her until tomorrow to give her answer? How generous of him. But she was not about to change her mind.

To her relief, Og left her standing alone in the hall with no attempt to show any kind of affection toward her. But a light footstep running toward her, startled her. She turned and saw her friend, Kersta, headed for her in a dither. Her brown curls, nearly black they were so dark, once bound in blue silk ribbons to match her gown, dangled loosely over her shoulders, and her black eyes were wide with excitement.

"I've heard the news. Oh, Talamaya, all the gorgeous young men are leaving on this quest tomorrow."

Talamaya rolled her eyes.

Kersta grabbed her hand and yanked it. "Is it true what they say? Is it true that whoever claims the scepter, claims the throne?"

"Yes," Talamaya said dryly. "If the men have to risk their lives to protect our kingdom, whoever accomplishes the quest will rule over her next."

"And your brother is leading them?"

"Yes."

Kersta pulled her toward the gardens. "It's been rumored, Saqualian asked Prince Grisom to wear her amulet on the quest."

Talamaya nodded, her heart pounding in her ears every time she considered Saqualian ruling beside her brother. The woman never had a kind word for any of the servants. In that regard, she'd never been nice to anyone no matter what their status.

Kersta shook her head. "Bad days lie ahead for us then."

The fragrance of lilies, roses, and the minko flower filled the gardens as they strolled down one of the stone paths. Butterflies flittered about the girls' heads, confused with the sweet waters they wore.

Talamaya walked over to a pond filled with crescent fish. The rainbow-scaled fish surfaced. Reaching into a pouch tied to her belt, she pulled out fenim seed and sprinkled it over the surface of the water. "I never knew he had any interest in the lady. Why her, of all people?"

"Who knows? Her biting tongue chases most away. You are not the only one who despises her." Kersta took a deep breath and changed the subject. "There's to be a feast tonight in the men's honor. When we attend it..."

Talamaya glanced up to see a star streaking across the sky. Silently she murmured the words, "I wish my father to rule proudly over Damar for the rest of his days."

"Anyway," Kersta continued and Talamaya only now realized her friend had been speaking the whole time, "I've been trying to figure out who to give my favor to. Three have asked me for it, you know. Gynt, Hauk, and Zornan. I just cannot decide who the lucky man should be."

"If you give your favor, it's to show how much you care for the man. If he survives the trials, most would assume you would marry him upon his return."

"If he brings home the scepter, I would be proud to." Kersta sputtered suddenly, "Oh, pardon my saying so, Princess Talamaya. Whatever made me say such a wicked thing? Of course, your brother must claim it and bring it home. Your family has ruled well over Damar forever." She glanced at Talamaya's amulet as she held it tightly in her fist. "Are you going to give your necklace to Og to wear? Everyone expects you will, since your father—"

"Like you, I am not certain who should wear my favor. I would not wish the warrior to get the impression I would marry him should he survive the quest."

Kersta twisted her mouth. "You're right of course, my lady. Are we still to meet in the arena to spar with Mexia?"

"Yes."

"I thought all of this talk of war and—"

"If we're to go to war and the scepter isn't returned, the young women will have to fight alongside the men. None of us will give in to the barbarians."

Kersta nodded, then whispered, "They say they are rough on their women."

The memory of Talamaya's father's words caused chill bumps to erupt on her arms. "The barbarian men are like dogs."

Mexia stood waiting in the jousting and sporting arena as Kersta and Talamaya joined her. All three wore soft leather breeches and shirts secured with leather straps criss-crossed to keep their clothes from flapping in the breeze and hindering their aim.

Kersta smiled as Talamaya faced Mexia first, their quarter-staffs held at the ready. "We have company again, ladies."

Talamaya said, "Even though my father forbids the gentlemen to watch our activities whilst we spar in men-like fashions."

"They still cannot believe three ladies of the royal family of Damar could fight properly." Kersta tucked an errant curl back into the rest of her bound hair.

Talamaya struck at Mexia's staff. She jumped away from the blow, lessening its impact. Twisting her body, she followed up with a strike aimed to block Talamaya.

Talamaya struck again with catlike precision, twice to throw Mexia off balance. "More of us will have to learn to fight to protect ourselves, should the barbarians get a foothold in the royal city."

Mexia jumped back to regroup.

Kersta said, "Talamaya says the barbarians are like dogs with regard to their women."

Talamaya nearly lost her staff. "That's what my father says." She struck Mexia's staff, causing it to slip from her grip and fall several feet away with a thud on the soft earth.

Distant laughter and clapping followed. The three ladies glanced at the stadium and found several more knights watching them.

Talamaya shook her head. "They don't think we could ever fight anyone, if we had to."

Kersta stepped in front of Talamaya to take her turn. "Ah, and maybe they're right. We only spar with one another. What if we sparred with one of them?" She quirked a brow.

"My father would not permit us to spar with a man. Once our trainer showed us the most basic of moves, Father promptly dismissed him from teaching us further." Talamaya hit Kersta's staff hard.

"Because?" The sun shimmered off Mexia's blond hair and vivid green eyes.

Talamaya smiled. "He didn't wish for a man to fight with a woman, even just to train one. In fact, Mother had to convince him to allow our instruction in the first place."

Kersta concentrated on Talamaya's thrust. "You're better at this than either Mexia or me. I wager you could stand your ground with one of the knights. Maybe not defeat him, but at least keep your staff without losing it."

Mexia shook her head. "Any of them would be careful with the princess."

"Oh?" Kersta blocked another of Talamaya's hard hits, then attempted retaliation. "You don't think to show the others how easily he could beat a woman, he wouldn't try? Do you believe any of the men could bear to let a woman best him?" She gave a ladylike snort. "That would be the day."

Talamaya twisted, then banged her staff against Kersta's and sent it flying. Stepping back, she allowed Kersta to fight Mexia this time.

"Besides, it wouldn't be fair. They have been sitting on the stone benches resting all this time. The princess has sparred with each of us already." Mexia readied her staff against Kersta's blow.

The wood cracked against wood as Talamaya glanced back at the men. Several smiled at her. Anyone of them would have wished her hand in marriage. But would any of them spar with her against the king's wishes?

She headed to the stands where the men quickly stood to attention. The sound of Mexia and Kersta's staffs striking one another behind her, stopped.

When Talamaya drew close to the men, they all bowed. She lowered her head in greeting, then looked up at the group. "Who amongst you wishes to spar with me?"

Chuckles ensued.

She raised her brows and folded her arms. "None?"

"You and the other ladies make fine sport, Princess Talamaya. But you are no match for any of us." Lord Gynt, one of the tallest of the young men, motioned with a broad sweep of his arm toward the other knights.

Lord Hauk, two years her senior, but still wiry and not as well-muscled as an older man, cleared his throat. "Not only that, but your father would more than frown on any man who took up a staff against you."

She tapped her foot on the ground. "You, Lord Hauk? Have you never done anything the king might frown on?"

His ears tinged red and he combed his fingers through his dark brown hair resting at his broad shoulders.

She smiled.

He stepped down from the seven-tiered stands. Was he worried she would tell of his folly with a pheasant girl? What if it reached Lady Kersta's ears? He still wished Kersta's favor as evidenced by his asking her for it earlier that morning.

"A sparring match?" he asked, his tone cocky.

Gynt grabbed his arm. "If you do this and injure the princess—"

Hauk shook loose of him, his dark brown eyes sparkling with enthusiasm. He replied with a smirk, "I'll be gentle."

2

Talamaya smiled at the knight as he flexed his muscles. "I'm glad you plan to be gentle with me, Sir Hauk. Rest assured, I won't be with you."

Kersta and Mexia joined them and Kersta handed her staff to Hauk.

Talamaya readied her staff while Hauk glanced back at his friends. She figured he sought their approval, but the look on their faces showed mixed emotion. They wanted him to best her, she was certain, but they feared he might hurt her in the process.

"Ahem. Are you sure you want to do this, my lady?"

She nudged his staff. "Prepare yourself, Sir Knight."

Raising his staff diagonally across his body, he waited for her to make her move. She struck, wishing he'd do something more than stand like the padded wooden dummies the men attacked in swordsmanship practice.

Still, he barely moved with her decisive blow, and at once she realized how much harder facing a male opponent with heavier muscles and weight could be. Undaunted, she struck twice so quickly in succession, he jumped back.

The men chuckled and the ladies clapped. Hauk smiled, undoubtedly amused she could force his defensive reaction. Pleased with her efforts, she smiled back.

"The princess has already sparred with the two ladies, Hauk. Remember," Gynt goaded.

Spurred on by his companion's ribbing, Hauk thrust his quarterstaff at Talamaya, but her quick reaction blocked his move. The wood vibrated through her hands with such ferocity, she realized long term she never could match his strength. She retaliated, striking with as hard a blow as she could manage, only he turned slightly, and her staff struck his knuckles to her horror.

"Ahhh," he cried out, and lost hold of one end of his staff.

"Oh." She dropped her staff and grabbed his hand. "Whatever made you turn—"

King Sal shouted, "Princess Talamaya! You will leave the arena at once! To your chambers!"

"Yes, my lord father." She hurried off, hoping to the heavens she hadn't harmed the knight's reputation with the king...or injured the knight too badly.

"And you, ladies, leave at once, too," the king added.

Talamaya glanced over her shoulder and saw the ladies grab their staffs, then race after her.

"What will your father do to Hauk?" Kersta asked as she and Mexia joined her, then exited the arena.

"Not much of anything, I imagine. After all, my father needs Hauk to accompany my brother on the quest tomorrow."

"If his hand isn't too badly injured," Mexia said.

Talamaya's body heated in shame. "I hadn't meant to hit him. He turned, I guess when he caught sight of my father entering the arena. Just that slight move when I dove forward to strike his staff was enough to cause the accident."

Kersta patted her shoulder. "He knows you wouldn't have

tried to hurt him. In fact, Hauk has teased me that I should be more kindhearted like you, then he'd consider marrying me."

Talamaya smiled. "He won't call me that any longer. Besides, I thought he *had* considered marrying you."

Kersta smiled. "Yes, but you know me. I cannot decide which of the three knights I like the best."

Mexia shook her head when they entered Talamaya's chambers. "Here, no one is interested in *me*."

Talamaya motioned to the silk-cushioned benches. "There's interest, but you don't...encourage it."

Kersta sat down on one side of Talamaya while Mexia sat on the other. "She's shy with the men," Kersta said. "And Princess Talamaya has the Vice Couns—"

Her words ceased when footsteps approached the chamber in rapid succession. A guard announced the king's imminent arrival, and the ladies all rose from their seats.

"My lord father," Talamaya said, curtsying when he stepped into her room, her heart pounding furiously.

The other ladies quickly curtsied and hurried out of her bedchambers like mice fleeing a feral cat in their midst.

"You won't spar with my knights any longer, Talamaya. It was one thing that I permitted my instructor to teach you ladies the basic moves, but I don't wish you injuring my knights any further." His eyes twinkled and his lips turned up considerably.

"Oh, Father, I'm so sorry I hurt Hauk."

"He'll be all right. The healer will mend him well enough that he can leave with Grisom tomorrow. However, this business about marriage—"

"I don't wish to marry."

"Grisom will marry, too."

Talamaya folded her arms. "A woman of his choosing, Father. You're not giving me such a choice."

"Grisom doesn't need to marry a woman of the highest rank.

You know this very well. With you it's different. I won't permit you to marry someone beneath you."

"All right then. I wish to marry Lazarion."

Her father's brown eyes narrowed. "Don't mock me, child."

"He's a king." She tilted her chin up.

"He's my enemy and a barbarian."

She paced across the floor. "As daughter of the ruler of Damar, I have the right to choose a husband for my own, don't I?"

"Within reason. Ultimately it's up to me."

"Unless I invoke the trial."

Her father's eyes widened briefly, but he quickly couched his look of disbelief, then snorted. "It hasn't been used for five hundred years, since Princess Aralias—"

"And the king, her father, couldn't agree on a suitable mate for her."

"Why do you choose to be so difficult?"

"I won't marry the Vice Councilor, my lord father." She kissed his cheek and patted his hand. "I have always been a dutiful daughter. And I will have to be a dutiful wife for a husband next, but at least let me choose him for my own."

"I didn't think you had any interest in the men in our realm. That's why I chose Og. He's widowed and experienced in how to handle a wife."

Turning away from her father, Talamaya tugged on her belt tassels in annoyance. "I'm not interested in *any* man. And least of all, your Vice Counselor."

"He hoped I could convince you otherwise, marry you at the feast tonight and spend the remaining hours with you as your husband before he left on this most dangerous of quests."

"Father!" Talamaya couldn't contain the hurt and anger welling up inside that he wouldn't consider her feelings concerning marrying Og.

"It's up to you, my daughter, for now." He sighed. "I wouldn't wish for you to marry him, then have him die and leave you widowed."

Taking a deep breath, trying to quell the upset his words had caused her, she reached for her father's hand. "For you to give up the kingdom to the one who accomplishes the quest, must rest gravely on your mind."

"It does, Talamaya. But whoever completes the quest will have saved our kingdom and deserves to rule her in my stead."

"Even if it isn't Grisom?"

"Yes, even if he fails the quest."

Talamaya knew then, her father feared losing his son. Only if she had a suitable heir then, could the family remain in power. She rubbed her temple. Unless one of the other men brought home the scepter and became ruler. But if none did, then the barbarians would overrun them.

What if Damar prevailed through the barbarian invasion *even* if they didn't have the scepter? And what if the despicable Saqualian married her brother that evening at the feast? Then if their union resulted in *her* having a son...

Talamaya's head throbbed with the thought. She squeezed her father's hand. "Grisom isn't marrying tonight at the feast, is he?"

3

Talamaya sat quietly at the long white-clothed table at the feast that night wedged in between her mother and Og. No matter how much they tried to force the Vice Counselor on her, she wasn't changing her mind about him.

The mood remained solemn while the servants served the best of the foods. Steaks of roasted wild boar coated in succulent spices, shellfish from the Neferon seacoast garnished with onion pearls and garlic cloves, freshly killed gryphon served in spicy soups...all offered to celebrate the departure of the warriors who would make the journey the next day, with the knowledge most, if not all of the men who were sent on the quest, could die.

Talamaya turned her attention to Saqualian. The woman hovered over her brother, smiling like the two-headed spotted cheetaur just before it ate its next meal. Her dark hair draped over her shoulders as she kissed his cheek. What had she done to catch his eye so all of a sudden? Grisom had never mentioned liking the woman at all. Was it that he'd turned of age and the woman made her move? Saqualian raised a grape to Grisom's lips, making Talamaya lift a brow.

Suddenly, she saw Grisom slide from his bench to the floor in a groggy state. She stood, concerned and anxious to see to him.

Her mother took her hand and tugged at her. "What's wrong, Talamaya? Talamaya, what's the matter?"

The queen's words dripped with worry, and Talamaya stared at her mother for a moment, then looked over at her brother. He still sat on his chair and continued to nibble at selections of fruit Saqualian hand fed him.

Talamaya shook her head and sat down. What was the matter with her mind?

"Are you all right, daughter?" her mother asked again, running her hand over her arm.

"Yes, my lady mother." Talamaya rubbed her temple. "I...I must be tired."

Her mother frowned. "We'll talk about this after the meal tonight."

Talamaya nodded, then glanced at her companions, Kersta and Mexia. Both watched Saqualian with Grisom. Nothing good could come of a marriage to the dragon.

Og touched Talamaya's hand. "You have not eaten hardly anything this evening."

She quickly pulled her hand into her lap. "I worry about my brother and of course you and the others leaving our kingdom tomorrow. It weighs heavily on my heart."

"You have not decided about me, then? Your father said he would speak with you about us."

"I cannot give my favor to any. I beg your pardon." She stirred her broth, dipping chunks of gryphon and potatoes about in the thick mixture.

Og leaned back in his chair. "I meant about our marrying. Your father said he would discuss our marriage tonight."

Had Og not been listening? She'd already said he wouldn't

have her favor. Certainly he couldn't have her hand in marriage. No way would she marry the brute. He'd rule every second of her life with an iron will, just as he ruled his men. Not once could they have any say in any matter. She wasn't about to be treated like that by him, or anyone. She shook her head as she tried to crush her growing irritation.

"I'm a patient man, Princess. I'll wait a little longer." He smiled and pointed to her broth. "That's the gryphon you were intent on making short work of with your dagger in the council chambers, by the way. You really ought not carry a dagger on your person. It's inappropriate for a young woman of your rank to be armed in such a manner."

She stared at the soup for a moment, then glanced back at her brother, the vision of his collapsing still fresh in her mind.

All at once his face turned colorless, and he slipped to the floor in a faint. Several shouted in alarm, and she knew then it was for real.

"Grisom!" she shouted and bolted from her seat.

TALAMAYA'S MOTHER sat with her in her bedchambers later that evening while healers saw to Grisom in his room. Her mother took Talamaya's hands in hers. "What is it that you saw concerning your brother before it happened?"

Talamaya's gaze shifted to the floor. How could she tell her mother she'd seen the strangest things all day? Was she going as mad as the poor knight Malachon, the only one to return alive from the failed quest for the scepter, his mind shattered into a thousand fragmented pieces?

She'd never kept secrets from her mother before, well, except for kissing Lord Zornan beneath the sparkle of the moon one night. And she'd had some fantasies about kissing two of the elf queen's sons, but other than that...

"Talamaya, what is it that you see?"

She'd seen the most gorgeous of men, his hair blond like the color of elmarion wheat ripening in the sun, but more golden, thicker, and coarser than the elves' paler blond, fine stranded hair. Tall, like her father, the man was built like him, too, sturdier, not finer featured like the elves. Yet his tanned face was naked. Was he human? She couldn't be sure. His long hair covered his ears and she couldn't see if they were elven or not.

In a forest, he sat perched on a horse the same color as his golden hair, its mane and tail slightly paler. Sunlight filtering through the thick grove of trees highlighted the man's green garments, richly brocaded, but nearly blending with the color of the woods.

Except for the rustle of leaves in the slight breeze, she heard no other sound except for the pounding of her heart in her ears. But when the man turned to see her standing there, gawking at him, awestruck, she'd nearly died.

"Talamaya?"

She turned toward her mother and choked back the tears. Her words were no more than a whisper when she blurted them out. "I think I'm going mad, my lady mother."

Her mother gathered her in her arms just like when she was little when the world seemed all at once too overpowering for her. "Tell me about it."

"I saw Grisom collapse from his chair, only he had not. Not until later."

Nodding, her mother stroked her arm. "Yes, and what else?"

Talamaya hesitated. Nothing else worried her more than her brother's health. "Nothing really."

"What else, Talamaya?"

"Just that Og would follow me out of the council chambers

and I had to...to escape him. But I knew he would come after me, so it was not exactly that I saw it beforehand."

"And?"

"Really, my lady mother, it is my brother who should warrant your concern."

"The healers are seeing to him. They are trying to determine the poison that has weakened his body."

"Poison?" Talamaya's head swam. Why would anyone have poisoned her brother?

Then the thought occurred to her. The scepter. If Grisom had traveled with the other men and succeeded in obtaining the scepter, he would rule. No one else would have a chance then. With him unable to ride, someone else could claim the scepter and the throne. Who in the group of thirty men would have done such a despicable deed?

Og was the only one who came to mind. But then again where he was concerned, he always met with disfavor in her eyes.

Saqualian fed Grisom the food. Was she to blame? Perhaps she felt as Talamaya and most of the rest of their people did, whoever rode on the quest would never live to return home again. Saqualian wouldn't want to give up her role as queen when the time came. If it was her, would she poison the king, too? After all, unless Grisom retrieved the scepter, the kingdom remained under King Sal's rule.

"Is Father safe?"

Her mother kissed her cheek. "Yes, dear. His advisors believe someone does not wish Grisom to take part in the quest. That's all."

"Saqualian," Talamaya said under her breath.

"Everyone is under suspicion."

Talamaya looked up at her mother.

"Except for the royal family, though one of the advisors

commented you had spoken with your brother about not wishing him to go."

"Og." Talamaya folded her arms.

"Yes, well, neither your father, nor I suspect you would have done such a thing. Your knowledge of herbs and poisons is extensive, but you would never have risked harming your brother, despite wanting to protect him from future danger. It isn't in your nature." She gave Talamaya a squeeze. "But I worry about this other business. Tell me what else you see."

"Nothing, really important. Just..." She paused. Could she jeopardize her secrets by telling her mother the most bizarre thing she'd ever seen? Would they lock her away somewhere in one of the outlying palaces, far from the capital city to hide their witless daughter?

"Talamaya, whatever you say is important. We have never kept secrets from each other before. Yet, I feel we are drifting apart."

"You'll think me crazy."

Her mother's brown eyes softened, and she squeezed her hand with reassurance. "No, my daughter."

"I saw the strangest creature never before beheld by man. A half-woman, half-fish basking on a moss-coated rock in the southern seas." She took a deep breath.

Her mother grew stiff all at once and her eyes widened.

"I told you it wasn't important. Just my imagination wreaking havoc with my—"

"What did she look like, this mermaid that you saw?"

Mermaid? Talamaya had studied as many books on the creatures found across the region as she could, fascinated with the subject, but she never remembered reading anything about such a race.

Her mother looked down at the floor for a second, then back to Talamaya. "It's important, daughter. What did she look like?"

"Her red hair, braided with pearls and seaweed, dripped over her shoulders." Talamaya whispered, "Her breasts were bare."

"Yes, go on." Her mother twisted the ties to her pouch at her waist.

"She had a silver green tail like a fish and it flopped up and down on the colorful coral rock. And...and she slammed a shellfish on the coral, then devoured it, shell and all."

"Where were you?"

Talamaya stared at her mother, not sure she understood her. The vision of the mermaid resulted from something strange she'd eaten at the evening meal, she was certain.

"This is important, Talamaya. Where were you when you saw the mermaid?"

"I don't understand your question, my mother. I was here, in my bedchambers. I saw her early this morning."

Tears filling her eyes, her mother shook her head. "Think, Talamaya. Were you swimming in the water, or standing on the shore? Did your body rock with the motion as though you rode in a boat? Where were you when you saw the mermaid?"

Talamaya rubbed her forehead and attempted to conjure up the vision. "I was sitting on my horse, Cristana, when I saw the mermaid resting upon the coral. The swells of the sea licked the surface of her island rock."

Her mother stood. "For five hundred years, our family has not had the gift. Only when Princess Aralias lived, did she have the ability to glimpse visions of the future. She invoked the trial to choose a husband. It was the only way she could find the one who suited her special needs."

Her mind flooded with confusion, Talamaya stared at her mother. "I don't understand."

"Your father told me you mentioned invoking the marriage trial, just the way she had done." Her mother paused. "Tell me you don't wish the barbarian king to be your husband, Talamaya."

Talamaya rose from her seat. "I only said such a thing in poor jest, my lady mother. I said it only because Father wishes me *not* to marry beneath our rank. The barbarian king was the only human who came to mind, who outranked a crown prince, even. But I meant no harm by it. I would not wish to be...be married to a dog."

Her mother's eyes couldn't have widened any further and her mouth dropped open in surprise.

Talamaya quickly said, "Father said the barbarians bred like dogs."

Her mother's mouth clamped shut, her face contorted with a mixture of surprise and irritation, then she took a deep breath. "I shall speak to your father about saying such a thing in front of his daughter. But what I believe he was referring to was the way in which their kind have litters of children, not that they..." She closed her mouth. "I will speak to your father about this. He won't wish you to go, but it is inevitable that you speak to the soothsayer. She will advise you."

"But women are not allowed to see her. It is forbidden."

"She will expect you. Tonight. Take Mexia and Kersta with you."

"I don't understand. None of the women are allowed to leave the palace grounds at night. The guards won't let us pass."

"Word will be sent at once."

"Do you not think we should take a couple of knights with us?"

Her mother patted her hand. "The knights will never get as far as the three of you will, I predict."

Talamaya wasn't certain she understood her mother's words. "The way to the soothsayer's cave isn't too terribly dangerous, is it?"

Her mother sighed deeply. "No, but the way to Lanai and retrieving the scepter will be fraught with danger. The sooth-sayer will guide you best." She wrapped her arm around Tala-maya. "Queen Aralias was a great leader. You will follow in her footsteps."

"Queen? Through her husband, you mean."

"She was the only woman to ever reign over Damar, and she ruled well."

Talamaya's skin tingled with worry. "I don't understand. The history books didn't say that." She considered her mother's words further. "You don't mean for me to retrieve the scepter...as a...a woman?"

"Aralias held the scepter during her rule. A rift grew between her twin sons upon her death. Her most loyal advisor stole the scepter and returned it to Lanai, the place she had retrieved it from in the first place to avert war."

Talamaya stared at the floor. "The history books kept it secret? Because...because the men didn't want any to think a woman capable of ruling?" She groaned with disgust. She looked up at her mother, whose face appeared wearied now with concern. "But if I were to retrieve the scepter, I would give it to Father so that he would remain in power."

"He has decreed—"

"That a man rule, not a woman, should they retrieve the scepter."

Her mother nodded. "Hurry and get ready. You must go now before anyone discovers the three of you are leaving for Lanai."

4

Talamaya still reeled with the news she would go in her brother's place to attempt to retrieve the scepter. Had the soothsayer told her father this? She squeezed her mother tightly. "Why did Father have me sit in on the council meeting today?"

"He knew you were the one to go on the quest."

"Why did he not say something to me?"

"He didn't believe what the soothsayer said was true, not until you spoke about invoking the marriage trial. When you had the vision concerning your brother, we both knew the soothsayer spoke the truth."

"Og or the others who are going? Do they know?"

"No, my dear."

"What do we do? Join the men? I would think this a breech in our etiquette. Unmarried women don't sleep out in the open with unattached men. But if we go alone, how can three women survive alone in the wilderness?"

"The soothsayer will tell you what you must do."

"But what about Mexia and Kersta? Why are they to go with

me? I wouldn't wish them harmed on such a dangerous journey."

"They have special gifts, too. That is why the three of you were drawn to each other. The soothsayer has said so. The three of you will face great peril, but between you, you shall be able to outwit the evil that exists in your path."

Talamaya shook her head. "They would have told me if they had special abilities. Neither have said a thing to me about it."

"And you, dear Talamaya? Did you confide in your friends concerning the visions you have had?"

She rubbed her temple. "No, my lady mother. I thought I was going crazy."

"As I am certain they have felt as well. Speak with them and leave tonight to see the soothsayer. From there, you will begin your journey."

"But why did Father wish me to marry Og if I were to seek the scepter?"

"He still had hoped the soothsayer was wrong. You have to realize your father holds with the old ways. He fights the notion his daughter, not his son, would save our kingdom."

"And Kersta and Mexia's parents?"

"They have already been advised their daughters must travel with you to a distant place. Everything else remains unspoken." Her mother took a deep breath and patted her hand. "Food is already being prepared for the men for their journey tomorrow. A special portion has been set aside for you and your companions."

Her mother kissed her cheek and gave her one last embrace. "I will pray you will return soon to me, my child." Then she hurried out of the room, while Kersta and Mexia ran into the chambers.

Both wide-eyed, they grabbed Talamaya's hands. "Is it true?"

"Seems the feast for the warrior's departure was also meant

for us." Talamaya brushed the feelings of anxiety that churned deep inside away and hurried into her clothes' room. She grabbed a cloak suitable to repel the rain and chill, her sparring clothes, and two traveling gowns. One, green velvet, for their trip through the Wildwood forest and the other white wolverine wool for the snow pass of Mount Elan. Both were basically trousers, with legs as full fashioned as a skirt for modesty, but with the advantage of trousers for riding and fighting...and the only type of clothing permitted for women traveling through the countryside.

"Is that what we are to take?" Kersta asked.

"I'm trying to think. Our sparring clothes will be good for the desert plain of Marsa. We'll need the wool for warmth and to blend in through the snow pass. The green will suffice for Wildwood."

Kersta said, "We'll dress like the barbarians do. Hiding against the setting like the cat-creature cheetaur camouflages itself against the reddish-orange and gold speckled rocks of his homeland."

"Yes, we need every advantage we can get. Though I don't believe we'll dress as poorly as the barbarians do."

"The dogs," Kersta said. Mexia nodded.

"Ladies, concentrate. We must pack our things and see the soothsayer before our journey begins. We won't return until we find the scepter."

Mexia's mouth dropped open as Kersta said, "The soothsayer? We have to see the soothsayer? She is a witch! No woman is permitted to see her."

"She awaits us." Talamaya considered her clothes, then pulled out a lilac travel gown.

Mexia shook her head. "That doesn't match any scenery I've ever read about."

"It doesn't matter. Besides the gown I wear now, it's my

favorite, and always brings me luck. Go, pack now, ladies, and we shall be on our way." As the ladies headed for the door, Talamaya halted them. "Wait, what special powers do you possess?"

Mexia folded her arms and smiled at her. "Well, I can tell you right now, Kersta has a way with men. But, as for me, I'm afraid, except for making up a great batch of potions, that's about it."

Talamaya turned to Kersta. She shrugged. "Like Mexia said, I can talk my way around the fellows, if that's what you mean."

Groaning, Talamaya motioned for them to leave. "Pack and meet me here as soon as you're done."

Once Talamaya finished, she called for a servant. "Pack these on my horse and have Lady Kersta and Lady Mexia's horses saddled as well."

When the servant hastened down the hall with her bedroll and bundle of clothes, Talamaya sought audience with Grisom.

Barely awake, he lifted his eyelids halfway and attempted a smile. "Yes, sister, what is it you...you wish of me?"

"I wish you to be well. If Mother has not informed you, I'll be away for a while. Try not to miss me too much."

His face pale and drawn, he nodded slightly. "I am sorry... about the way...I acted toward you...earlier." His words were spoken haltingly slow and drifted off into whispers in places.

"I worried I...would not save the kingdom...in time, and resented...carrying the burden...on my shoulders." He paused, and she waited patiently for him to continue. "I feared...not the...dangers, but failure. And now...I have failed before I even... have begun." Talamaya gripped her brother's hand tightly. A tear slid down her cheek to her annoyance and dropped on his. He shook his head. "The healers said...I would be fine. But...the recovery may...take as much as...the full circle of the moon."

"By the new moon," she whispered.

"I want you to...know, I would...have given the...scepter to Father. I am not ready to rule...in his place."

"You'll be a good ruler, someday, my brother."

"You must...not marry Og."

She smiled and kissed her brother's cheek. "*That*, you don't have to worry about."

"He would not...suit...your disposition."

"Agreed." She noticed Kersta motioning from the entrance of Grisom's chambers. "I must go. The gods be with you, Grisom. I will keep you in my prayers."

He closed his eyes, and she kissed his cheek. Her heart was torn with staying with him and helping him in his recovery and leaving to find the scepter. She was not certain she was prepared for facing the dangers she now had to conquer.

Saqualian strode through the door, her brown eyes narrowed with hatred. Talamaya brushed past her and grabbed Kersta's hand. Once they were out of Saqualian's hearing range, she said, "Is Mexia ready?"

"Yes, my lady. We are both ready to go."

"Not yet. We have one other to see before we leave."

"Who, my lady? My mother said we went in secrecy."

"One who will never tell anyone of our secret."

When they arrived at Malachon's father's humble residence, Kersta whispered, "Are you certain this is such a good idea?"

"He's the only one who made it back from the quest alive. If he has any valuable information, we must use it."

"They say he cannot have a thought that isn't muddled and confused," Mexia said.

"This may be so, but we must seek him out, just the same."

Talamaya knocked on the solid oak door. Silence followed her light knock, and she tried again, harder this time. After several more moments, the door squeaked opened. A white-haired man peered back at them over the flickering flame of a lantern. "What ye seek at this late hour, young miss?"

"To speak with Sir Malachon, kind sir."

"Ye be the Princess Talamaya?" He squinted his eyes, trying to recognize her.

"Yes, and you are Malachon's father, are you not?"

"I be. What wish you of young Malachon?"

"A word, sir, if I might."

"He speaks of nothing that most understand."

"Yes. Still, I wish to see him."

The man nodded, then opened the door farther to allow the ladies passage. When they entered the modest room filled with wooden chairs and a table for dining, Talamaya took a deep breath of the aroma of calomeran tea. Heavenly scented, the fragrance drew her in and at once relaxed the tension from her spine.

He motioned to three wooden chairs seated before a golden fire. "I will fetch Malachon for you."

The ladies sat, each exchanging glances that betrayed their nervousness, then stood when Malachon walked into the room.

His father motioned to them. "Sit, ladies. Sit."

Malachon stood before Talamaya and smiled. His brown eyes appeared glazed, and she wondered if he took some drug to lessen his pained memories. His brown clothes were disheveled as if he'd been sleeping in them for days and even his long brown hair appeared tangled and unkempt.

"Sir Malachon," Talamaya said, and instantly his lips turned up slightly. She assumed he appreciated someone who would address him as a knight still. His simple smile touched her heart. "I wish to know everything you can tell me about the quest to Lanai. The quest for the scepter, if you could, Sir Knight."

"My lady," Malachon's father said, "must ye trouble the lad with this business?"

She continued to look into Malachon's eyes. Reaching up, she took his hands and held them lightly. "I must seek the scepter for the kingdom. Can you help me in any way?"

Malachon's father gasped and whispered, "King Sal cannot expect his daughter to fetch the scepter. 'Tis too dangerous for the likes of a lady. Wild boar, there have been no men who could bring it back either."

"Sir Malachon," she asked again, ignoring his father's interruptions, "can you help me?"

"Red sea at night, sailor's delight, red sea in the morning, sailor's warning."

"He has it mixed up," Mexia whispered. "And it is the sky not the sea—"

Talamaya shook her head. "No, he is right. The mermaid of the sea, the one with the red hair. She is deadly to the men in the morning. But at night, she is well fed, or sleepy or something and isn't dangerous. Is that right?"

A spark of recognition appeared in Malachon's eyes. The smile returned to his lips.

If she could help him to remember all that he must have encountered on the way during his quest for the scepter, would he be cured of his sickness? She hoped it would be so.

"Sir Malachon, what else can you tell us?"

"Sticks and stones will break your bones, but words will hurt you...more!"

She hadn't seen any other visions of their quest so far. What did he mean? He waited, like a child, hoping she'd recognize the muddled words he spoke. So hopeful, her heart ached for him. And then the vision came.

Three-headed, one eyed...Cyclops? Yes, uprooting trees and tossing boulders, but not at them. At whom? Their men? She didn't recognize their garments. No, at someone else.

"The Cyclops, Sir Malachon. What words would hurt you

more than the trees and boulders they toss at you like a child throws sticks and stones?"

"The wizard's words that command them to do it."

Malachon spoke plainly this time, and his words cheered her. A glimmer of hope...she may pull him from the darkness yet. She nodded and squeezed his hands. "Anything else, Sir Knight? Anything else that will aid us?"

5

A new concern wormed its way into Talamaya's stomach. Why would a wizard command the Cyclops? She'd never heard of anything so bizarre.

"He is the rock, bears his teeth, only seconds before he rips out your throat...rips out your throat." Malachon growled.

For a second, he confused her. Then she realized he'd moved on to describe another obstacle that lay in their path.

"The cheetaur?" Mexia asked. "The cheetaur blends in with the speckled rocks of the plain. For the unsuspecting, he will go for the throat."

"The speckled rocks." Malachon nodded.

"And?" Talamaya prompted him.

He pulled his hands free and rubbed his temple. "The cave... black as Soren's shield and twice as ugly. Deadlier than any venom, deadlier than the devil himself."

"The Cave of Sorrows?" Kersta whispered as if the name would cause the evil to appear before them.

He nodded and strolled toward his bedroom.

"Thank you, Sir Malachon, for helping us in our quest,"

Talamaya called out to him. "Upon my return, I'll visit with you again."

"Thank you, Princess Talamaya. The gods be with you," he said under his breath.

His father stared at her, then grabbed her hands and held them tightly. "You have healed him in part, my lady. You have treated him like a knight of the realm, duly earned, and you have helped him to relive some of the painful memories. I cannot thank you enough for helping him like this. He has not spoken so clearly since the day he made his way home."

"I didn't know until today what ailed him. But I'm pleased beyond words that he's so much better. We must go now, though." She stood, then turned as Malachon's footsteps padded toward her again.

"Take this amulet, my lady. Wear it with honor and pride. It saved me once; it will aid you now." Then he handed her a map. "May this also aid in your quest."

He kissed her cheek, and the other ladies' mouths gaped open, then he frowned. "Be wary of the blinding snow of Elan Pass. It can devour you alive."

LATER THAT EVENING, the women traveled in silence along the path to the soothsayer's cave through the neutral zone. Overhead, the stars glistened against the black night like millions of diamonds sparkled against velvet. Woodland fairies glittered around them, casting sparks of rainbow-colored light, here, then there, greeting them as they made their way.

Well-worn, the path to the caves proved easy to follow. Except for the beetles singing their raucous noise, the horses clip-clopping at a steady pace, and the sturdy breeze shaking the new green leaves of the trees, the woods remained peaceful.

Finally, Kersta spoke up. "Is he cured, do you think? Malachon, I mean?"

"He seemed much better. Even his father said so. I still wish to speak with him longer upon our return though."

Then Talamaya saw the man of her vision, his face stern while he considered the woods, listening, watching, and concentrating.

She motioned for the ladies to stop. They paused.

"What is it?" Kersta whispered.

"Shhh." Talamaya held her finger to her lips.

He turned his head in her direction, and she thought he saw her. But he twisted his horse back south toward the soothsayer's cave. She realized then, he hadn't detected her in the woods at all. Then he motioned to someone farther away, someone she couldn't see. They galloped off. Were they hunting something?

The warm air circulated around Talamaya's face, and she sniffed the air. Besides the heavenly odor of pine needles twisting in the breeze and an occasional wisp of fragrance from the sweet waters the ladies wore, something else caught her attention. Whispering, she said, "Do you smell something?"

The women raised their noses slightly to sniff the breeze. "Like what, princess?"

"Smoke. I think I smell the faint odor of smoke."

"To the south," Mexia whispered. "The direction we must go."

"From the soothsayer's cave, do you think, my lady?" Kersta asked, her voice darkened with concern. "It is in the same direction, is it not?"

"No," Talamaya said with a hushed voice. "The soothsayer's cave is slightly to the east."

Then, she glimpsed the same man in a new vision, now standing in a clearing, his golden hair let loose about his shoulders while he stood before a campfire. The same man that she had envisioned sitting on his golden horse moments earlier in the woods before her.

The flame flickered light off his tanned, chiseled face.

"Who is he, my lady?" Kersta asked.

"What?"

"The gorgeous man with the golden hair."

Talamaya twisted in her saddle to look back at Kersta, riding slightly behind her on the trail. "What did you say?"

"I visualize the man you described to me. He stands by the fire. The golden flames flicker blue with the heat of the coals. His golden hair ripples over his shoulders, loose, slightly tangled. You wish to draw your fingers through them to comb them out."

Talamaya's face burned with mortification, and she pulled her horse to a stop. "I said *no* such thing."

Mexia stared at her, then remarked to Kersta, "She said no such thing, Kersta. Where did you ever get that notion?"

"Shhhh." Talamaya looked south. "They will hear us." She headed in their direction.

"Where are we going, my lady?" Mexia asked. "Should we not follow the trail southeast? We're going out of our way. No telling what danger lies in our path this way."

Kersta smiled. "She wishes to see the golden-haired man, stripped naked to the waist. How much more will he remove before he beds down for the night, eh?"

"Shhh." Talamaya waved for her companions' silence, her annoyance perceptible in the tone of her voice.

Talamaya raised her hand for the ladies to halt their horses, then she dismounted. Kersta slid from her horse and joined her. "What are we doing, my lady?" she whispered.

"I fear they travel in our direction. I see them again later, in Wildwood forest. Would it not make sense to attempt friendship?"

"And if they are not friendly?'"

"They won't harm us."

"How do you know, my lady?"

"I just do. We'll tether our horses here. On foot, they wouldn't see us as a threat."

"But we'll take our staffs."

"Of course." She glanced back at Mexia. "Do you wish to watch over our horses instead?"

"Heavens, no." Mexia dismounted. "I must see what the naked blond male looks like that everyone else has seen."

"If they head in our direction, is that not a bad thing?" Kersta asked.

"We won't travel with them. But when we run into them again, they will know us as friend not foe." In reality, Talamaya wished to see what he looked like in the flesh and what beautiful flesh that was, at least as far as she could tell in her vision.

"Ah." Kersta smiled. "You just wish to see how far the man will undress."

"How *do* you know such things, Kersta?"

"How do *you* know what he looks like, princess?"

Talamaya stopped walking. "I see glimpses of the future."

Kersta shook her head. "I don't."

"Then how is it that you see what I see?"

Mexia poked Kersta. "You read her mind?"

Talamaya frowned.

The ladies chuckled.

"This should be an interesting trip," Mexia said.

"When did you begin to see my thoughts?"

"When we began the ride on the trail."

"At the moment you turned eighteen?" Talamaya asked.

They both looked at Mexia.

"In another hour I will reach the age of majority," Mexia offered.

"I wonder what you will be able to do," Kersta whispered.

"Shhh," Talamaya said. "Can you hear their voices? They are close."

All at once, the woods came alive with men, rushing them from all sides.

"Hey! What have we here?" one asked his companions as he grabbed at Mexia's skirt. She readied her staff but looked back at Talamaya for her approval to whack the hand of the offending man.

Talamaya quickly counted their numbers. Ten men dressed in green tunics and breeches of butternut surrounded them, blending with the woods.

She bowed her head in greeting. "My name is Tala, and these are my companions, Kersta and Mexia. We are traveling through the neutral zone to see the soothsayer."

"Who goes there?" a man shouted from a clearing in the woods several yards away.

It was him, the man from her dreams. What part did he play in her quest for the scepter? Friend or foe?

6

The man's voice boomed from a short distance away, and the deepness and darkness of his words made Talamaya reconsider at once her desire to make friends with whoever these men were.

"Women, my lord," the man shouted back.

"Bring them here."

Talamaya held her staff at the ready while one of the men led them through the woods. The rest followed behind them as if to make sure none escaped.

"What have we here?" the man said, pulling a tunic over his head.

In awe, Talamaya studied the man's lightly muscled arms and the way his breeches form-fit his legs, then disappeared into thigh-high boots.

"Well?"

Talamaya tilted her chin up to show she wasn't afraid of this man, or any other, but when she proceeded to speak, her throat was as dry as the dusty plains. "Tala is my name, and these are my companions."

"No others? No men accompany you?" He looked at his soldiers.

One shook his head. "They seem to be alone. The others are still checking."

The man circled the women, then faced Talamaya. "Your hair and clothes are like what the Damar women wear. Yet you cannot be Damarian because the men's rules imprison the women."

Talamaya's cheeks grew hot, and she tightened her grip on her staff. Make friends, she urged her mind while her emotions threatened to rule her better judgment. "Who do I have the honor of addressing?"

"Lazarion."

Her breath caught in her throat. The barbarian king? She feared looking at her companions lest they give themselves away. Easily this king could take them hostage and ransom them for great concessions from her father.

"Where are you from and why have you come here?" he asked.

"We are travelers like you and have come to seek the word of Modi, the soothsayer."

"Ah." He motioned to the fire. "Join us and share some drink."

Talamaya nodded. "Thank you."

The men hurried to serve the ladies goblets while Lazarion motioned to a makeshift seating of logs. The ladies sat on one together, attempting to make themselves comfortable on the knotted wood. He sat opposite them, and his men stood in a semicircle observing.

Sipping his drink, he then pointed in the direction of the caves. "I have just come from there."

Talamaya smiled. "I hope she brought you good tidings."

Only once did he take his eyes off her to consider the other ladies' appearances, but then his gaze returned to Talamaya and remained there.

"I found her words more...riddle-like than usual."

"Oh? Perhaps I can help to clear up the meaning for you."

His stern face brightened and his mouth curved up considerably. His men laughed.

Did he think as a woman, she could not make sense of the words of the soothsayer? Or was it something about the riddle itself that made them see the situation as so humorous?

He lifted a stick off the ground and drew a strange symbol in the earth. "How do I know you are not my enemy?"

"I don't know you, therefore, I cannot be your foe. To be your enemy, I would have to find fault with you."

"Yet, the Damarian hordes have raided our border without provocation." He pointed to her gown. "And you wear the Damarian dress."

Talamaya stared at him in disbelief. Their people would never start a war without good cause. She looked down at the ground for a moment and considered the implications. Then she faced the king. "What did these men wear?"

"They didn't wear Damarian uniforms, if this is what you seek to know." He tilted his head slightly. "Do you know something of these people?"

"Certainly not. My...I understand the Damarians would not attack unless provoked." Her whole body heated. Had Og caused the conflict? She'd have him branded a traitor and thrown into the Elgin Sea.

"That was my understanding, but someone has changed the rules."

"Can you describe this man who led them?"

The king leaned back on his log slightly. "You seem to know something of this."

"Of course not. I would like to know who this man is who

violates peace between...the Damarians and the barb...your people."

He raised a brow. "It is late. After you have seen Modi, please feel free to bed down with me...us."

His men chuckled in response. Talamaya's body tensed with irritation. Had he made the slip of the tongue to amuse his men, or had he really been thinking it and made an honest mistake? Either way, his words made her wary of his intentions toward her.

She hadn't thought she'd reacted any, but even then her lack of response must have made him rethink his words.

"You'll be safe at our camp. Three ladies as attractive as you are shouldn't be traveling alone."

Ten more soldiers walked into camp. "No sign of any others who came with these, my lord."

Lazarion rubbed his smooth chin. "What kingdom of humans do you belong to? Though we don't have the restrictions on our women that the Damar do, we would never allow our women to roam the wilderness unaccompanied without protection. It is too dangerous."

The only female society Talamaya had read about where the women were self-sufficient were the Amazons of the Maken Peninsula. But they were too far north and never ventured into mid-Inherian where only men ruled. Plus, they were said to be as tall as her brother, Grisom. Talamaya and her friends stood only a little over half a foot shorter than her six-foot tall father.

"Resilion," she made up.

Lazarion sat taller, his green eyes sparkling in the light of the flame. He raised his blond brows in question. "I've never heard of it." He looked over at his men, all of whom shook their heads. "Where is it in relationship to Malaron?"

"Malaron?" Inwardly, she laughed. No one in Damar called it

Malaron. To the Damarians, the people who lived in Malaron were too barbarian-like to have a name for the place they lived.

"The land east of the Salanta River. To the west is the Kingdom of Damar and even farther west, the elf kingdom of Mesa. The land after this drops into the Ebolon Sea. The uninhabited plains are south of us. Malaron rests along the Damarian border and on our eastern coast lies the Pala Sea. So where is this kingdom in relationship to any of these?"

Talamaya hadn't expected to get a geography lesson from the barbarian. How did he know so much?

"Our settlement is between Damar and the elf kingdom. We are travelers who were allowed to settle there and self-rule."

Did he believe her? She glanced at Kersta. Did Kersta's wrinkled brow mean she read his mind and if so, he didn't believe her?

Talamaya finished her wine, trying to curb her nervousness. "Thank you for your generosity. We must see Modi, then be on our way."

She rose to her feet and the ladies did, too. For a moment, Lazarion remained seated. Then he stood and walked over to her. The smile returned to his lips, and his gaze drifted from her face all the way down her long skirts to her boots, then back up again. "Anytime, Tala."

Her face warmed. Just the way he spoke her name, made her worry she'd given herself away. She doubted the barbarian king would know any, other than her father's and maybe her brother's names, but still she feared Lazarion was suspicious of her.

He drew closer. Slipping her hand under her cloak, she touched her jeweled dagger. His gaze shifted to her subtle reaction. He brushed away her cloak and smiled to see her hand resting at the handle of her dagger. His fingers wrapped around hers. The heat rose to her cheeks again, but this time her whole body warmed.

Lifting her fingers to his lips, he kissed them, his gaze never straying from hers. His green eyes challenged her to take their relationship farther. Pulling her hand away with a jerk, she headed out of camp with her friends following close behind. "The impudence of the man," she muttered silently to herself.

"Later, my lady," Lazarion called after them.

Ten of Lazarion's men escorted them back to their horses. When they mounted, they were surprised to see several mount theirs, too. When the women began to canter, to their horror the men rode behind them. Talamaya imagined then, the barbarian king either wished to ensure they had spoken the truth and were bound to see Modi, or he worried still for their safety.

The women rode in silence as Talamaya fumed about the barbarian king's actions. She was dying to know what Kersta had read of his thoughts, but with the men following so closely behind them, she couldn't ask.

When they arrived at the cave, the men hurried to help the ladies to dismount. Mexia smiled at Talamaya and thanked the man who helped her down.

"We will wait here and watch your horses," one of the men said to Talamaya.

"There's no need."

"Lazarion requires us to do so."

"Thank you then."

He nodded, his mouth turned up in a quirky grin. The look made Talamaya uncomfortable as her stomach fluttered uneasily. Did Lazarion think she'd bed down with him for the night? Thinking they were not Damarian women put Talamaya and her companions at a disadvantage. Perhaps he thought the women of this tribe who traveled without male companionship would seek it wherever they could. Certainly, she had sought him out, kind of. She steeled her back.

Kersta grabbed her hand, and they stepped into the dimly lit cave. She whispered, "He didn't believe there was any place called Resilian. From what I could tell, he is well traveled. I thought he was the barbarian king, yet nothing he did or said indicated this was so."

"But he didn't believe me?" Talamaya asked while the ladies made their way through the tunnel. Icy groundwater dripped on their heads like an intermittent winter rain. Her heart pounded with apprehension at facing the soothsayer.

"No. He thinks we're Damarian, but he cannot understand it. He assumes men always accompany our women when we journey beyond the confines of the castle. Not only that, but he knows, too, that our women are forbidden to see Modi. So he's thoroughly confused. Oh, and your name. He immediately drew a likeness between Tala and Talamaya. Only again, the confusion reigned in his mind. King Sal would never allow his only daughter to wander alone through the wilderness with just two lady companions. He considered though, we had run away from home, not wanting to marry someone our fathers wished us to wed."

Talamaya stopped walking. "I wouldn't have thought he would have known anything beyond my father and brother's name. What does he intend for his men to do after we leave the cave tonight?"

"He had it in his mind that they would escort us back to his camp. Beyond that, I don't know."

Talamaya breathed deeply, the cold damp air filling her chest. "I feared as much." She squeezed Kersta's hand. "What words of wisdom did Modi offer him when she spoke with him earlier tonight?"

A voice as sweet as the fragrance of the minko flower swirled toward them from the depths of the cave. "Modi tells him to befriend the dark-haired ones who will be his greatest allies, or his downfall, *if* he isn't careful."

"Modi?" Mexia whispered.

"Yes," the feminine voice responded. "Seek council ye do. Tarry no longer. Come, sit with me, Princess of Damar."

"And my companions?" Talamaya asked without moving a foot in her direction.

"Welcome, they are. Come."

The women walked through two more passages before they arrived at a cavern cloaked in green moss. Lanterns washed the room in light, and the walls glistened with moisture. The woman smiled at them, her hair shimmering with silver highlights as if rays of the moon shown on it. Otherwise, her hair was as white as the freshly fallen snow of Elan Pass. Yet her face was devoid of wrinkles, perfectly smooth and youthful as if she'd recently come of age in Damarian society.

She nodded. "Seven and ten. But add another seven hundred and my age you will have." She motioned to stone benches cushioned with moss. "Sit and drink."

She passed a cup between them.

Talamaya smelled the fragrance of tea, the same scent that filled Sir Malachon's abode.

"Drink," Modi prompted.

"Malachon has seen you?"

"The tea aids him to see the light."

Talamaya took a sip, then handed the cup to Kersta.

"No!" the soothsayer said sharply.

Startled, Talamaya turned her attention to her.

Modi softened her voice. "All of it, you must drink."

Taking a deep breath, Talamaya drank the rest of the tea.

"Now to your friend, offer it."

Talamaya did as she was told, and Kersta smiled. "The cup is full again."

Modi nodded. "Give me your water pouches." She poured the warm water out onto the rock floor. Instantly, the water vanished. Then Modi raised the spout of a vase into each pouch and filled them with the sweet tea. When she finished, she motioned for Kersta to take them back. "What do you seek, princess?" she asked, then motioned to their staffs.

Mexia gathered them up, then handed them to her.

Talamaya ran her hands over her lap. Shouldn't the sooth-sayer have already known what she was there for? "A way to retrieve the scepter of Lanai, Modi."

"You already have the way." Smiling, Modi ran her hand from one length of Talamaya's staff to the other. "Danger fills the path, however."

"Yes, I have spoken with Malachon—"

"Clever you are. Your warriors waste not their precious time on a feeble mind. But you...you sought him out and now on to recovery he is." She waved her hand toward the exit to the passageway. "Follow the path of righteousness always, princess. Any other path, fateful will it prove." She ran her hand over Mexia's staff, her slender fingers caressing the oak with a gentle touch, then proceeded to do the same to Kersta's.

"Righteousness?"

"You or one of your companions will know the way. Afraid you are not to seek advice. Afraid you are not to make new alliances. Courage you have when it counts." She nodded and said under her breath, "Like Princess Aralias did." She motioned for Mexia to take their quarterstaffs back.

"The ruler of Damar, five hundred years ago?"

"Rewrite your history books, you will. Remember, the path of righteousness. Choose well."

She clapped her hands and to the women's surprise, they stood near the cave's opening again.

"The path of righteousness?" Mexia asked.

Talamaya motioned toward the cave's entrance. "She said we

would know the right way to go. Hopefully, she knows what she speaks of."

Melodic laughter echoed off the cave walls. The women looked back toward the cavern.

"Now what?" Kersta asked.

Talamaya tapped her staff on the cave floor. "I guess we bed down with King Lazarion for the night and try to keep our wits about us."

7

Talamaya turned to Kersta. "Was it a slip of his tongue or had Lazarion made jest of us bedding down with him?"

"Not us, my lady, you." Kersta shook her head. "You wouldn't wish to know what he truly was thinking."

Talamaya stared at her. "What?"

"Perhaps, Mexia shouldn't hear this." Kersta whispered, "She isn't of age at least for a few more seconds."

Mexia hmpfed. "Of course I want to hear this."

"What?" Talamaya asked again, her voice growing agitated.

Kersta couldn't contain the smile on her lips. "He wished to snuggle with you close and kiss those full lips of yours that he knew burned with unspent passion. Oh, and that he knew for certain your lips wished his kiss in return."

Talamaya smoothed down her skirt, trying not to reveal to Kersta how she really felt about the man who stirred her blood with fervor. How could Lazarion know what she felt after all? He couldn't read her mind, too, could he?

Her cheeks burned with mortification. Her feelings were becoming as transparent as the silk curtains that were draped around her bed, and she didn't like it...not one bit. Her mother was the only one who truly ever sensed how things were with her, now everyone could? Was it her coming of age that threatened to undo her?

"That is it?" Mexia asked. "Nothing more?"

"For heaven's sakes, that's enough," Talamaya said, hoping the annoyance she felt that the barbarian could feel such a way about her wasn't too evident in her voice.

"Naked," Kersta added.

Talamaya stared at her as if she'd lost her mind. Incensed beyond reason, she clenched her staff in her fist. Yet, hadn't she wished to see him that way also? Yes, seeing but not...touching. It wasn't the same, after all.

Kersta shrugged. "That is what he envisioned. The two of you naked. I cannot help it."

Talamaya and Mexia headed outside. "Barbarian," they both said at the same time.

The ladies returned to their horses and to their astonishment, found no sign of the men. Talamaya's skin chilled. "Where are they?" she whispered. In her heart, she knew the men wouldn't have left them alone without good reason.

Then she saw it in a vision, some distance from the cave, the men attempted to kill two enraged boars. "Come," she said, "let us be on our way. Poor King Lazarion won't have us warm his bed tonight."

Kersta looked at Talamaya. "They're fighting wild boar?"

Mexia smiled. "I was thinking how we needed a distraction. Amazing how miracles can happen, now and again."

Talamaya and Kersta stared at her. "Nah," they both said and mounted their horses.

At a canter, they headed for the village of Kern, the last place they could safely stay before they ventured through Elan Pass.

T<small>ALAMAYA</small> <small>STUDIED</small> the town as they drew close. Still part of the neutral zone, dwarves, elves, and humans from the three major kingdoms visited and dwelled in peace here.

Cluttered with mostly one-story buildings, there was no uniformity in the materials or style of the abodes mostly owing to the different inhabitants' taste in workmanship and materials. Mud, thatch-roofed homes squashed up against stone houses. Some of the buildings were built of neatly squared bricks. Three two-story buildings stood out amongst the shorter dwellings. The first of these was the tavern for lodging and food.

The ladies headed straight for the tavern in the center of town. But when they entered the two-story stone building, a dwarf several inches shorter than the women greeted them with a stern look and a gruff voice. "What do ye want?"

Talamaya tilted her chin down and considered the bearded man. Black beady eyes glared back at her. He folded his arms and raised his chin higher.

"We wish lodging for the night, sir," Talamaya said.

"Women don't stay here."

"Where may we seek lodging then?"

Though she'd ridden a horse since she was old enough to, the thought of sitting one more second in the saddle made her want to risk walking the rest of the way to Lanai.

"The merchant, Salden, may allow ye to rest at his place for a price. If not in his house, the stable, mayhap. 'Tis the last two-story house that lies at the end of the main road through Kern."

He stared at Malachon's amulet resting at Talamaya's throat and frowned. "Where have I seen that before?"

"A great Damarian knight gave it to me to wear for protection."

"Malachon? The mad knight?"

"No longer." Talamaya turned with her friends and headed for the door.

"It won't protect ye either, if ye seek the scepter," he grunted.

Talamaya turned. "Who says we seek the scepter?"

His eyes narrowed to nearly slits. "Malachon treated me well, of all the uppity knights of Damar. He wouldn't have given it to anyone for any reason, unless..." He scratched his wooly brown hair that reached to his elbows. "Unless he deemed ye pure of heart and needed protection on the quest."

"A woman would not risk such a dangerous venture."

His white pearly teeth glistened in the bed of dark whiskers. "Ye are of the Damar. Women there are kept in chains, but ye, ye are different somehow." He wriggled his bushy brows banded together in a bridge across his nose.

The notion both the barbarian king and this dwarf of Kern thought the Damarian men kept their women enslaved irritated Talamaya to such a degree, she clutched her staff making her knuckles whiten in anger.

Mexia touched her shoulder. "Come, we're tired. Let us find shelter."

Talamaya nodded and left the lodging without a backward glance at the dwarf. "I cannot believe so many feel our men rule us."

Mexia smiled and wrapped her arm around Talamaya's shoulders and gave her a light embrace. "Yes, how can they think such a thing? Only this morning, I considered how before long, my father would marry me off to some gentleman whether I wished it or not."

"Yes, and as for me," Kersta broke in, "my father warned me to choose amongst my three gentleman suitors, or he would make the choice for me."

Talamaya shook her head. "If I am able to retrieve the scepter, I will return it to my father's rule. But on one condition...there will be some major changes in the woman's role in Damar."

Mexia laughed. "Dear princess, do you not see, there already has been?"

They mounted their horses and headed toward the two-story building where lanterns illuminated a sign swinging slightly in the breeze.

"And what, pray tell, has changed, my friend?" Talamaya asked.

Kersta laughed. "You're right, of course, Mexia. Why, no Damarian woman has ever met Modi, for one."

Talamaya sighed. "Except for Aralias."

"And no Damarian woman has ever spoken with the barbarian king," Mexia added.

Talamaya's lips inched up.

"And no Damarian women have ever traveled on a quest like this before."

Talamaya turned to Kersta. "Except Aralias."

"So you see, dear princess," Mexia said, "already the tide of change moves in our favor. If we're able to bring home the scepter, the odds are your father will have to make sweeping changes in the house of Sal. If not, he'll lose face."

"The men won't like this."

"You only *now* considered this?" Mexia asked.

"Yes. I had only wished to keep my father as our ruler because my family's rule has maintained peace and prosperity for a thousand years. Only recently have we had problems with the barbarians at our borders. But I never realized how much my, or any Damarian woman for that matter, bringing the scepter home could affect the balance of power between men and women." She smiled. "Though, it's certainly about time."

When they reached the merchant's house, Talamaya slipped off her saddle. "Wait here, ladies. If you are like me, if he has no room for us, you'll never be able to mount your horses again tonight." She walked stiffly to the door, then knocked.

A dwarfish man opened the door and frowned at her. "Aye?" He shifted his gaze to Mexia and Kersta.

"We seek lodging, good man. We have coin to pay for it."

"Come in." He motioned inside.

"And our horses?"

He said to a young boy, "Fetch the horses. Feed, water, and bed them down for the night."

Talamaya waved at her companions to join her.

Within minutes, he walked them down a long hall, then stopped before a door. Pulling it open, he motioned inside. "In here ye may sleep." He stepped into the room and lighted a lantern.

"Thank you."

"My wife will prepare morning meal at dawn."

Once the man closed the door to the room, the ladies hurried to pull off their garments. The large bed easily would accommodate the three of them. Sleep was all any of them wished more than anything else in the world.

They washed some of the dust off their skin using a basin of water provided for guests. Wearily, they pulled the covers aside, then crawled into bed. Mexia extinguished the candlelight, and Talamaya drew the covers underneath her chin.

"This may be the last comfortable bed we sleep in until our return," Talamaya said, then shut her eyes.

Mexia turned onto her side, making the mattress rock like a ship on unsettled seas.

Kersta snored in response and Mexia and Talamaya chuckled.

Talamaya rubbed her temple. Would their knights catch up to them in the morning? Then what? Og would certainly try to have them sent back to the palace. If the ladies woke too late, the men undoubtedly would overtake them.

Just as Talamaya's mind relaxed before she drifted off to sleep, the door opened a crack with a slight creak. She opened her eyes and stared at the opening where a dwarven lady stood, the candlelight casting light on her dark beard.

"My lady," the woman whispered.

"Yes?" Talamaya responded.

"May I speak with ye?"

"Certainly."

The woman drew close to the bed, then dropped to her knees. "A scout from the Damarian palace came an hour before ye and said thirty knights would seek food for morning meal. I inquired if they could help me with a task. He said they had the most ponderous of journeys to make and nothing could make them deviate from it." Her words turned to sobs.

Talamaya took the dwarf's stubby hands in her own and held them tightly, attempting to reassure her. "What is it you wished of them?"

"My daughter was taken to the dwarven mines. We are half-dwarven, my lady, but one of the dwarves in the mines took a fancy to Alist. But she loves another. The one who runs the tavern."

Talamaya struggled with the notion. She had to get the scepter quickly, yet, she wished to help return the daughter to her mother. If she were a mother, wouldn't she wish the same?

The dwarven woman spoke again. "I recognized the king's seal on your horse's saddle. Rather, my son did. Ye are of the royal house of Sal. I'd hoped ye could convince the knights to help us when they come through in the morning."

Talamaya squeezed the woman's hands. "I cannot promise you anything. But I'll do my best to have your daughter returned."

The woman kissed Talamaya's hands, handed her a map of the dwarves' caves, and thanked her all the way to the door, then hurriedly shut it on the way out.

Talamaya closed her eyes again. Though getting the scepter was uppermost in her mind, if she was able, shouldn't she at least make an attempt to rescue the dwarf's daughter?

Sleep came slowly that eve, but in that sleep another vision manifested itself.

The damp cold air and the smell of wet earth surrounded Talayama. In the distance, the sound of rocks crashing and dwarves cursing and shouting filled her ears. Suddenly, she felt hemmed in, suffocating, fearful of being buried alive.

8

B efore the rays of sun filtered through the burlap sack curtains hanging crooked against the wall, Talamaya dressed.

Kersta peered at her with a sleepy eye. "Is it already time to rise? I feel as though I had too much wine last night in celebration. Did I?"

Talamaya shook her head. "Wake our sleepy friend. It is time to grab a sweet cake, then head into the dwarven mines of Danate."

Kersta bolted upright. "I studied Malachon's map after we left Modi's cave. The mines are at least an hour's ride out of our way."

"We'll make time."

"What has happened now?" Kersta rolled out of bed.

Mexia groaned and rubbed the sleep from her eyes. "Why is it that I hear all this talking so early in the morn?"

"The princess wishes to view the gem mines before we journey any further to Lanai."

Mexia touched the purple stone at her throat. "At Danate?

Disagreeable dwarves. They charged Father twice what the jewel was worth."

Talamaya smiled. "Are you always this grouchy when you fall out of bed first thing in the morning?"

Mexia unbraided her hair. "A morning person, I am not." She combed out her hair, then proceeded to rebraid it.

Kersta smiled. "I see we shall learn many things about each other on this journey. For one, the princess wishes the barbarian king's kiss."

Talamaya threw a pillow at her, making the two ladies laugh. "Hurry, ladies. You're taking longer than even my brother does to go on a hunt."

"Why are we going to the mines, my lady?" Mexia asked, as she hurriedly pulled on her boots.

Kersta answered for Talamaya. "We're seeking to free a dwarfling from a particular dwarf's greedy grasp. Am I not right, princess?"

Talamaya refastened her braids close to her head and grabbed her cloak. "You are right, Kersta. Though I don't think I'll ever get used to you reading my mind."

They both paused to look at Mexia who grabbed her cloak and turned to see the expressions on their faces. "What?"

"Exactly what power do you possess?" Talamaya asked.

Mexia shrugged.

Talamaya grabbed her staff and the ladies retrieved theirs.

Kersta said, "Perhaps she's a late bloomer, my lady."

WITH SUGAR CAKES IN HAND, the ladies rode to the end of town, then headed east toward the mountains ringing the neutral zone to the northeast. When they reached the first of the caves, a sign posted at the opening warned them, "Danate Mines. Trespassers stay out!"

Talamaya finished eating her cake, then dismounted. "I must alert you, ladies, a welcoming committee is nearly upon us." She and the others tethered their horses to a tree, but Talamaya couldn't suppress the dread she felt in going into the caves this time.

They grabbed their staffs and headed quickly into the cave. Well-lighted, the purple gems sparkled with sprinkles of water in clusters across the otherwise moss-covered walls. A musty odor permeated the air from the constant groundwater that seeped down the walls and through the ceiling. Grumbled voices and heavy footfall echoing off the walls some distance away warned of the impending miners' arrival.

"Where are they?" Mexia whispered.

"They're coming." Talamaya headed down one corridor, then switched off to another.

"How do you know the way?"

"The girl's mother gave me a map and marked where she thought she was imprisoned."

"Halt!" a dwarf shouted, his war hammer held threateningly above his head as he trudged toward them as fast as he could from an adjoining tunnel.

Soon he was joined by three more blocking the path Talamaya wished to go. She folded her arms. "Is this not where the Damarians buy gemstone?"

"Why didn't ye say ye wanted to buy gems?"

"I have been told the best quality is this way." She pointed to the path she wished to go.

He glanced back that way, then looked at her again. "Who told ye that?"

"A gem dealer. But it is my money and I wished to see the gems for myself."

He eyed her warily.

She raised her brows at him. "What? You believe three help-less women would be capable of stealing gems from such strong dwarves like yourselves?"

He looked back at the path she chose and one of the men shifted nervously on his feet.

"Either that, or I shall see the dwarven mines farther south." She touched the burgundy crystal at her throat. "I like their gemstones, too." She motioned to Mexia's amulet. "But I like my dear friend's stone also. And that came from here."

"All right. Don't touch anything!" He led them through the tunnel, pointing at clusters of the crystal glistening in the lantern light. She touched it despite his warning, not out of spite, but just a natural reaction, the beauty of the crystals luring her. Then she motioned to continue on their way.

After shaking her head at all the gems the dwarf pointed out along the entire length of the tunnel, they finally reached the end of the passage where a door barred their path. The dwarf growled, "Never have I met such a picky human."

"Female," another grumbled.

"All right," the first said, "that's enough, human. Ye are out of here."

Talamaya touched the wall as she thought she heard the rocks rumble. "Is there a cave-in?" Her heart thundered. To be buried alive...

She turned her head in the direction of the entrance of the cave, wanting to dash outside into the fresh air. But her mind warred with her over Alist. She was this close and couldn't leave her to her fate now.

The dwarves shuffled their feet as if trying to decide which was the lesser of two threats, a cave-in, or the human women, who left on their own might steal from them. Then with war hammers raised, they ran past the ladies to another tunnel.

"A cave-in ought to keep them busy," Mexia said, reaching for the door. She twisted the handle and swung the door open, while the others readied their staffs.

Inside, a dwarf paced across the floor in a small cavern and behind him, another door cut into an adjacent wall.

"Who are ye?" he shouted out in surprise. Before he could grab his weapon, Talamaya darted across the floor. Slamming her staff into his chest, she knocked him to the floor with a jolt. He grunted and passed out.

The three women stared at him. Kersta whispered, "What did you do to him?"

"I hit him, like I would any man who threatened me bodily harm."

Mexia reached down and touched his cheek. "He's breathing."

"Hurry, then we must free the dwarf girl."

They dashed across the floor to the next door. Kersta yanked at it, but found it locked. Before Talamaya could react, Mexia ran back to the guard and searched through his garments for a key. Soon she jiggled a ring of keys in her hand, then she ran back to the door. Shoving one of the keys into the keyhole, she twisted.

The lock ground open and Talamaya pulled the door aside. Inside, they found a kitchen, not a prison as Talamaya had assumed they'd find. A young dwarf woman stirred a pot of some kind of broth over a fire. She turned with a start to see Talamaya and her companions, her blue eyes widening.

"Are you Alist?"

The girl nodded. Talamaya motioned to her to come. "Hurry, your mother has sent us to bring you home."

"Oh, oh," the girl cried out with joy, not being able to say anything more as she dashed across the floor to join her, sending the ladle clattering to the floor.

Talamaya led the way while Kersta stayed with Alist in the middle of the party and Mexia watched their back.

"They'll never let me leave," the girl whispered.

"They have no choice," Talamaya whispered back.

When they reached the place the dwarves first met them, a dwarf slightly taller than the rest, stepped into their path. "My men say ye come for gems." He nodded at Alist. "I see ye have my special gem. Ye pay for her?"

"She isn't yours to sell." Talamaya readied her staff.

His beady eyes tightened with anger. "Ye cannot have her."

"She isn't yours to have."

"Ye think ye can get by me then?"

"Another cave-in!" a dwarf shouted in panic from a tunnel some ways away.

"If you don't let us go, your gem mine will be a pile of rubble," Mexia warned.

Talamaya steadied her staff, but she couldn't squash the need to leave the cave at once.

The dwarf eyed Mexia warily. "Ye are not wizards." He motioned for one of his dwarves to take care of Talamaya.

Certain his war hammer would shatter her staff, she cringed when he struck it with dwarfish might. To her astonishment and everyone else's, his hammer split in two. The vibration jolted his arm, and he cried out, jumping back.

The leader of the dwarves stepped back. "Ye are wizards?" he growled. Turning to the girl, he snarled, "She's not worthy of being my wife. A lousy cook. Be off with the likes of ye."

The women maneuvered around the dwarves, their ale breaths and odorous clothes making the women wrinkle their noses in disgust as they attempted to back out of the cave.

When they were again in the fresh air, Kersta and Mexia helped Alist onto Mexia's horse. Then the women mounted their ponies and headed back to the village of Kern.

"What happened back there?" Kersta asked, her voice ragged.

"You mean with regard to my staff?"

"Yes."

Talamaya took a steadying breath. "Only one thing I can think of. Modi gave us a little going away present."

Kersta ran her hand over her staff. "Do you think mine will do the same thing?"

"Only time will tell."

Kersta gave an evil grin. "Maybe now you could best Hauk. Would he not be surprised?"

"It would not be the same. Skill is one thing. Using special powers to give you an advantage, another. Of course on our journey, I would prefer to have the advantage."

Her companions smiled back at her.

Then she and Kersta turned to Mexia. She shrugged. "I don't know. I had a thought that if we could distract the dwarves enough, they would leave us alone."

"Like the wild boars distracted the barbarians?" Talamaya asked.

"No more guessing at what you can do, eh, Mexia?" Kersta smiled.

"Now what, princess? Do we finally get on with our quest?" Mexia asked.

"As soon as we take Alist home."

"I cannot thank ye enough, my friends, for helping me." Alist sighed heavily. "That idiot Mendon planned to marry me tonight, when I was already betrothed to his brother, the tavern keeper."

"His *brother*?" Talamaya shook her head.

When they arrived in town, Talamaya motioned to the horses tied up to the hitching rail at Alist's parents' home.

"Our men," Talamaya said. "They were supposed to breakfast at Alist's home. They cannot know that we are here. Alist, we will leave you off here."

"But, my mother...my father, even my betrothed will give ye something for saving me."

"Tell them to wish us well on our journey."

Alist waved goodbye to them, then turned and ran back toward the house. But as Talamaya and her friends headed out of town, she glimpsed the sight of the golden horse, and the man who rode it, tall, grand, handsome as ever, his golden hair tied in a knot at the back of his head. As he entered the main avenue, his men followed behind.

She kicked her horse at a gallop and rode out of town with the ladies rushing to keep up.

When they cleared the village limits, Kersta said, "You saw him again. The king. Is he following us?"

"I fear he seeks the scepter, too."

Kersta glanced back. "He saw us and for an instant wished to chase you down. For an instant. Better judgment made him lead his men to the tavern for food and drink. But that's *not* where he wished to go." Kersta looked over at Talamaya and seeing she waited for more news on the barbarian king, added, "He seems to be rather frustrated, where you're concerned."

A sense of heart-warming satisfaction filled Talamaya all at once. Pleased she could entice him in such a way, but keep him at bay at the same time, gave her a strange sense of power. Had reaching womanhood given her that strength?

She patted her horse, but her thoughts focused on Lazarion's smooth chest as he'd pulled his tunic over his head in the light of the fluctuating flame. She took a deep breath. If he'd stopped her from retreating from him in Kern, then what? Would he have kissed her hand again before they parted? She touched her lips with the tip of her finger. Or would he have pushed for more than that this time? She glanced over to see Kersta smiling at her. *Quit reading my thoughts!*

Kersta laughed. "Sorry, my lady. This is a side of you I have never known. It brings a cherry coloring to your cheeks. Quite pretty, really."

"We're still close enough to home, that I could send you back there."

Kersta shook her head. "You need me, so the soothsayer said."

Mexia shook her head. "What am I missing this time, ladies?"

For several miles, they rode through piney woods. When they reached the lower level of Elan Pass, the mountains rose high above them, the peaks barely visible in the snow-laden clouds.

Talamaya dismounted. "Already I can feel the air grow colder. Smell the crispness in the air? We must change into our woolen garments."

Mexia's eyes grew big. "Out here? In front of the gods and everyone?"

Kersta pulled off her cape. "There's not a soul out here, but the three of us." She glanced over at Talamaya who watched them but listened for sounds of anything unusual. "Is that not true, my lady?"

Talamaya yanked off her cloak. "Yes, it's true. But we'll find trouble ahead soon enough."

Mexia stared at her. "I'm not sure I like that you can see things that are going to happen." She pulled off her cloak. "Will you not tell us?"

"White devil wolves, but something else exists in the snow, too. I cannot make it out, but it's there. Waiting."

"But we make it safely through to the other side. You do see this, do you not?"

"Yes, we'll make it to Wildwood Forest."

She pulled off her skirt, then slipped the white wool one over one leg, then the other. Pulling it up to her waist, she tightened it with a leather belt. Flipping her cape to the reverse side, she was instantly cloaked in white.

When the three had finished dressing, they remounted their horses.

Talamaya paused. "We'll become separated in the snowstorm, ladies. I wish for you to wait for me beyond the pass."

Mexia shook her head and tightened her grip on her reins. "We cannot leave you behind, my lady. We go together or not at all. Modi said so."

"We'll become separated, ladies. There's nothing we can do about it. I promise you, I'll meet you where the snow line ends, beyond the pass. Make a campfire to warm us after our trek through the mountains and wait for me. For now, we must stay together.

"The wolves haven't had enough to eat in recent days. Though we're not as meaty as other creatures, in a pinch, we'll suffice for their morning meal if we don't keep our wits about us," Talamaya said.

She nudged her horse forward and took a deep breath. She'd never envisioned she'd have to fight her way through the pass alone. The thought chilled her even more than the cold air that clung to her cape, forming ice crystals across the white wool.

Her breath and her horse's produced puffs of smoke as they entered Elan Pass.

9

For twenty minutes, the ladies rode at a walk along the snow-covered trail. Only in places did Talamaya catch glimpses of ice where the snow had blown away. She wondered then if they rode on top of a sheet of frozen water. She quashed the growing anxiety rising in her heart.

Snowflakes fell lightly at first, but when they reached higher elevations, the white crystals turned into blankets of blinding snow. The air smelled fresh like it had been born brand new only minutes before.

Above the sound of the wintry wind whipping through the jagged peaks of the pass, Talamaya swore she heard a low growl, then two more. "The wolves...they surround us, ladies."

Their horses softly whinnied their distress. When the first of the wolves pounced, Talamaya swung her staff. She struck it hard, sending it flying with the impact. A yelp, then silence followed.

A wolf attacked Kersta, and she used a similar maneuver with the same result. The wolves retreated slightly, blending with the snow-covered boulders.

Her voice shaking, Kersta said, "You're right, my lady. Modi has aided us well."

"Modi," the word whispered on the frosty breeze.

Talamaya shivered. What evil lurked in the cold surrounding them, unseen, and unpredictable, deadly? "Go, ladies. Head through the pass as quickly as you're able."

A slight rumbling underfoot made the horses balk.

"Mexia?"

"The wolves won't like the earth shaking, princess."

"Good. Ride, ladies. I'll be right behind you."

The growls of the wolves vanished as the dark brown tail of Mexia's horse swishing in the breeze disappeared from Talamaya's sight. She nudged her pony to catch up to the others, but a low groan met her ears. She pulled her horse in the direction of the noise.

"Watch out, blast ye!"

She recognized at once the short, thick tongue and brusque voice of a dwarf. "Where are you?" she whispered.

"Come, no closer, ye," he threatened.

"I'm not here to harm you."

"Ye will steal my spirit away. Off with ye or I'll split your skull with Ren."

She couldn't see him in the blinding snow. How could he see her? "I am Damarian, from the royal family of Sal. I mean you no harm."

"Ye nearly trampled me with your snow beast!"

Why didn't he wield his hammer at her? "Are you injured?"

He grunted in response.

She slid from her horse. Using caution, she approached the direction his voice had come. "I am Princess Talamaya from Damar. I have just come from the village of Kern. Do you know Mendon there?"

"Mendon." He glowered at her.

"And Alist," she quickly added.

"Alist." He grumbled under his breath. "Ye are not a snow spirit?"

When the figure of the dwarf came into view, half buried in the snow, she tried to rush forth. Concerned he was injured beyond her healing capabilities, she trudged through the snow mass piled up around him as quickly as she could. Crystals hung from his brown whiskers where his breath moistened his beard.

"How are you hurt?" She laid her staff to the side, then began to dig the snow away from him, her heart beating wildly, the fear whatever danger existed in the pass could attack at any time plaguing her.

Tugging at his war hammer, the dwarf tried to wriggle free of the snow. "The wolves got a bit feisty."

When she'd freed his legs, she found one soaked with blood. She pulled a healing pack from the inside of her cape pocket. "I will start the healing process, then we must go."

"Well, hurry it up, woman."

She couldn't help smiling. There was nothing like earning a dwarf's gratitude.

He gritted his teeth when she applied the compress to his injured leg.

After tying leather straps around the medicated bandage, she reached for his arm and gave him a slight tug. "Can you stand? We must leave here at once. The medication will help your leg to mend quickly, but something evil lurks here in the snow. I wouldn't wish to find out what it is."

The sound of horses snorting behind them as they drew closer, made Talamaya hurry the dwarf as she grabbed her staff. "Come, quickly, someone's behind us. Can you climb onto my saddle?"

"Bring your horse over to this rock."

She did as he ordered, but as soon as he had mounted her horse, the growling began again. Then shouts from men behind her sent icy panic racing through her. Were they Damarian knights? Or the barbarian king and his men?

Yelps from wounded wolves pierced the frigid cold as she imagined the beasts met the sharp ends of the men's swords. Before Talamaya could climb onto her horse, the animal spooked, and charged down the pass.

"Cristana!" she yelled in utter disbelief and frustration.

She ran after the horse trying to keep it within sight as the dwarf hollered, "Stop, ye blasted witless, four-legged..." His words faded into the distance as the horse made its way through the narrow passage at a deadly gallop.

She only hoped when the dwarf made it to her friends at the end of the path—if it didn't throw him from the leather before he got there—her companions wouldn't kill him, thinking he'd harmed her and stolen her horse.

She gripped her staff tighter in her clenched fists. Her leather boots sent powdery snow into gentle ripples with every footfall. Her boots tread silently, except when she stepped on crusted snow, making her flinch. Would whatever evil lurked nearby know exactly where she was? Then what?

Taking an icy breath made her lungs ache from the cold. Her legs cramped from riding and running. She fought the urge to stop to catch her breath. But the panic filling her heart as to what waited for her hidden in the snow, spurred her on.

"Tala," a voice shouted from behind her. She turned but saw only a blur of white. It had to be Lazarion. Had he heard her shouting for her horse?

Running forward again, she knew her only hope was to get through the pass before the wolves amassed for another attack.

"Princess Talamaya," the wind whispered.

She stopped. Standing in the swirling particles of ice crystals stood a creature, her hair, skin, and gowns as white as the snow. Her pale blue eyes shimmered like shards of ice as she gazed at Talamaya. Her pale lips remained unmoved.

Talamaya stood frozen to the spot. What had she read in travelers' journals concerning their experiences as they journeyed through the pass? The woman was a snow goddess who blinded them with her beauty...that's what they all said.

Talamaya's mind grew numb. Her legs quit aching, her breathing slowed. Blinded by the light reflecting off the snow, Talamaya watched, awestruck.

"Talamaya," the creature said. Her lips never moved, only the breeze carried her word to Talamaya's ears.

"Blasted, four-legged, hard-headed mule!" The dwarf's crusty words broke the spell.

Talamaya turned to see the dwarf still riding her horse, returning for her, to her relief.

"Come on! Come on, woman! What are ye waiting for?"

He reached down, his short arm grabbing at her shoulder. With his help, she swung onto the saddle.

After riding back down the pass toward Wildwood Forest for several minutes, the dwarf shook his head. "We should have made our way out of here, by now. It took me half this much time to reach the end of the pass the last time." He tugged at his beard, evidently exasperated.

"You'd already made it that far?"

"Aye, saw two women, dressed like ye. They came after me with staffs like ye carry. With room to maneuver off the rocky path, I was able to turn around and come back for ye."

"Good thing you did."

"Why weren't ye farther along the path? I didn't think I'd have to ride so far back to find ye. And dressed all in white like ye are, I thought ye the snow devil herself."

"I was blinded by the snow."

The white blankets continued to pelt them with fresh snow as if the tears of the enchantress froze as they fell from her mountain peaks. And then Talamaya saw her again. Silent, exquisite, waiting, watching, deadly.

"What is your name, Dwarf?" Talamaya asked.

"Gallant."

If she wasn't so cold and worried about getting free from the pass, she would have laughed. "Gallant, how long were you lying there injured in the snow pass?"

"Several hours. What of it?"

"I wonder if she feels you were hers to keep. Maybe she believes since I saved you, I have to take your place and remain here with her. Only one of us can leave here now, perhaps. Unless, we find something else to appease her."

"Who are ye talking about, woman? Dumbest thing I ever heard."

Gallant kicked the horse to move again, but after another twenty minutes, they'd still made no progress. The sky, ground, and every fragment of space between, was filled with snow. Except for the wind, winter crystals, and the biting cold, nothing else seemed to exist.

"What would the snow enchantress take as a substitute? I believe she feels cheated. What can we give her instead?"

The dwarf grunted.

Talamaya looked back in the direction she thought Lazarion had come from, but there was no sign of him or his men. An overwhelming sense of despair gripped her...an inescapable heart-wrenching hopelessness of ever getting free from the pass. "I wonder what happened to the men who were coming up the path behind us."

"I heard no one."

"No, it was after you'd left. Yet they should have been here by now. It's like we're lost in a blizzard and cannot find our way out of the storm."

"Nonsense. The path is straight ahead. We'll find our way soon."

Talamaya guessed another hour had passed when she finally urged Gallant to stop the horse. "We cannot keep going in circles."

"How do ye know we are going in circles? Nothing looks the same to me."

"Everything looks the same to me." She lifted her flask to her lips and drank of the tea. Suddenly, she could see a clearing in the snow.

"Modi," the enchantress groaned.

Talamaya shook the dwarf's arm. "To the left, Gallant. Take the path to the left."

"I don't see a path there."

"Trust me. I can see the way clear." She added silently, "Just as Modi helped Sir Malachon to see through the fog of his mind with the aid of the tea."

"Blasted, woman, there is no path."

"To the right now."

Despite grumbling his objections, he turned the horse every time she bade him to and after what seemed like hours, they finally glimpsed the clearing. They headed down toward the base of the mountain where the grass grew green.

Talamaya breathed a deep sigh of relief as she spied the trees of Wildwood forest, and smelled the campfire burning that would warm her to the core of her being.

Then her stomach churned with concern. Were her friends all right?

As they drew nearer to the fire, they saw no signs of them.

When they pulled into the camp, she dismounted. "Here, let me assist you." She reached up to help the dwarf down.

He groused at her. "I need no help from a woman." He jumped down from the horse and snarled in pain.

She turned her attention to the woods. "Mexia! Kersta!"

"We're coming, my lady!" Kersta shouted, running from the forest carrying more kindling.

Before Talamaya could say another word, Mexia and Kersta dropped their sticks and embraced her warmly.

"What happened?" Mexia asked. They looked over at the dwarf and frowned. "He came back with your horse. We feared he'd—"

"Watch your tongue, woman," he growled.

Talamaya shook the snow from her cloak. "Wolves had injured him. I found him half frozen in the snow."

Mexia said, "But he came here with your horse, without you."

"Wolves spooked Cristana and she left me behind. How long have we been separated?"

"Only a few minutes. We were gathering more wood for the fire." Kersta pulled Talamaya to the flame. "You're half frozen, my lady."

"You need to change," Mexia said.

They all looked at the dwarf.

He shrugged. "Don't mind me."

Kersta shook her head and motioned for the dwarf to be gone. "We no longer need you."

"He can stay with us a while longer, ladies. We have to make sure his leg heals adequately."

They looked down at his leg.

Talamaya quickly added, "We'll erect a quick shelter between the trees. We must hurry. The barbarian king follows close behind."

The dwarf smiled. "Who is the barbarian? Your father?"

Talamaya's face grew hot. They'd have to watch their tongues in the future when they referred to the barbarian king while the dwarf was in their presence. "Of course not."

With her luck, Gallant was a friend to Lazarion and would tell him what she thought of him. She shuddered from the thought, or the cold, she wasn't sure which.

The ladies tied their cloaks to trees, then Talamaya changed into her green gown. Then they grabbed their cloaks while Mexia headed for the campfire. After she doused the flames, they heard horses approaching from Elan Pass.

"Come, ladies, we must go." Talamaya headed for her horse.

"What about him?" Mexia asked, pointing at the dwarf.

Talamaya turned back toward him. "Do you wish to ride with us?"

Kersta groaned. "He'll slow us down. And his gruff speech won't make our journey any the more pleasant."

"Debt of gratitude," Gallant replied. "I stay with ye, woman, until I repay my debt."

"You saved me when you came back for me," Talamaya said. "You owe me nothing."

"Orc dung. Not once did I raise my war hammer in your defense, did I?"

"No."

The ladies climbed into their saddles.

"Then I have not repaid my debt."

"Come, then, we must go."

The dwarf mounted Talamaya's horse. "Ye don't want to travel through Wildwood Forest...not just the three of ye women."

"We have you, remember?" Kersta said, her voice haughty.

"I journeyed through here a fortnight ago. The dark elves have taken a foothold in the woods."

"Dark elves?" Talamaya urged her horse into the forest.

"They live on the continent of Albion, I understand. But as far as I know, they've never come to Inherian."

"I have seen them with my own two eyes. The dark elves." He waved his war hammer at the trees. "A dark-haired version of their cousins, the elves of Mesa, they are the opposite in temperament. Ill tempered. Ye meet them and they'll kill ye first then ask who ye be, afterward." He chuckled at his own dark humor.

"Do you wish to stay behind then, Gallant?"

"I told ye, woman. I have a debt to repay. But if it were me, I would not go this way."

"It's the only way to..." Talamaya paused her speech, not trusting the dwarf with their plans. "It's the way we wish to go."

Everyone remained silent while they made their way into the forest. The breeze swished through the pine needles, the pleasant whooshing sound belying the evil that lurked within. The dappled sunlight sprinkled over the ladies' green gowns as they rode deeper into the woods. The fragrance of pinesap scented the air. And birds filled the woods with songs and chatter.

High overhead, a gryphon soared, searching for food, casting a shadow over them briefly. Talamaya glanced up at it.

"Headed for the plain," the dwarf said.

"I have never heard of a dark elf. What else do you know about them?" Mexia asked of him.

"It is best to stay out of their way. They attack on foot with their short swords, wiry and full of the devil. If they now claim the woods to be theirs—"

"The woods are owned by none, but the four-legged beasts that prowl it," Kersta replied.

"Says ye. They say differently."

"How did you manage to travel through it before then?" Kersta asked.

The dwarf grunted. "They busied themselves with bigger prey. They couldn't be bothered with one little dwarf."

"Who was the bigger prey?"

"Amazons."

"The women of the Maken Peninsula?" Talamaya said in disbelief. "They never come this far south of their lands."

"Maybe like ye, they had something they were after that lay in the path somewhere ahead."

Talamaya considered his words. The Amazons never left their home as far as she knew. "What happened to the women?"

"I told ye, I didn't wait to find out."

"You let them fight the dark elves by themselves?" Mexia asked, her voice rising in irritation.

"Have ye seen the Amazons? They probably wiped out half of the elves' kind, by the time they were through with them. They have no love of dwarves either."

Talamaya twisted in her saddle. Something in the woods had changed.

Like the stillness before a storm, she realized then the woods had grown graveyard quiet.

10

"Y"ou sense something is wrong, do you not, Princess Talamaya?" Kersta asked. "I can tell it's on your mind. Shall we dismount?"

"Yes, the woods have grown quiet. Some beast of prey is close by. If the threat is the elf kind and they don't ride horses, we can wield our staffs better against them if we're on foot also."

Talamaya slipped off her horse. Everyone else followed her, dropping to the spongy floor without a sound, except for Gallant's groan as his leg still pained him. The four formed a circle, each facing out as they watched for their foe.

Gallant griped, "I told ye we shouldn't have come through Wildwood."

Suddenly, male elves surrounded the party of three women and one dwarf, three to one. Just like their cousin counterpart in Mesa, they were tall, slender, and stately. They wore suede-like breeches the color of dried pine needles, and thigh-length tunics as green as when the needles still hung fresh on the tree, making them blend with the forest. The elves' nearly black hair was bound behind their heads in long tails, showing off their pointed ears and permanently arched eyebrows. Their eyes, dark as the bowels of an unlighted cave, almond-shaped and otherwise attractive, glowed with hatred.

The short swords each elf held caught the filtered rays of the sun as they twisted the blades back and forth, taunting the women and their dwarf companion.

"Hmpf," Gallant grumped. "That's all they have to throw at us?"

Talamaya fought the urge to punch him with her staff if she hadn't needed him so much. Twelve elves could quickly overcome their small party of four, depending on how skilled the men were at fighting.

Her heart thundered and her palms grew sweaty in anticipation. What were they waiting for?

"I was thinking the same thing myself, my lady," Kersta replied.

"What?" Mexia asked.

Gallant turned to Kersta. "Ye read minds?"

"Yes, dwarf. Even yours."

He gave a look of disdain, then faced the menace before him.

A horse's hooves clip-clopped at a quickened pace as it hurried toward them. Upon the ebony horse rode the most regal of elves. His clothes sparkled in the faint light while a gold belt shimmered at his waist. Like the others, his face wore no whiskers. Despite how youthful he appeared, he seemed to be in charge of the elves on foot as many nodded to him in greeting. His equally dark eyes glowered at the party of humans and their dwarf friend as he seemed to take every bit of the women's appearances in.

Gallant cleared his throat. "A dark elf lord. The minions had to wait for his appearance before they could proceed. Like the tourneys where your knights injure each other for sport and wait until the king is seated to continue. Only in this case, the elves kill their opponent, dead."

"Our jousts are done in sport, not to injure one another," Kersta retorted with bitterness, her words on edge, betraying her nervousness.

"If we take out the lord, will the others give up?" Talamaya whispered to Gallant.

"No, woman. They came here to kill ye, and me, and the others. If they leave any of us alive, they'd be sent away from their people, banished from their society for being cowardly. Not a dark elf quality."

"Then why are they waiting still?"

"The elf lord is curious about us," Gallant replied. "He wonders why three human women, who are obviously not warriors, are traveling with a dwarf alone in Wildwood Forest."

The elf lord unsheathed a long sword and cried out, "*Carunth me, thun ale sease, my lady.*"

"Seems I am wrong. They wish to spare your life, woman, but the rest of our lives are forfeit. He assumes ye are in charge, which means when the rest of us are dead, he will force ye to tell him who ye are and what quest ye are on." The dwarf readied his war hammer. "Come on, ye devils. Let us see who the best of us is!"

Immediately, the elves attacked Mexia, Kersta, and the dwarf, avoiding contact with Talamaya. But as soon as the elves slashed their swords at her companions, Talamaya jumped into the fray.

Thrusting with her staff, she connected with the first elf's chest she could reach. To her astonishment, one swift hit, sent him sprawling to the ground, the life snuffed out of his being in an instant. For a moment, she stared at him, expecting him to jump to his feet as any spry elf would do and return to the fight.

But he remained motionless. She quickly turned her attention to another who thrust his sword at Kersta.

As soon as Talamaya blocked his movement, his sword struck her staff, and shattered. For a moment, he stared at her in disbelief, then he reached for a dagger sheathed at his belt. She struck him once, not hard, as he was slightly beyond a good staff reach, just enough to knock him off his feet. But like the other, he crumpled to the ground, and didn't make a move afterward.

Mexia cried out in pain, the sound of anguish ripping at Talamaya's heart, and she rushed to help her. Mexia dropped to her knees. Her hand gripped her bloodied shoulder. Her eyes glazed over in pain.

Talamaya struck an elf, and then another, sending them both sprawling on their backs. Her back bumped into a body, and she swung around to strike at her foe. Seeing it was Gallant, she turned again to protect Mexia.

As Kersta felled the last of the elves, Gallant ran after the elven lord, who disappeared into the forest at a gallop.

Talamaya dropped to her knees to assist Mexia. "My healing kit will aid her," she said to Kersta as she applied the patch, "but the wound is too deep. Mexia is the best healer amongst us, but she's barely conscious."

"A healer's hut appeared on the map, my lady. Perhaps we can take Mexia there."

"Too deep in the woods. It takes us too far out of our way," the dwarf mumbled as he ran back to the women, having lost the elf on horseback.

Talamaya helped Mexia to her feet. "Help me get her to her horse. We must reach the healer's hut at once."

"Ye will get us all killed," the dwarf said.

"You need not stay with us, Dwarf," Kersta said.

Mexia groaned as they helped her onto her horse.

"What do you say, Gallant?" Talamaya asked, climbing behind Mexia. "Do you continue with us, or will you leave the forest on your own?"

He looked around at the woods, still once again. He stomped over to Talamaya's horse. "I will ride your horse then, woman?"

"Do. We must hurry."

Once he sat in the leather, they maneuvered through the trees while Kersta led the way using the map to guide them. Again, the songbirds sang their alluring tunes and the bugs made their own kind of music. The sounds couldn't have been more welcome, knowing with the pleasant tunes return, the dark elves existed somewhere well away from their location.

"Have you ever been to the healer's hut before, Gallant?"

"Aye. Though I don't know why they call it a hut. It is more like a dwarven home."

Kersta glanced back at Talamaya. "How's she doing, my lady?"

"She has nearly passed out. The healing patch has stopped the blood from flowing from the wound, but it'll take too long for the medication to work. The healer will quicken the process." Talamaya took a deep breath and wrapped her arm tighter around Mexia's waist. "Hold on, dear Mexia. We'll have you in a bed before you know it."

The dwarf grunted. "We could have gone straight through the forest in the time it'll take us to visit the healer's hut and return to the path."

Kersta shook her head. "We should've left him behind, my lady."

"Shh." Talamaya waved her hand to the trail they had just passed. "Do you hear something?"

"The birds and the bugs have begun to sing again."

"No. Something else." Talamaya strained to listen, attempting to hear what sound she thought she'd perceived.

Kersta frowned. "What did you think you heard?"

"Metal striking metal."

"Swords against swords?" Kersta asked.

"Aye, steel against steel, it is," the dwarf said, nodding his head. "Faintly ringing out at the fringe of the forest near where we first entered."

"Between us, our men and Lazarion's, we'll keep the dark elves busy," Talamaya said, relieved they might have some assistance after all.

Gallant scratched his beard. "Why are ye traveling alone if men of the Damar also head in this direction?"

Talamaya glanced over at Kersta who waited for her answer. She turned to Gallant. "They travel too slowly for us."

Kersta smiled at her and nodded.

"Aye. The lot of ye are impatient then."

Talamaya took a deep breath. "When we arrive at the healer's hut, we must eat and rest."

Kersta wrinkled her nose at the dwarf. "I don't suppose you brought your own food with you." She turned to Talamaya. "We don't have enough food to feed him, too."

"We'll make do, Kersta."

"I kill what I eat. Ye don't need to feed me," he grumped.

"Good," Kersta said. "Our cook's sweet bread speaks to me, and I cannot wait to wash it down with some more of Modi's tea."

"Bread?" the dwarf asked, eyeing Kersta's leather saddlebags.

"You said you would kill your own food."

"Not here, when everywhere lurks danger. I would be the prey then, not the beast I meant to eat."

"We cannot share our food with him, princess."

"How far to the hut, Kersta?"

"I know this ploy of yours. When you don't like the subject, you change it." Kersta unfolded the map and measured out the distance with her finger. "He cannot have *my* bread." She paused. "Several more minutes at the slow speed we're traveling."

"Then nudge your horse faster. We must move more quickly. I fear we're being followed."

The party listened as Kersta tucked the map away in her cloak pocket. "The woods are quiet again."

"Yes. The birds ceased their chatter only seconds ago."

Talamaya wished Mexia rode with Kersta. Then she would have stayed behind to stop the dark elves who followed them now. But what if they had been ambushed ahead? Stay together, the best they could...that was the best plan.

An arrow zinged into a tree behind them. Gallant snorted. "They cannot reach us now."

Talamaya shook her head. "They're afraid of our staffs. If they use arrows to bring us down—"

"We're under the healer's protection now." Gallant waved his arm around. "She has a ward spell that circles the whole area several hundred yards from her home."

"A ward spell?"

"Aye, woman. Three wild boar chased me after I killed one of their brethren for dinner. I ran for a short distance, then turned to kill as many of them as I could. They stopped all of a sudden. It was like a glass wall had been erected between us. They snorted and pawed at the ground but couldn't come any closer."

Talamaya glanced back. "I see no sign of them."

"The elf lord probably gathered some of his archers to pick us off, only they didn't get to us in time. He probably figured ye would have been heading on the right path, straight through the forest, and not have taken this detour."

Kersta shook her head. "Good thing that we came this way then."

The dwarf scowled at her. "And when we have to leave? They'll be waiting for us."

"Not that you're afraid, or anything," Kersta responded.

"I'm not afraid of anyone or anything, beast or..." He glanced at her staff. "What is in those staffs of yours? I have never seen an elf keel over dead like that with one blow. They are sinewy devils built to withstand a hell of a fight."

"Modi gave us some extra protection."

"Modi? The soothsayer? Heap of troll's dung."

"You don't believe in her?" Kersta asked.

"Nay. I believe in me, myself. That's what I believe in." He cleared his throat and held up his war hammer to examine it. "So, do ye think Modi could add a bit of spark to the old Ren?"

Kersta laughed. "But you don't believe in her, Dwarf."

He cast a glaring look in her direction, then looked straight ahead.

They walked for several more minutes before they exited the heavy brush and entered a clearing in the woods. The healer's hut sat in the middle of a green glade, one-story high with a wooden roof and thick stone walls. Surrounding the home, the blue minko flower, its five petals fully opened to show off its spotted throat, scented the whole area with its sweet fragrance. A golden flower as brilliant as the sun mixed with these. Hidden nearly from view a shy purple rose peeked out amongst them, adding additional color to the fragrant blossoms.

Kersta hopped off her horse first and rushed over to help Talamaya with Mexia. Gallant jumped from his high mount, and for the first time didn't groan from the wolves' injury to his leg, when his feet hit the ground.

Talamaya glanced over at him. "Are you healed?"

"Aye, seems to be."

"No thanks?" Kersta asked as they helped Mexia to the door.

"The woman knows she is appreciated," he said, disdain evident in his voice.

"Hmpf, and you expect me to share my bread with you for as much gratitude as you show the princess?" Kersta asked.

"He helped us when we were attacked by the dark elves, Kersta," Talamaya said, her voice anxious with concern for Mexia.

Kersta knocked on the door, but Gallant butted past her and shoved it open. "It is a healer's hut, woman. Not a private abode."

They stepped inside and a dark-haired, thin woman hurried out of a back room and greeted them. "Come, bring your companion inside and lay her there in my bed." She hovered over Mexia as they lay her on the mattress. "Have some trouble with the dark elves, I see? They are pesky vermin; best be rid of. If I could, I would—"

"Will Mexia be all right, miss?" Talamaya asked.

"Kralof is my name. She'll be fine. By the morrow, she'll be as good as new. I will serve you a hearty boar stew upon your return." The healer pulled the bandage from Mexia's shoulder.

"Upon our return?"

"Yes, yes. Go find her and bring her here. She has tried for several days to reach my shelter, but they overwhelm her. I can sense her struggles. She's a healer amongst her people, just as your young friend here is a healer. But I knew you'd bring Mexia to me safely." She turned to see Talamaya's eyes wide with confusion. "You're from the adventurers' guild, are you not? You ride with Gallant, so this must be so. Go aid the lady and bring her here."

"Who?"

"A woman from the Maken Peninsula."

Gallant shuffled his feet. "An Amazon?"

"Yes. The dark elves killed her companions some time ago. And only because of her healing powers has she been able to stay alive. But she cannot make it here on her own. Go, go, straight south. Bring her here."

Gallant folded his arms. "I don't rescue Amazon women. They would not pay me the same courtesy."

Talamaya grabbed Kersta's arm. "Come, we'll find the woman and bring her here."

When they rushed out of the home, Gallant followed them, his stubby legs running twice as fast to keep up.

"I thought you didn't wish to come with us," Kersta said.

"I have not paid my debt of gratitude yet. I would not have it said that I let the woman out of my sight. Then if she were to get killed, where would I be? I cannot protect a ghost."

Talamaya smiled. "Come, Gallant, ride Mexia's horse. We'll make sure the Amazon woman isn't too hard on you."

She knew they had to help the woman survive the onslaught of the elves. But she hated to leave Mexia behind, though she realized they could do no more for her.

"I agree, princess. I don't wish to leave her either. But what if we get killed? Then what?" Kersta asked.

Gallant grunted.

"I guess we cannot let that happen then, Kersta."

"The elves will expect us to leave the way we came, not in the opposite direction." Gallant chuckled to see humor in the situation as grave as it was.

The party grew silent as they reached what they imagined to be the outer boundaries of the healer's spell ward to her lands. For several miles they rode through the thick forest, detouring around boulders, sloshing through a rivulet, always heading south. Then the sound of metal hitting metal reached their ears.

"This way," Talamaya said, and galloped her horse toward the sound of the fighting.

In the middle of six dark elves, a woman stood at least six inches taller than any of them. Her golden hair, hanging loosely about her shoulders, whipped around every time she swung at her opponents.

Talamaya and her companions slid from their horses and ran into the midst of the fighting. Gallant's war hammer struck at the first elf he could reach, while Talamaya twisted her staff to strike one who turned to face the new enemy at his back.

"I don't know who you are," the Amazon shouted, "but you're most welcome."

Gallant mumbled something under his breath.

"Even your small friend there."

"I am not small," Gallant argued. He struck another blow at the elf who thrust his short sword at him. "You are just unbelievably tall."

The woman laughed, a deep throaty sound, mixed with relief that she had found companions to help her in her time of need. "Is the healer's hut near?"

"Yes," Talamaya responded, sending a second elf to his knees. "And she told us you needed our help."

"I have been so besieged by these creatures almost constantly. In fighting them, I have been sidetracked so often, I had gotten turned around."

Kersta finished off the last of the elves and Talamaya waved at their horses. "Hurry, we must return at once to the healer's hut. The birds have not begun their singing. Dark elves must still be nearby."

"You sense this, too? It's the only way I have stayed alive for so long. Well, that and because of my curative powers. But every time the woods grew silent, I knew the elves encroached upon my space. By the way, I am Sessel."

"Princess Talamaya and Lady Kersta of Damar. Gallant of Kern," Talamaya offered.

Before the dwarf could climb into the saddle of Mexia's horse, the dark elves swooped down on them from a knoll farther south. With speed and agility, the elves surrounded them, and Talamaya and Kersta dismounted.

"I cannot see how you made it this far, Sessel." Talamaya readied her staff. She silently counted twenty this time.

Kersta nodded. "They sent more because the word must have reached them that Sessel had new companions to fight with her."

Talamaya struck two elves in quick succession, but though her staff gave her a mighty advantage, her movements slowed with the weariness her body felt. In time, she knew, one slowed reaction to a dark elf's thrust of a sword could cause her serious injury. She noticed, too, Kersta had faltered twice while blocking the slashing movement of a sword. They all required rest and food. There was no way they could outlast the hoards sent to attack them. If they managed to kill these, a new wave would surely be the death of them.

"I must sharpen my sword," Sessel said. "Though it can still separate a dark elf's head from his scrawny neck, it takes twice the effort to do so now."

"And we must eat," Gallant said. "I can hear my stomach grumbling from lack of food even over the sound of the swords clanking."

"We must rest," Kersta said. "I almost wish I was Mexia lying in the healer's hut."

"You have a friend who's injured?" Sessel asked.

"Yes, another lady companion from Damar."

"Ah. We'll see her soon, then."

Gallant snorted. "The healer promised us boar stew upon our return. At this rate—"

"Shh," Talamaya prompted, knocking down another elf. "Do you hear something?"

"Other than the thud this elf made as he fell dead to the ground—"

The elves held their weapons at bay for a moment, their attention riveted to the woods around them. Everyone stilled their actions momentarily.

The ground rumbled beneath their feet and Talamaya worried, her stomach clenching with concern. If they were dark elf archers, they were doomed.

11

"Look!" Kersta shouted, pointing to the men on horseback, suddenly appearing from the green of the trees. "The barbarian king and his men!"

Gallant laughed, then swung at the elf who made a stab at him once more. "So Lazarion is the barbarian king you refer to."

Sessel laughed, too. "I have never heard him called that. He has visited our people many times. I have always thought him chivalrous."

Talamaya knew one of them was bound to slip. Her skin heated as she grew concerned the word would slip from the dwarf's lips to Lazarion's ear.

Lazarion motioned to his archers. Immediately, arrows sung through the air at an incredible speed making a whapping sound as they met their mark in elves' chests and backs.

Kicking his horse, Lazarion rode toward the party of four. He extended his arm, offering Talamaya the opportunity to ride with him as his men decimated the dwindling number of elves still left alive.

"I have my own horse, thank you, sire." She hurried off toward her own mount.

Kersta ran for her horse and Gallant headed for Mexia's.

Sessel smiled. "May I ride with the small one?"

"Gallant, is the name."

She chuckled. "Gallant, then."

"If ye must."

"We'll escort you back to the healer's hut," Lazarion said, swinging his horse next to Talamaya's. "We only just came from there. The healer said you were in need of rescue."

"Sessel was."

"Yes, and once you sought to help her, you were in trouble."

Without looking at the king, Talamaya said, "Thank you for the rescue." She couldn't look at him. Every time she did, her heart beat out of control. She had no time for such nonsense. The notion he was after the scepter didn't sit well with her either. There was no way she could allow the barbarian king to claim it for his people.

"I saw you briefly in Elan Pass. What happened to you? I called out your name, but you vanished."

"I heard you call my name, but I never saw any sign of you. The snow blinded me."

"Had I known you and your lady friends were going that way, I would have escorted you through there."

"There was no need."

He patted his horse's mane as if he were trying to think of what to say next. Finally, he said, "My men were besieged by wild boar when they waited for you at Modi's cave. After they killed the boar, they returned for you, but your horses were gone, to their surprise. I thought we had agreed you would stay with us for the night...for your protection."

"Again, I say there was no need. And only *you* had agreed to our staying with you, as I recall."

When he didn't speak for several seconds, she looked at him

to see him studying her face as if he were remembering every detail or trying to read her mind.

"Are you from Langdon?" he asked, his brow furrowed as if he was concerned she might be.

"On the continent of Albion? No. Why do you ask?"

"A coven of wizards rule and train there. I wondered if you might be sorceresses. Of course, at first, I considered you were Damarian women, but the women there wouldn't be allowed to leave the castle grounds without an escort. Nor would they have been trained in weaponry. And from what I understand, they are not allowed to see Modi. So then my thought was, where were you from really? How else could you manage to survive so well in the wilderness if you were not mages?"

"Do you think of me a lot?" Talamaya looked over to see Lazarion's reaction to her words said in jest.

His mouth inched up as if he couldn't contain his amusement. His eyes sparkled with mirth. Changing the subject, he said, "I understand you rescued Alist from the dwarf, Mendon, in the dwarfish mines near the village of Kern. We ate at the tavern there. The keeper was extremely grateful to you, though he couldn't understand why you left so quickly without his being able to pay you a reward."

"I did what was right. I sought no reward."

"You don't run from *me*, do you?

"Of course not."

"Who do you run from then?"

"No one."

He rubbed his smooth chin. "The Damarian knights were in town as well."

"Why would you think we're running away from anyone?"

He chuckled. "Forgive my saying so, but when you saw us arrive in Kern, I detected a bit of a rush in your rapid departure."

"And?"

"I wondered then if the Damarian knights sought to return you home. Why else would you not travel together?"

"Because we are not Damarian possibly?"

Gallant stifled a laugh. Talamaya attempted to ignore him as Lazarion glanced back at him.

"How are you, old friend?" Lazarion bowed his head to Gallant.

"Fine, your lordship."

"And the family?"

Gallant grumbled under his breath.

"Tell me, Gallant, have you learned much about your female companions?"

Gallant nodded. "Sessel is from the Maken Peninsula."

"This I already know. What about Tala here?"

Gallant's bushy brows rose. He cleared his throat. "I owe her a debt of gratitude."

"She saved your life?" The king raised the question in such an incredulous fashion, he instantly aroused her ire. "Tell me, how did she do such a thing?"

"More dark elves," Talamaya said.

The men readied their arrows as Lazarion and his soldiers formed a circle around the women and Gallant to protect them.

"We are nearly to the protected area," Gallant said. "Just a few more feet."

Arrows zinged through the woods as the party continued forward. But once they were within the protected ward, the party relaxed again.

"So tell me, Gallant, how did the lady manage to rescue you?"

"I was wounded by white devil wolves. She healed my wound and bade me ride the rest of the way through the mountain pass on her horse."

"She was alone?"

"Do you never tire of asking questions?" Talamaya asked.

Lazarion smiled. "Not when they have to do with the most mysterious of women."

Then she worried, would the dwarven girl, Alist, have told Lazarion who Talamaya really was? Talamaya twisted her reins in her hands. When he caught her action, she quickly stiffened her back. "We're back at the healer's hut. I must see to Mexia."

"I'll go with you."

She looked at him in disbelief.

"Three of my men were wounded. That's the reason I came here in the first place. Then I was told you needed rescuing." He jumped from his saddle and hurried to help Talamaya down from hers. "We'll see to our wounded, together."

"What? Are you afraid I'll 'run' away again?"

He smiled at her, his hand nudging her elbow, guiding her into the house. "You would not leave your companion behind."

Her whole body heated with that one little touch, annoying her. "You're right, of course."

"That much, I can speculate about you. The rest, is still unknown."

Mexia smiled at her as Talamaya hurried to her bed. "How are you doing, dear Mexia?"

"Oh, my lady, much better. My head swims with the medications I have been given, but by tomorrow morning, I can ride again."

Lazarion was watching them, then he turned to the healer. "And my men?"

"The poison tipping the dark elves' arrows was nearly deadly, my liege. Your men won't be ready to leave until at least tomorrow eve."

He folded his arms. "Are you certain?"

"Yes, of course, sire."

"Should not Mexia stay until then, too?"

The healer smiled. "If you wish the ladies to remain in your company for longer, *you* will have to convince them. Not me."

"They should not leave here with the danger of the elves all about."

"I agree, sire. But the ladies will do what they must."

Talamaya considered the weakened condition of Lazarion's men. Their gaunt eyes and pale skin made her shiver. There was no way she could risking losing her friends to some deadly poison. "We'll ride out together, when you're ready, sire."

He offered a small, conceited smile. "Good. Let us eat a meal together now." He ran his hand across his stomach in a circular motion. "I'm famished."

Talamaya looked at Mexia.

"I have already eaten, my lady."

Sessel stepped into the hut.

"Welcome," the healer said.

"Thank you. If you had not sent the ladies to my aid, I would never have made it."

"And me," Gallant retorted, stalking into the healer's house with Kersta. "We have seen to the horses, but where is the stew that we were promised?"

The healer motioned outside. "If everyone will find seating outside and some of your men help me to serve the food, we'll sup out there. The wounded have already been fed."

Not long after everyone took their seats on blanket rolls in several small groups, the women, Gallant, and the king sat together.

"What do you plan to do now, Sessel?" Lazarion asked.

"I'll return home. If some of your men can escort me to the fringe of Wildwood, I can make it home from there."

"And you, Gallant?"

"I stick with the princess."

Lazarion smiled broadly. Talamaya got a glimpse of the look

of pure delight on his face, then she locked her gaze onto her bowl of soup. Gallant had not once called her princess or Talamaya the whole time they'd been together. Only *woman*. Now of all times...

"Ahem." Lazarion winked at Talamaya, then poked his bread into his stew.

Did he know who she was really? Or did he assume she was a princess from somewhere else? She frowned. He had to have known. But why didn't he say so? Maybe he was still confused as to why she and her friends rode through the wilderness alone. Kersta nodded.

Talamaya raised her brows. As soon as she could, she'd learn from Kersta what else he had been thinking.

"I'm curious about the route you take, *princess*," the king said. "I wonder if we are to ride in much the same path, if we couldn't ride together. Safety in numbers...that sort of thing."

"I'm sure we're not headed in the same direction."

"Yet so far, we've managed the same path." He pulled out his map and traced a line with his finger. "Next is the plain. Littered with boulders the size of the healer's house, the place is a great refuge for cheetaurs. Deadly creatures. And above the plain, gryphon pick off the unsuspecting as they soar above, unimpeded by trees, all except for an occasional shrub."

Talamaya shook her head. "There are many ways to cross the plain. I'm certain our way won't be close to your path."

"You're probably right, my lady. However, we would not mind delaying our journey a bit to secure safe passage for you."

Sessel laughed. "I do believe the king has taken a liking to you, Princess Talamaya."

Talamaya felt the blush rise to her cheeks. Now he knew who she was beyond a shadow of a doubt.

The king smiled. "I thought so," he said under his breath. He motioned to one of his men to refill his bowl, then leaned back on his bedding. "Why would King Sal's daughter be trekking across the wilderness alone, my lady?"

"The woman isn't alone," Gallant objected. "I ride with her now."

Now he called her woman.

"So you're running away from home?" Lazarion scratched his chin. "Yes, you just came of age. And your companions must have, too. Your fathers decided you must wed some ogres for husbands and you chose to run away. But why in this direction? Why not seek shelter with the ladies of the Maken Peninsula? They would sense your frustration and keep you safe."

"Why are *you* traveling this way, sire?" Talamaya asked.

He took a deep breath. "There's much instability in the region. If we retrieve the scepter of Lanai..." He paused when Talamaya choked on her tea.

"Are you all right?" Kersta patted her on the back.

Talamaya's eyes filled with tears as she attempted to clear her throat of the tea that had slipped down the wrong way.

Lazarion studied her curiously.

Sessel nodded. "We had the same quest in mind. We understood some powerful wizard from the continent of Albion wished it for his own. If we had the scepter, no one else could change the balance of power between the peoples of Inherian."

Lazarion agreed. "If the knights of Damar are not attempting to bring you home as I once thought, perhaps they seek the scepter as well. Is this true, princess?"

"It is," she said, her voice still strained.

"You cannot seek the scepter for yourself," he said finally.

She folded her arms. "A woman of Damar would not seek something as important as that, hidden in such a dangerous place, now would they? Not when their women are chained to their beds—"

He chuckled.

"Their...their castle," she rephrased her words, her cheeks blossoming with heat again.

"Has your father chosen a husband for you?"

"I'll invoke the trial before I wed..." She paused when Kersta gasped.

"The trial, my lady?" the king prompted, sitting taller.

"Nothing." She handed her bowl to one of his men who offered to refill it for her.

Kersta's eyes were wide.

"I assume the man your father wishes you to marry isn't such an agreeable sort."

"He's much too old."

"Oh." Lazarion finished his stew and handed his empty bowl to a soldier. "And how much is too old?"

"Two and a half times my age, is too old."

"Ah. So you seek another...someone closer to your age then."

"Absolutely not!"

Sessel laughed. "You would find a home with us, my lady, should you choose to give up men."

Lazarion smiled. "You don't give up men entirely."

"Of course not. We have to have children to carry on our traditions. But the men don't tell us how to live our lives."

"And they won't in Damar if the princess has any say in the..." Kersta stopped speaking when Talamaya's mouth dropped wide open. Kersta turned to the healer. "Your stew is some of the best I've ever eaten."

Lazarion nodded, his gaze never shifting from Talamaya. "I've never eaten such good stew with such interesting dinner companions."

Talamaya rose from her bedding. "Come, Kersta. A word with you, please."

Kersta hurried to join her, but before they had moved very

far from their dinner partners, Lazarion said, "So, Gallant, tell me more about the princess."

Sessel laughed. "Why King Lazarion, I have never heard you take an interest in any female before."

Talamaya walked Kersta far away from the camp while the men began to set up the area for sleeping. "I cannot believe the barb...Lazarion plans to steal the scepter."

"Not steal the scepter, my lady. Lay claim to it, like we plan to do."

"Of course. But he cannot have it. He plans to fight us after all."

"Who has said this?" Kersta asked.

"Our advisors."

Kersta nodded. "Og would lead our men. He's the one who claims the barbarians are creating skirmishes at our borders. Lazarion says our men are creating the clashes, not his."

Talamaya folded her arms. "Yes, you're right. Neither can be trusted. We'll travel with him as far as the plain. Safety in numbers...that sort of thing."

Kersta took a deep breath. "I'm so relieved you have said so, my lady. Have you seen how sick his men look who were poisoned?"

"Yes, Kersta. I wouldn't wish for us to be afflicted with the same malady. We'll ride with them. Pull out your map."

Kersta unfolded the map. Talamaya looked back at Lazarion and to her surprise he watched her as one of his men spoke with him.

She turned her attention back to the map. "Perhaps we can take a different path somewhere on the plain."

"Can we not stay together while we cross the plain? The cheetaurs are the most vicious of creatures."

Talamaya glanced back at Lazarion who raised his brows at her and smiled. "All right. We'll stay together to cross the plain.

Beyond that is the village of Miekal. There, we'll go our separate ways. Four paths lead out of town. All paths eventually make their way to the seacoast."

"What about Gallant?"

"He may remain with us until he wishes to go his own way."

"He is...is...is..." Kersta clenched her fists until her knuckles turned white.

Talamaya smiled. "He irritates you. But his rough way grows on you, do you not agree? Besides, he has been a great help to us already."

"I'll not share my bread with him." Kersta crossed her arms.

"You won't need to. We have been fed twice and saved our own rations. I'm sure Lazarion's men will help to provide a meal for us on our journey across the plain. In Miekal, we can buy food. We're doing well with our rations."

Kersta glanced back at Lazarion. "You know, he wants to speak with you alone. Like you and I are doing. Just the two of you."

"Then what?"

Kersta's face brightened into a smile. "You could not have hooked him any harder than if you reeled him in from the sea. I have never seen you blush so. Yet, if you could have read his mind, I do believe your cheeks would have even turned redder."

"Don't tell me he saw me with him, naked, again."

Kersta chuckled. "In truth, my lady, he contemplates how he can ask your father to permit him to court you. He really is smitten with you."

"You're not serious."

"I am. He worries about your safety foremost. He's concerned that you do intend to try to retrieve the scepter. It's not that he does not wish you to have it, but he feels you would never make it there alive."

"Well, he does not know everything."

"No, but he wishes to. He's dying to find out everything there is about you. What you like to eat, what you enjoy doing, what kind of characteristics impress you about a man. He was much relieved when you said you didn't want a man much older than yourself and said Og was more than twice your age."

"And he is?"

"Twenty-three."

"Oh."

Kersta frowned. "I cannot believe you said you would invoke the marriage trial, my lady."

"It is my choice."

"Your father...was he furious?"

"I don't think he was pleased, but then again, my mentioning marrying the barbarian king even pleased him less."

Kersta's eyes widened. "You didn't say such a thing, my lady."

"I did, only to make a point. But of course I didn't mean it."

"Will you really invoke the marriage trial?"

Talamaya looked back at Lazarion. "Only if my father wishes to force me into marriage with Og or some other who displeases me. Come, let us see to Mexia."

When they headed back toward the hut, Lazarion bowed slightly to Talamaya. "I imagine you're looking in on your friend, but when you leave there, would you honor me with a moment of your time?"

12

After Talamaya and Kersta visited with Mexia one last time in the healer's hut for the night, Kersta said, "Princess, will you speak with Lazarion?"

Talamaya nodded. "Yes."

"Do you wish me in attendance?"

"Certainly."

They stepped outside to find the king speaking with several of his men while Gallant talked with Sessel. As soon as Talamaya walked outside, everyone grew quiet. The silence distressed her. At home, no one paid much attention to her...not like they did here. Was it the king's interest in her that made everyone watch her so?

She scolded herself. Nothing could come of his obvious interest in her. Not if her father had any say in the matter. Yet, here this man had reign over his own kingdom and no need to marry her to improve his status with the ruling family of Damar. The notion totally agreed with her that a man would be interested in her, not for power, or wealth or family position...but just wished to be with her, even before he knew who she really was.

Lazarion joined her. "Come walk with me, Princess Talamaya."

She hesitated, knowing she should have a lady with her at all times and in addition, realizing her father would not approve that she walked with his enemy. She glanced back at Kersta.

"We'll be in full view of your lady companion at all times."

"All right." Talamaya held up her arm to him. She really didn't want Kersta reading both of their minds while she walked with him.

This time Lazarion was the one who hesitated to react, amusing her. Then quickly overcoming his surprise, he placed his arm beneath hers.

They strolled away from the gathered men and women, and Lazarion asked, "Tell me, truthfully if you would, do your people truly see us as barbarians?"

Gallant must have told him she'd called him the barbarian king. How could she have been so rude about a people she had never met? She wanted to shrink into the ground like a rain droplet soaked into thirsty soil as her stomach tightened with fretfulness.

"My lady?"

"Some do. But there has been news that your people have crossed our borders and killed farmers' livestock without provocation."

"Ah. Yet the same thing has happened on our side of the border."

Talamaya stopped in place. "Really?" She pondered the news, then patted his arm. Taking a deep breath she continued to walk with him. "What if someone was causing problems for both our people? Not someone from either your homelands or mine, but someone else who would cause strife between us?"

"For what purpose?"

She shook her head. "Because of the problems...you, my

people, and the Amazons are making an attempt to retrieve the scepter."

"Why would someone wish us to do so?"

"To start a war? To distract us? Create a diversion? What if we fought over ownership of the scepter, then he could step in and conquer the divided peoples."

"One man?"

"Well, he and his armies, I do suppose."

Lazarion pondered the notion, his brow furrowed deep in thought. "Seems highly unlikely." He moved closer to her as they continued to walk around the perimeter of the clearing.

His closer proximity with Talamaya didn't go unnoticed. But she was clueless as to what to do. If she drew away, would he be offended? And if she didn't, would it mean she wished to show she had some...affection for the king?

She couldn't deny that she did as much as her mind warred with her heart over the matter. Even now her heart raced at a quickened beat as his body heat warmed hers. And his spicy scent intrigued her. In fact she couldn't remember a time that she stood so close to a man other than her father or her brother. But here, the man wanted her, lusted for her, wished to hold her naked against his body. She shuddered. If her father knew how attracted she was to the barbarian king, he'd have a stroke.

"Are you cold?"

"No."

Despite her denying that she was, he closed the inch gap between them and now they walked, their bodies touching with every step they made. She should have pulled away. Then she scolded herself. He only wished to keep her warm. But then again, she wasn't cold.

She looked toward the camp and noticed not only did Kersta keep an eye on them, so did the king's men. "Wagging tongues will greet you when you return home."

He smiled. "I'd hoped I could give them something really to talk about upon our return."

She pulled away from him as she came to a dead stop. "Oh?" The irritation was apparent in her voice.

"I know this is inappropriate to discuss with you, but under the circumstances—"

"Proceed." The suspense was killing her.

"I wish to ask your father if he would permit me to court you."

She took a breath of fresh air, not realizing she had been holding it at the first. "Court me?"

She couldn't have been more astonished and the look on his face...well, she couldn't tell what he felt. Almost wistful, hopeful that she'd assure him she'd put in a good word with her father. "Oh." She raised her arm and he slid his under hers, then continued to stroll. "My father would say no."

"How can you be so sure?"

"I have already discussed marrying you—" Talamaya stopped speaking as Lazarion pulled her to a stop. What was the matter with her? She couldn't believe she'd said that! To him!

"You did what?"

She stared at the ground. He was so easy to talk with. Was that the reason she said the one thing she'd never meant to mention to him, ever?

It was one thing to tell her lady friends, but she hadn't even known who the barbarian king was until she met him near Modi's cave. Or was it that secretly she preferred to wed someone so different from her own people? Someone who desired her, not for her position in Damarian society, but who wanted her as a man longed for a woman?

He waited patiently for her to speak but when she remained speechless, he lifted her chin and gazed into her eyes, willing her to speak further with him. "Talamaya?"

She began to walk again, and he took her hand in his this time.

"And he said?"

"I said it in jest as my father stated I would marry someone who was at least equal to my rank and status. So I said *you* were higher rank than me. What about marrying you? Or something like that."

He smiled. "Sometimes all we need is to sow the seed of an idea in one's thoughts, and when the time is ripe, the person will think the idea their own."

"I only said it in jest. And he was not pleased."

The smile on Lazarion's lips returned. "Yes. So tell me about this marriage trial."

"Only in the most extreme case would I invoke such a thing."

"What is it?"

"If my father and I cannot agree on a suitable mate for me, I can challenge a suitor to accomplish a quest. Whoever completes it, would be my husband."

"Can you choose only those who would contend in the contest?"

"Yes."

"Now that sounds barbaric."

"You mean you would not attempt such a quest for my hand in marriage?"

He chuckled. "I just thought I would ask your father permission to court you, Talamaya."

Talamaya's whole body warmed. She'd never embarrassed herself so many times in one man's presence as she did with Lazarion. Didn't he want to marry her after all? Or just get to know her better to see if she was compatible enough for him?

When she grew quiet, he kissed her fingers and changed the subject. "Tell me you're not going after the scepter, my lady."

"My brother was poisoned before he could make the journey. Modi told my father I would follow in Aralias's footsteps."

"Aralias?"

"The only female ruler Damar ever had. She retrieved the scepter five hundred years ago."

"Then it is you who I am to ally with."

"What?"

"Modi's prediction for me. I thought she meant I was to befriend King Sal, but now I see you are the one who is more open-minded than any of your people. I tried to speak with some of your knights in Kern. None wished to speak with me in return. Still, when some of my men return Sessel to the fringe of the forest tomorrow morning, I wish you and your ladies to go with her."

"I will cross the plain with you."

"You will? I mean, I wish you to return home. The way is too deadly for you and your ladies."

"We have Gallant." She smiled.

"He has the courage of a cheetaur, but he is but one small dwarf."

"We'll cross the plain with you when your men are ready to ride. It's all I can promise you."

THE NEXT DAY, Mexia was fully healed and while some of the men escorted Sessel back to the border of the forest, the rest sharpened their weapons while the women foraged for herbs to replenish their healing packs. That evening, Lazarion's men were completely healed and early the next morning, they began the next leg of their journey through the uninhabited Plain of the Ancients.

The land seemed boundless, stretching as far as the eye

could see as they reached the outskirts of Wildwood Forest. Parched red clay earth lay flat in all directions, dotted with red prickly stemmed shrubs, the leaves so small, they were hardly perceptible except close up. Boulders littered the entire area.

Legend had it, the Cyclops used the plain as a playground at one time, stacking boulders into towers, then tossing the rest in clusters, occasionally leaving a stray one behind, isolated from the rest.

Even the sun seemed red as it rested high above the plain. And the air had turned much hotter than in the shade of Wildwood Forest.

Lazarion turned to Talamaya. "My men can still return you to the fringe of the forest leading to Elan's Pass, Talamaya."

"I must cross the plain as you must, sire."

She distinctly thought she heard him mutter under his breath how she was the most stubbornly beautiful woman he'd ever met. She smiled and pulled her hood of her cloak forward to shield her face from the sun.

Lazarion motioned for his men to move forward. In a fan, they spread out, the women and Gallant riding in the center beside the king. Talamaya sensed Gallant wished to ride on the outskirts of the party, ready to do battle with whatever threatened them on the plain. But he kept his word and rode one of the king's extra horses in front of Talamaya, ready to protect her if need be.

The anxious looks on everyone's faces betrayed their concern cheetaurs would attack them at any moment. Talamaya was glad she and her lady friends had the king's escort to help them make the journey as she gripped her staff tightly in her fist with one hand and her reins in the other.

Periodically parched bones of humans, dwarves, and elves littered the ground, their weapons still clutched in their bony fists, their fight forever finished.

Though everyone watched the rocks for movement, it was an archer who first noticed the threat overhead.

"Gryphon!" the man shouted.

The archers immediately readied their crossbows and shot poisoned bolts of steel into the air. At once, three gryphons plummeted to the ground barely missing one of the knights on horseback.

The sky blackened briefly with a multitude of gryphon wedged together in a v-shaped formation like Damarian geese flew south for the winter.

Talamaya gripped her staff harder, ready to do battle if one flew close enough to her. "I don't understand. Gryphon never flock together." Then the image of the gryphon who flew into her father's council chambers came back to her. Were the creatures poisoned with some kind of madness, or being controlled?

The wings of the gryphon stirred up the red dust into a frenzy as several fell to the ground, wounded fatally. But somewhere in the red choking dust, lurked a new threat.

"Cheetaurs!" a man yelled as the cat creature lunged at him.

The scene was Talamaya's worst nightmare. Similar to the blinding snow of Elan Pass, the visibility on the plain was no better. But though the cold made her lungs ache to breathe in the air in the pass, here she could barely breathe at all in the powdery red dust.

She could see neither the king nor Mexia now who rode on either side of her. Yelling laced with panic and anger from the knights filled the air, mixed with the screams of the gryphon in their death throes.

Fearful of striking one of her companions with her staff, Talamaya held it ready, close to her body as her horse whinnied and twisted its head, stomping its hooves with fear.

Then the talons of a gryphon knocked Talamaya from her horse, and she lost her staff. For an instant, she panicked. Then she groped around in the dust for her staff. Her fingers touched the wood and she grabbed her staff and jumped to her feet.

She moved toward where her horse last stood. Instead, she found a cheetaur ripping out the throat of a knight lying still on the ground. Her heart leapt out of her chest. For a second, she wondered why she hadn't stayed home, safe to be a female in her realm. Then her anger boiled over.

No matter what obstacles lay in her path, she would return the scepter to Damar and discover who was behind all this madness. Now she was certain, one man more powerful than any she'd ever known was at the source of all the evil. Now, she wished she'd known why Aralias had sought the scepter in the first place. Had the madness been unleashed during her time also?

Talamaya dashed forward and struck the cheetaur with one blow, paralyzing it instantly. Fewer bolts whizzed into the sky now and the dust began to settle. In the haze, she spied another cheetaur, this one wounded, blood soaking its front legs making him deadlier than any uninjured cat. Without waiting for it to attack anyone else, Talamaya dashed across the plain to put an end to its misery.

With her staff readied, she fully intended to strike it when a growl from behind her warned her another sought her as prey. She swung around and struck the cheetaur, all four of its paws airborne, as it lunged at her. He dropped to the ground, instantly killed. She turned, wondering why the other hadn't attacked from behind. To her relief, Gallant finished him off with his war hammer.

"Princess!" Kersta called.

"Here, Kersta! Mexia!"

"Here, my lady!"

In the clearing dust, the women sought each other out,

stumbling over rocks, and finally grasped each other in warm embraces.

Lazarion rode up to them. "The three of you are all right?"

"Yes, sire," Talamaya said.

"Stay here then. We'll find your horses, and I must regroup my men."

Shaking his war hammer, Gallant hurried over to the women. "Now that was a fight."

Mexia wiped a tear away.

Talamaya squeezed her hand. "We'll get through this together."

"Yes, my lady," she sniffled. "But I cast a spell and...and I did it wrong."

Talamaya's chest constricted when she heard the despair in Mexia's words. "What are you saying, Mexia?"

"I meant to turn it into rock, only, my spell didn't work."

Talamaya patted Mexia's shoulder. "It's all right. It's your father's fault for not allowing you to study his books, except for those on potions. You could be a great mage like him if he would ever let you be."

"Hey!" a knight shouted. "What happened to Rupert?"

"Fairy magic!" another hollered.

Talamaya took hold of Mexia's hand and whispered, "You turned a man into stone?"

Mexia nodded, two more tears dribbling down her cheek, barely restraining the floodwaters that threatened to spill from her tear-laden eyes. "The cheetaur had leapt for him, its fangs bared to rip the man's throat out. I cast the spell, but it attached itself to the man instead of the cat. He would not have survived, my lady. He wouldn't have. I couldn't reach him quickly enough, and his back was turned to the cat while he fought another at his front."

"Oh," Talamaya said, her head swirling with thoughts. "Can you change him back?"

"I'm afraid to try, my lady. If I haven't already killed him, I might do so with trying to bring him back."

"What happened here?" Lazarion shouted.

"A wizard must have attacked him, my liege. Nothing else could have done this."

"I'll kill the mage who has done this to my brother!" another yelled.

"Sire, may I have a word with you in private," Talamaya asked the king.

He lifted her to his saddle and rode her away from the rest of his men. "You know something of this?"

"Mexia is a mage apprentice. The knight was attacked from behind by a cheetaur as he fought another in front of him. She could not reach the cheetaur with her staff in time. She cast a spell to turn the beast into stone, only instead she turned your knight into stone."

He stared at her, his face hard. "My people don't like wizards, Talamaya. Can she return him to his former self?"

"She's afraid to try. Can we not take the knight with us and find a sorcerer in the next village who might be able to undo her spell?"

"Wizard apprentices are worse than wizards themselves," he darkly responded.

Talamaya slipped off his horse. "She attempted to save his life the only way she could. Had she not turned him to stone, he would be dead." She turned and stormed off toward her companions.

When she joined them, she said, "Mexia, do you not think you could change him back?"

Mexia shook her head. "I never practiced the reverse spell."

"What did you turn into stone then?"

"Poisonous frogs."

Talamaya nodded. "Like the stone frogs at market. I never would have thought you'd created them and not a stone mason."

Gallant shuffled his feet nearby. "There's a wizard in the next village. Perhaps he can undo the spell."

Lazarion rode up behind them. "Get Sir Rupert," he commanded his men. "We ride to Miekal."

Mexia squeezed Talamaya's hand, her eyes sodden with tears. "I'm so sorry, my lady."

"You saved his life. If the men cannot see that, then well, it isn't your fault. The knight still has a chance at life when he had none before."

If the barbarians were afraid of mages, so be it. Talamaya knew then, nothing could ever come of a relationship with Lazarion.

The women mounted their horses and stuck close together, their staffs ready for further fighting if need be. Lazarion rode with his men at the outer perimeter of the party.

Twice more cheetaurs attacked, and both times the knights slew them. But no one sighted any more gryphon. Talamaya wondered if the whole species had rained down upon them at once, and now were eliminated forever in Inherian.

"Sessel spoke of a wizard being the reason for the Amazons trying for the scepter, my lady," Kersta said.

"Yes, I'm thinking the same. If it's a wizard, he could possibly wield such power as to control the minds of mindless beasts of prey."

They looked over at Mexia, but her thoughts seemed a million miles elsewhere.

"She's distraught over the knight."

Talamaya nodded.

"The king seems unduly disturbed."

"He says his people don't like wizards. To think I told my father I would marry the brute."

Kersta smiled. "Yes, well I can still see you have a great deal of affection for him, no matter how angry you are with him. He's upset because his men are afraid of Mexia. They'll come around, if they see how useful wizards can be."

"Only if the knight can be saved." Talamaya considered the plains reaching out to the edge of the earth. Then a stand of trees appeared upon the horizon.

Kersta pulled out the map. "The Grundgen Forest. Beyond that is the village of Miekal."

"If it were not for the fact that Mexia will have to visit with the wizard to undo her spell over the knight, I would have us travel on our own from here on out."

"The Grundgen Forest is safe to travel?"

"It's like our own from what I have read from journal entries of travelers to the region. Wild boar to hunt for food. Red wolves create a menace occasionally. Nothing more."

The men quickened their pace, evidently their spirits improved to see the forest so nearby.

Kersta raised her brows as she considered Talamaya.

Talamaya smiled. "We look a sight, do we not? Your hair is as red as I imagine mine is."

"Yes, my lady. And you wear a red mask."

"Is there a river where we can cleanse the dust from our skin? We could change into clean gowns then, too, before we reach the village tomorrow," Talamaya wondered aloud.

Gallant glanced back at them.

"We would have to separate from the barbarians," Kersta said.

Yes, they were barbarians once again. Anyone who could not tolerate wizards in their realm *were* barbaric. What did they think of the healer who cast a protective spell over the land and kept them safe while they slept there the two nights? What of Modi and her special powers?

"What about Gallant?" Kersta asked, pointing at the dwarf.

"I will act as sentry while ye ladies bath. Neither beast nor man would come close while I'm in charge."

Talamaya agreed to the plan. "Well, I for one would give anything to be clean again."

Despite the woods appearing so close, it took several hours before they arrived at the perimeter of the forest. Immediately, the air turned cooler, still warm, but pleasant.

The leaves of the oak trees filtered the dust from the air, and Talamaya took a deep breath. "I can breathe again."

"But he cannot," Mexia said softly.

"We'll do what we can for the knight, Mexia. Don't continue to dwell on the matter. By tomorrow afternoon, the latest, we'll be in the village. We'll see the wizard there, first thing."

Lazarion rode back to Talamaya and said, "We'll camp near the river, two miles from here. There we'll eat, rest the horses, and sleep. Tomorrow, we'll journey the rest of the way through the woods and by the afternoon should make it to Miekal."

"All right, sire."

When Lazarion pulled his horse away from them, Kersta said to Talamaya, "You didn't tell him we were going to bathe in the river."

"I don't need his approval to do such a thing."

"Yes, but—"

Talamaya raised her brows at her.

"Yes, my lady."

Half an hour later, the weary party reached the river and while the men led their horses to the water and drank their fill, Talamaya and her party headed west.

"We'll not stray too far from them, will we, my lady?" Kersta asked, worry clear in her voice.

"We'll not be long. But we must be far enough away to have our privacy, ladies."

Where the river made a sharp turn and snaked north, Talamaya dismounted. "Here at the bend in the river, we're well-secluded from the men."

"We have traveled nearly three miles, my lady."

"Yes, well…," Talamaya hopped down from her horse, "if my horse could have held out a bit longer, I would have made the distance greater."

She walked over to Mexia's horse and reached up to grab her hand. "Come, Mexia. Join us in the river. You'll feel better once you're clean."

"I will only feel better once the knight is his former self."

"Tomorrow, we'll take care of that matter."

"A cousin of mine lives in Miekal. I wish to see him before we leave the town," Gallant said.

"Of course, Gallant."

Talamaya and Kersta hung their cloaks across a cluster of trees while Mexia stared at the river. Kersta unfastened Mexia's cloak next, then tied it to the trees until they had a tent fashioned a foot off the ground without a roof and that reached to their chins. Talamaya and Kersta pulled Mexia into the shelter. Then they removed their boots and gowns, leaving only a slip for modesty.

Once they had unbraided their hair, Kersta grabbed a vial of soapy liquid. They all ran for the water, both out of concern they might be caught in their undergarments by the barbarians and worry they might change their minds and remain filthy for the remainder of the leg of their journey to the village.

When the women squealed, Gallant whipped around, his warhammer at the ready.

"Watch that way." Talamaya waved at him to turn around.

"Blasted, woman, I thought some kind of fish was eating ye alive." He turned his back to them again.

The women laughed. Dipping under the water, they cleansed the red dust from their skin and hair.

They played in the water, giggling and splashing at each other, like when they were young girls. But then, Talamaya caught Gallant waving at someone in the forest.

She held her breath.

"Get them out of there, now!" Lazarion called out from the woods, his words harsh, his command brooking no argument.

13

G allant folded his arms. "I cannot tell the ladies what to do, King Lazarion. Ye tell them what to do."

Mexia whispered, "What is going on? I have soap in my eyes."

Lazarion rode forth on his horse to the edge of the water, his cheeks blazing red with anger. "You're sure to get yourself and your ladies killed, princess. Come out of there at once."

"We will rejoin you when we are ready." Talamaya dipped down lower in the water, her skin burning with mortification.

"One dwarf cannot protect you should you need protecting. My men have set up a perimeter camp. You'll return at once where you'll remain safe."

"We'll return once we are done with our bath."

Talamaya turned her back to him and dove under the water.

When she rose, Kersta whispered, "Gallant told him we were as stubborn as dwarven women. Lazarion rode off in a huff."

Talamaya turned to Gallant. "Are they gone?"

"Aye, woman. Though ye would have been safer had they remained here."

Before she climbed out of the water, Gallant dashed into the woods. "Gallant?"

The ladies hurried out of the river. After pulling fresh gowns from their bundles, they returned to their makeshift tent and dressed.

"Where was Gallant off to, do you wonder?" Kersta asked.

They braided their wet hair, then secured it close to their heads.

"Probably wished further word with Lazarion."

They untied their cloaks from the trees.

"Do you feel better, Mexia?" Talamaya asked, shaking the dust from her cloak.

"Yes, my lady. Much. And I think I remember the reversal spell for the knight."

"Good. Let us return now then and see what we can do for him."

"But if it doesn't work?"

"We can still take him to the village."

When footsteps approached at a hurried pace, the women grabbed their staffs.

Gallant appeared, wide-eyed and shaking his head.

"What's wrong?" Talamaya asked.

"The king's men were shouting from some distance away, and he rode off to see to the matter. A flash of light blinded me momentarily. When I could see clearly again, the men and their horses were all gone."

"You didn't make it all the way back to camp on foot?"

"No, woman. The king and his men had ridden here to the river to find where you had gone."

"Hurry, then, we must return to camp."

The four mounted their horses, then galloped along the edge of the river until they reached the campsite of Lazarion and his men. "The woods are too still," Talamaya whispered, jumping down from her horse. "Not a bird or bug is making a sound."

With her staff in hand, she hurried into the camp while the others followed her. Boar hung on a spit over a blazing fire and the succulent pig scented the air. The men had laid bedrolls in a circle in the camp, but there was no sign of the men or their horses, except for the stone statue of Rupert.

Mexia ran her hand over his arm. "Where have they gone, my lady?"

"There's no sign of a struggle," Talamaya said, her skin crawling with dread, "but I can see no vision of what has occurred either."

"I sense something," Mexia said, reaching her hands out. "Something like a magic portal opened here, a doorway to some other realm."

"Could the men and their horses have been taken somewhere?"

Mexia squeezed Rupert's hand. "Yes. A great magician could move living creatures that were located within the portal opening. Rupert was stone so he would have been left untouched."

"Can you change him back, Mexia?" Talamaya asked, hopeful.

Mexia walked over to a tree and concentrated, then mouthed some words under her breath and wiggled her fingers at the leaf of a tree. The green leaf turned to gray stone.

Taking a deep breath, she glanced over at Talamaya. She nodded at Mexia to proceed.

Mexia said another incantation and moved her fingers in a different path. The leaf remained unchanged. She took a deep breath and looked stricken.

"Try again. It took several men to load Rupert onto his horse. Our party of three women and one dwarf could never lift the stone statue so that we could take him to the village. And we don't wish to leave him behind." Talamaya attempted to hide her feelings of hopelessness. She had to steel herself for what lay ahead.

"What are we going to do, my lady?" Kersta asked, twisting the ties of her belt through her fingers.

"We'll stay here the night. Our horses must rest. We must also. We still have a long ways to ride to reach Miekal."

"And then?"

She couldn't think of what would happen then. She wanted to ensure Lazarion and his men were safe, but if they couldn't find out about them, then what? They had to get the scepter. "Then we shall see."

"You don't think they'll return, do you?"

"No, Kersta. I think something more powerful than anything we have ever known is out there and is attempting to stop us from retrieving the scepter."

"Troll's dung," Mexia said, still not having any success with her petrified leaf.

Talamaya raised her brows in surprise as Kersta smiled.

"Would the wizard kill the men?" Kersta asked Talamaya.

"Maybe he's using them to get to us."

"How so, my lady?"

"If Modi is correct, I follow in Aralias's footsteps. What if the wizard existed way back then, and he did as he's doing now, causing a rift between our peoples, and she had to retrieve the scepter to keep peace? Modi knew, but we didn't know enough to question her about it. What if he was a powerful mage, and Aralias's fight with him drained his energy to the point it took him five-hundred years before he could return?"

"Then you'll have to fight him like she did."

"Yes." Though Talamaya couldn't fathom how she could ever win against a powerful wizard like that.

"Did she have two female companions?"

"Very little was written about her so I don't know. She retrieved the scepter. Nothing was said about who went with her to help her in her quest."

"Ah!" Mexia exclaimed.

Talamaya and Kersta ran over to the tree and touched the leaf, returned to its original green state. "But will it work the same on a man?"

"I don't know, my lady. I shouldn't have tried to cast the spell."

"You saved his life once, Mexia. You must try and bring him back to life again."

Mexia nodded, but her solemn face indicated her heart wasn't in it. Walking over to the statue, she ran her hand over the knight's cold cheek. "I'll do all in my power to bring you back to life, but whatever happens, I want you to know, I only cast my spell to spare your life from the cheetaur's bite."

Mexia stepped back from the statue and raised her hands. With a slight movement of her fingers, she spoke a spell and the stone began to change.

The grayness faded from his skin, his eyelids fluttered briefly, then his body became human once more, and he crumpled to the ground. Mexia knelt at his side. "He's breathing. What do I do now, my lady?"

"See if you can get some of Modi's tea down him, and we will lay him on some of the bedding. Maybe by morning, he'll be more conscious."

Talamaya turned to Kersta. "The pork must be done by now. I'll serve up the meat if you could see to our horses."

"I'll help the woman," Gallant said, then hurried off to pull their horses into the camp.

"I got some tea down him, princess."

"Good, Mexia." Talamaya finished slicing up the meat, portions for the four of them, then joined Mexia. The two ladies half dragged the six-foot tall, golden-haired male to the closest bedding near the fire that they could reach.

"You're right," Mexia said. "As a statue he would have been too heavy for us. Even as a man, he's unbelievably—"

He groaned.

"Oh." Mexia dropped hold of his arm as if he'd burned her.

"He's stirring. Help me to take him to the bedding, Mexia."

"Yes, my lady." Regrasping his arm, Mexia helped to lay him on the bedroll.

His eyelids fluttered open. Blue eyes, the color of azure, stared at Talamaya for a moment, and she smiled at him. He turned to Mexia whose eyes were full of tears. He reached up and touched her cheek. "Thank you, my lady, for saving my life."

"You know? I mean, you heard?"

"Everything. I would've punched my brother for getting angry with you."

"Are you all right? I mean, does everything work?"

His lips turned up slightly, and Mexia's cheeks reddened.

"I feel weary, but everything seems to be fine."

"We have some boar to serve you that may help you to recover your strength," Talamaya said.

"He was a wizard, princess," Rupert said.

Gallant and Kersta joined them.

Talamaya took a ragged breath. "A wizard?"

"A bright light swirled like a dirt devil of white, and the men began shouting. Suddenly, the men and their horses were gone. Then you ladies came back into camp."

"And me," Gallant said, folding his arms.

Talamaya said, "The king had discovered we had taken a different path and—"

"Yes, and he and some of the men rode off looking for you. They must have heard the shouting and come back. All were taken away.

"When the light faded, I figured I would be doomed to live the rest of my days in these woods. A resting place for the birds and a cloak of green moss. He patted Mexia's hand. "But I would never have held a grudge against you, dear lady. You saved my life."

"Let us eat!" Gallant said, digging into his food with a knife. "I'm starving."

"Do you really intend to get the scepter, my lady?"

"Yes, I must. Somehow, I have to fight whoever this mage is. I cannot do it without the scepter, I'm certain."

"Will you take me with you?"

She hesitated to answer. She was certain she could trust Gallant would not make an attempt to claim the scepter. But what if Lazarion's knight wished to rule in his stead? Men were so easily corrupted by power.

"We'll all travel to Miekal together."

LATER THAT EVENING as Rupert bathed in the river, Gallant and the ladies sat on their bedding and studied the iridescent flames of the campfire, casting shadows across the leaf-covered ground.

"Have you ever wondered what life would be like in Damar if we had more say, ladies?" Talamaya asked.

Mexia tucked a loose curl behind her ear. "I for one would take mage training in Langdon."

"On the continent of Albion?"

"Yes, my lady. My father has never felt a woman should receive training from the high wizard. But if I could, that's where I'd go."

Kersta cleared her throat. "But do you not have to pass a test for admission?"

"Yes," Mexia said. "I've studied all that I can of Father's books, even the ones he has locked away."

Talamaya arched her brows in surprise.

"I didn't understand more of the complicated spells. And I wouldn't attempt to use them without knowing the consequences. Well, except as I did with Rupert in a panic. But I could be as good as my father, if he'd let me be."

"As great as the wizards in Langdon, even," Talamaya said.

Mexia smiled at her. "Thank you for saying so, my lady."

"It's only because I believe so. You can do whatever you set out to, Mexia, once your mind is made up."

Mexia's eyes sparkled with determination. "It is."

"Good, then when you take this trip to Albion I wish to accompany you."

"Because?" Kersta asked.

"I'm curious about this continent. Not much is written about the people who live there. I was interested in finding out more about them."

"And making more history at the same time?" Mexia smiled.

Talamaya smiled. Remembering her mother's words warmed her. Already, she had changed the history of her people. She turned her attention to Kersta. "What about you? If women had more of a say in our affairs, what would you do?"

Kersta tore a piece of bread off her loaf and noticed Gallant watching it. She handed him the piece. He smiled and shoved it into his mouth. She broke off another piece for herself this time. "I know what I wouldn't do. I would not marry right away. What if I settled down and discovered the man I married was not the right one for me?" She unbraided her hair for the night. "No, I would have to join you and Mexia on the trip to Langdon. Who knows who I might meet there? Someone even more enlightened than our own men, maybe."

Mexia laughed. "Sure, the way you are, you would have half the men on the new continent interested in you."

"And me?" Gallant asked. "What about me?"

Talamaya smiled. "What about you, Gallant? What will you do once you part company with us?"

"What? Ye don't like my company?"

"We've appreciated your being with us."

Kersta humpfed.

Talamaya ignored her. "But where do you go after this?"

"I don't look far into the future. Just recently I quit working for my brother, Mendon."

"In the mines?"

"Aye. Disagreeable dwarf." He poked the toe of his boot in the earth. "Though my kind rarely serves in the adventurer's guild business, I earn money from solving people's problems. It makes for interesting work."

"But not Alist's?" Kersta asked with an edge to her voice. "She had a problem, but you would not aid her?"

"Alist?"

"Did you not know Mendon was forcing her to marry him?" Kersta asked, her voice rife with suspicion.

"And your fathers are not doing the same with ye women? Women don't know enough to know what they want out of life."

"Alist loved the tavernkeeper," Mexia said. "And besides, it was not her father who was forcing her marriage to Mendon, but Mendon himself."

"Aye. But then, Alist said she loved me, too."

"As a brother," Kersta said, guessing.

"She said that?" Gallant eyed each of the women as if trying to determine if Alist had indeed said that. When none responded, he said, "Oh. Maybe so."

Kersta rolled her eyes.

He grunted and pointed at her. "Even ye, like me."

"Oh?"

"Aye." He smiled. "That is why ye are always so mad at me. Ye are afraid to show how much ye care for me."

Mexia and Talamaya laughed.

Kersta reached over and touched Talamaya's hand. "May I speak with you in private for a moment, princess?" She glanced over at Gallant, then smiled at Mexia.

"Of course." Talamaya rose from her bedding and walked with Kersta a short distance from the camp, both armed with their staffs. "What's wrong?" she whispered.

"I don't trust the knight. Mexia feels some kind of a bond with him for turning him to stone, then returning him to a man. But I don't trust his motives where the scepter is concerned."

"He's a man, and men lust for power, often."

"Yes. He wants to go with us. He feels three women and one dwarf are all too weak to stop him in his quest. Now that the king and his men are out of the way, he intends to claim the scepter. He assumes we can help him to make his way into the Cave of Sorrows, but after that—"

They heard Rupert speaking to Gallant and Mexia when he returned to camp.

"I felt the same thing, Kersta. I believe he'll not live long then. Let us get some sleep. We'll deal with it tomorrow."

When they walked back into camp, Rupert held Mexia's hand. Talamaya worried the situation could only get worse. As shy as Mexia was, no one had ever gotten close to her, but now, she'd opened her heart to a man, and Talamaya hoped he wouldn't break it.

Talamaya motioned to Gallant. "Would you take first watch, Gallant? I'll take the one after that, then Mexia, Kersta and Rupert, if you're feeling rested enough by then." She'd purposefully made Mexia follow her, with Kersta taking the next shift to ensure Mexia and Rupert didn't stay up the rest of the morning together.

The night passed without incident, but when they woke later than they had intended, they realized at once, their horses were gone...and so was Rupert.

14

"Rupert," Mexia hollered. "Rupert!"

"He is gone," Gallant grumbled. "And with it our horses and food packs, everything."

"Not our weapons." Talamaya bundled her bedding. "And we still have our pouches filled with Modi's tea. Come, we must start our journey at once. If we can get close enough, we can whistle for our horses."

"But not mine," Gallant said.

"Rupert will undoubtedly be riding yours as he is one of the king's own. I imagine he won't drag our horses with him all the way to the village though. It would slow him down too much."

"Why did you not tell me this would happen?" Mexia grouched. "Did you think I couldn't handle his deception?"

"Sorry, Mexia. Kersta read his mind, but could not see what he had intended to do exactly. I sensed he'd try to claim the scepter."

"He's going after the scepter after stranding us alone in the wilderness?" Mexia asked, her voice highly agitated. She shook her head.

They trudged across a narrow wooden bridge that creaked

with every step they made over the rushing river. Then they headed into more woods on the other side.

"I believe he intended to use us to help him get to the Cave of Sorrows, except when I was hesitant about taking him with us, he decided to go it alone. He doesn't really believe three women and a dwarf would be capable of the journey. He thinks the men kept us safe all along," Talamaya said.

Mexia's brow furrowed so hard, Talamaya worried it would freeze permanently like that. She patted her shoulder. "Kersta had to tell me, but she was afraid if we all began to speak of it, Rupert would return to the campfire, and the secret would be out. No telling what he would have done then."

Mexia's eyes grew big. "You don't think he would have killed us."

"I believe he feels he's in the position of claiming the scepter and Lazarion's throne."

"No," Gallant interjected. "He cannot think that."

"Lazarion is gone, and so are all his men."

"My lady, what about *our* men?" Mexia asked.

She nodded. "Our men, too. In the middle of the night I had a vision. Locked in cells in the deep inner sanctum of the earth, our men and Lazarion's will rot away if we don't free them. Our knights must have bypassed us when we had to stay for an extra day at the healer's hut, and already made it across the treacherous plain. Then when they reached the woods here, the portal must have opened and taken them inside, just like with Lazarion and his men."

"Where?"

"That, I don't know. I also cannot decide if we should try for the scepter first, or try to find a way to free the men."

Mexia shook her head. "Claim the scepter."

Talamaya looked over at her, surprised to hear the venom in

her voice. "Remember, Mexia, we must always choose the path of righteousness."

"Yes, my lady. I'm sorry if I sound bitter. But we cannot help the men if you don't wield the scepter."

"I have felt this, too. And you, Kersta, what do you say?"

"Yes, princess. The scepter it is. Before we return home, we must free the men."

Mexia dug her staff into the ground using it as a walking stick while they hurried through the forest. "If I see Rupert again, he'll become a statue for my gardens, permanently."

The ladies smiled.

Talamaya asked, "Do you think that's the path to take, dear Mexia? The path of righteousness?"

"Yes," Kersta and Mexia said at the same time.

"And what about me? Do I not have any say in this little venture?"

"Of course, Gallant. Your words of wisdom are most welcome," Talamaya said.

"I say we see my cousin first. Then we seek out the scepter."

"Your cousin?"

"Aye, I wish word of my wife."

"What is the matter with your wife?" Talamaya asked, surprised to learn he even had one.

"She ran off with a dwarf from Langdon."

"Oh." Talamaya didn't want to hear about it, feeling it was none of her business.

"She contacts my cousin from time to time. I wish to have word of her."

Surprised, she assumed he still cared for her. Though she couldn't imagine how. "You still love her then?"

"How could I love a woman like that? I want word of her is all."

"Oh." Talamaya smiled. There was no understanding a dwarf.

"Ye say ye have visions, woman?"

"Yes, Gallant. Not all the time, but just sometimes I can see glimpses of what lies ahead for us."

"Aye." He looked over at Kersta. "And she can read minds." Facing Mexia, he said, "What do ye do?"

She frowned at him. "Turn unchivalrous knights to stone."

He smiled. "The woman holds grudges."

Talamaya turned her attention to Mexia. "Are you all right?"

"Of course I'm all right. I shall have a handsome man-sized statue in my garden for free."

Kersta chuckled. "The man does not know how badly he fouled things up for himself when he hurt Mexia."

A rustling in the woods nearby made Talamaya motion for everyone to stop. She whistled, but nothing happened. Kersta did the same, but no response. Gallant shook his head and folded his arms across his chest. Mexia took a deep breath and whistled, and her horse cantered into view.

"Yes!" the three women shouted unanimously. After tying their bags to the horse's saddle, Mexia climbed on. She motioned to Talamaya.

"Kersta, you next. We'll take turns riding."

Periodically, she and Kersta whistled for their horses and half an hour later Kersta's horse came out of the thicket.

"Oh, yes!" Kersta cried with enthusiasm. She hopped off Mexia's horse, and Gallant headed to hers to join her. She wrinkled her nose.

Gallant waited.

"Well, all right, then."

They mounted her horse, and Talamaya joined Mexia. After only another few minutes passed, Talamaya's horse came to her call.

"Well, my lady, it appears we are where we were in the beginning. Three horses and one extra rider," Mexia said.

"Yes, but at least we're no longer walking."

By the time they reached Miekal, it was early evening instead of afternoon from all the walking they'd had to endure. Mexia still fumed about Rupert stealing their horses in the first place. But the first stop they had to make was at Tanner's Blacksmith's Shop, owned by one of Gallant's cousins.

As soon as they walked into the shop, a dark-haired dwarf eyed the women suspiciously. "What are ye doing here?" he asked Gallant.

"No hearty welcome for yer favorite cousin, Tanner? What is eating ye?"

His cousin lay down his hammer and walked over to Gallant, his gaze never moving from watching the women, and he gave his cousin a warm embrace. "Ye are always welcome, cousin of Kern."

Gallant pointed to Talamaya. "Princess Talamaya saved my life. I owe her a debt of gratitude."

"Aye."

"And the others, Kersta shared her bread with me."

Tanner's lips twitched in amusement.

"Ahem, aye, and the other, is Mexia. She has an interesting way with humans. She turns them to stone, then brings them to life. And threatens to return them to stone, when they steal her horse."

Tanner laughed. "Ye must be hungry."

"We are. The knight stole our horses, and we had to walk from the river quite a ways before we recovered our mounts."

"I know ye have come for news of your wife. She is well."

"And still in Albion?"

"Aye, Gallant. And still in Albion. She isn't returning. Ye need to find a new woman."

Gallant glanced at Kersta who raised her brows at him. He smiled. "I am working on it, my cousin."

They walked into his house through the back of the shop. Tanner motioned to a dwarf-sized table. The women sat down in the short chairs. It reminded Talamaya of the children's table in the dining hall.

"So what adventure are ye on this time?"

Gallant stole a look at Talamaya, then said, "We're trying to find out where the princess's men have disappeared to."

"If ye are speaking of the single knight who slipped into town earlier, he has already left and headed on the path to Lanai."

"He's one of Lazarion's knights. We seek him, too, and his knights as well," Talamaya said.

Tanner served up pigeons on oyster shells, and goblets of wine, then sat down at the table. "How many?"

"There were thirty Damarian knights, at least at the outset," Talamaya said.

"Twenty-nine, my lady, as your brother didn't make it," Mexia corrected her.

"Pardon, twenty-nine."

"Perhaps they didn't survive the journey."

Talamaya lifted her goblet. "I'm certain some of them didn't. But the remainder are locked away in a dungeon somewhere."

"How would you know this?" Gallant's cousin asked.

"She has visions," Gallant said.

"Aye. Well, there is no place like that in the village that I know of." Tanner chugged down his wine. "And the others?"

"The same. They started out with around thirty knights. Lazarion must have lost two in Elan Pass. Then six more died on the plain. The one became separated from his men, so the king and the rest of his men would total about twenty." Talamaya lifted a strip of meat off her bird.

"Who would have the force required to take all those men?"

"A wizard," the four companions said.

Tanner looked at each of them in turn, then poked at his fowl. "Aye."

"Do ye know of someone like this?"

"Ye know me, cousin, and ye know I am not one who listens to rumors."

"Aye, but ye have heard something?"

"We have no wizards here."

"I thought there be one."

"Nay, not now." Tanner guzzled his wine, then looked Gallant straight in the eye. "It is rumored that a new one has been floating around these parts for months."

"Floating?" Mexia asked.

"Well, ye know. He appears, then disappears."

"Asking questions?"

"Aye. He has been asking about three women, human, youthful, Damarian. He never mentioned one would be King Sal's daughter."

Talamaya's skin crawled with worry. "He knows we are coming."

"Aye. And he will be waiting for ye."

"Where?"

Tanner leaned back in his chair. "Do ye seek the scepter?"

"Yes."

"Then the rumor is, he waits for ye in the Cave of Sorrows."

"Can ye aid us at all?" Gallant asked.

"I would not get involved with this, cousin. The women are on an impossible quest and ye can only get yourself killed."

"After the princess claims the scepter, we must free Lazarion and his men. They have always been good to us."

"Aye, bought a sword from me, he did. I will question a few I know who tend to deal on the other side of the law. Maybe one of them will know something."

"Thieves," Gallant said, wrinkling his nose in disgust.

"Aye. And they have saved my butt a time or two when ruffians have shown up in town."

"Find out what ye can then."

"I will take care of your horses for the night. Ye will stay with me, cousin, will ye not?"

"Overnight. Aye. We leave in the morning at first light for Lanai."

"Ye will need two bedrooms?"

"Yes, with one bed big enough for the three of us ladies," Talamaya quickly said in the event there was any misunderstanding.

Tanner slapped Gallant on the shoulder. "Ye have far to go with this one."

AFTER TAKING baths that night and cleaning their gowns, the ladies slipped under the covers, enjoying the softness of the goose-down mattress.

"It isn't good that he knows we're coming, my lady," Kersta said, rolling onto her side to face Mexia and Talamaya.

Mexia shook her head. "Why did Modi not warn us about this wizard?"

"Maybe she realized we had to handle him in our own way," Talamaya said.

"And what way is that?"

"Follow the path of right, always."

"I suppose that means I cannot turn Rupert back into stone."

Talamaya smiled. "Certainly you can."

Kersta chuckled. "You cannot be serious."

"Mexia did what she felt was right to save the knight's life. If she was faced with a similar choice, and now knowing she can bring him back to life when he's out of danger, I would see no reason why she couldn't do the same deed."

"How can we fight the power of a wizard?" Mexia asked. "I cannot even fight my father and though he's powerful, he has never conjured up portals or anything."

"We still have a long ways to go, ladies, before we reach the island. The land of the Cyclops is in our path once we leave this village. Let us concentrate on one obstacle at a time. But first, we must get a good night's sleep."

She rolled onto her side, but before she could close her eyes, the door creaked open a crack.

Gallant stepped into the room as Talamaya sat up in bed, her covers pulled to her chin. "What's wrong, Gallant?"

"We must leave at once. I cannot say, but I have known my cousin forever, and all evening I have suspected he has acted oddly. I didn't wish to worry ye, woman, but once he left the house, I figured, we needed to leave at once."

"He left the house?"

"Aye, for no good reason, I am certain."

"We must dress, Gallant."

"Oh. Aye, of...of course. I'll get the horses."

When Gallant closed the door on his way out, Talamaya jumped out of bed. "Ladies, have you heard?"

"Yes," they both said.

Slipping into her gown, Mexia added, "But I would almost not care, if I could sleep one night in that soft down bed."

"Yes, only I fear we'd soon join King Lazarion in the dungeon."

The ladies climbed through the window with their staffs in hand, then headed to the stable out back. Gallant patted his cousin's horse. "I'll bring him back when I'm done."

"I wonder if Gallant has to always take the path of right as well." Mexia climbed into her saddle.

"Tanner owes me, for being traitorous to the core."

"Well, it's possible the wizard has threatened to harm someone Tanner cares for," Talamaya said.

"Aye, but his cousin should come first."

"A lady friend perhaps?"

"I...had not considered that."

They kicked their horses at a gallop and headed away from the land of the Cyclops. Kersta said, "This is the wrong way, my lady."

"Yes, and I venture to say, we'll get more sleep if we lay our bedrolls somewhere other than in the land where the Cyclops live."

"Oh."

"If Tanner tells the wizard where we're heading, he'll tell them in the direction of Lanai."

"All paths lead to Lanai. You said so yourself," Mexia said.

"Yes, but the one is the quickest way. The others add a week onto the time at least and other dangers lurk on those paths. Besides, I'm afraid our men and Lazarion and his men cannot hold out that long."

"You're worried about him, are you not?" Kersta asked.

"Yes, Kersta. We didn't part company in a very good way, for one."

"Yes, but if we had not left them and bathed in the river, *we'd* be in the wizard's dungeon with the rest of our men by now."

"You're right, of course."

"What path are we on, my lady?" Mexia asked.

"The one that runs through the land of the fairies. If we give them a gift, we'll be welcome to stay for the night."

"What kind of a gift?" Mexia asked.

"I'm not certain. For every traveler, it's different. In one case, a fairy wished a pearl from the sea. In another, anything that was uniquely different from anything they had ever seen."

"Do we each have to give a gift?" Kersta asked.

"Again, it depends on the gift. If it's something they love, it might suffice for our whole party."

"They cannot have Ren," Gallant grumbled.

"They wouldn't wish your war hammer."

"Our staffs," Kersta said. "They wouldn't wish our staffs?"

"No, Kersta. The staffs are way too big for them to handle. And they have no need of them. The fairies are only about three feet tall and slender like elves. In fact, they are cousins to the elves."

"Not the dark elves," Gallant groaned.

"A little mixture of both the elves of Mesa and the dark elves, I'm afraid. They're often generous, but can be mean-spirited if they don't get what they want."

"Like how, my lady?" Mexia asked.

"They can make you dance for days on end until they tire of the sport. They can make you forget who you are and lose years in their land, drifting about like a lost soul."

"Oh. Then we must offer the best we have." Kersta patted her horse's head.

"The best I have is my amulet," Mexia said.

"I don't have anything a fairy would want." Gallant tugged at his beard. "Unless she wants my war hammer. It's the only thing of value to me."

"Gallant, offer it."

"No." He tightened his grip on the handle.

"I promise they won't want it, but the gesture will satisfy them."

"If I lose Ren to them—"

"If you don't offer it, you may have to dance for days," Kersta said chuckling.

"How do I get myself into these predicaments?"

"Debt of gratitude," Kersta said.

"I believe Gallant has more than repaid the debt he feels he owes," Talamaya said.

"When?" Gallant asked.

The ladies all laughed.

"Can you turn them into stone?" Gallant asked.

"Heavens no," Talamaya responded for Mexia.

Kersta said, "Shhh, do you smell the sweet fragrance of the flowers?"

"And hear the tinkling sound of their fairy laughter?" Mexia added.

"Travelers," a fairy said, popping up amongst a bed of flowers. Her blue hair, skin and shimmering wings sparkled with fairy dust and were the same color as the petals she reclined against. "Why do you come here?"

"We're on a long journey," Talamaya said, "but we were not welcome in Miekal."

"Oh, and why not, human?" The fairy tilted her head to the side and stared up at Talamaya.

"A wizard wishes to imprison us."

"Talamaya," voices whispered amongst the flowers as if the buds had suddenly come to life.

"You seek the scepter?"

"Yes. We journey through the land of the Cyclops at dawn tomorrow on our way there. But we've traveled all day already and must rest first."

The fairy walked all the way around Talamaya's horse. "Would you come down here?"

"Certainly." Talamaya slid off her horse and stood in front of the fairy.

"Kneel."

Talamaya knelt before the miniature creature. "Aralias," the fairy said and nodded as she touched Talamaya's hair hanging loosely about her shoulders. "You look like her."

"You knew her?"

"She came through here, yes, a few years back."

Talamaya wondered if the fairy confused her with some other human. "Five-hundred years ago?"

"Hmmm, yes, that could be so."

"What was she like?"

The fairy smiled. "She was like you. Do you have something for us?"

"Anything we possess we would willingly give to you."

"Anything?"

"Within reason," Gallant grumbled.

Laughter rippled through the flowers. The fairy said, "Humans can be stubborn, but no more so than dwarves. What have you to give to me, dwarf?"

Gallant clutched at his war hammer for dear life. "Ren, if I have to."

"Ah, your war hammer? Well, dwarf, fairies have no need to wage war, however, we much appreciate the offer. We know how attached you are to such an item. What else do you have?"

"Nothing else of value."

She smiled an impish smile and pointed to his waist. "What about that leather belt of yours?"

"It holds up my pants, woman."

Laughter echoed across the valley.

"It is unanimous. The fairies wish your belt."

Gallant grumbled the whole time he unfastened the belt. Then he leaned down to hand it to the fairy. She examined it and nodded. "Yes, this will do."

She turned to Kersta. "And you, human? What have you for me?"

"My horse is the most precious possession of mine."

"Ah, your horse. We have no need of horses. They would eat all our flowers."

She turned to Mexia, "And you?"

"My amulet."

"It is a gift from your mother, only now she is dead."

"Yes," Mexia said, her voice breaking.

"Your companions serve you well, princess. They offer the gifts that mean the most to them. So what means the most to you, princess?"

"I treasure the amulet Sir Malachon gave me to wear on the journey for protection."

"Ah." The fairy touched the amulet and the gem sparked with light. "In the Cave of Sorrows."

"And the other my brother gave me when I nearly died of food poisoning."

"Yes, another treasured gift."

"My horse I raised from a colt."

"And as you know I don't wish a horse. Way too messy. They leave smells that are none too fragrant. There is something else, though, is there not?"

"My staff, now enhanced by a special gift given to me by Modi."

"Ah, Modi, yes. She could see the good in you and wished to aid you on your way also."

The fairy tapped her foot on the ground. "Something else though."

"My companions. They're more precious to me than anything."

"Yes, your companions. I knew you would finally come to them. You are like Aralias."

"Did she have two women companions also?"

The fairy smiled. "And a dwarf." She took a deep breath. "Of the ladies' possessions, I wish nothing. I will keep the dwarf's belt to humor me when I am low of cheer. But from you, I wish your companions."

Talamaya looked from one of her friends to the other, their eyes wide with concern, then she turned to the fairy. "Yes."

"For one night, I will keep your companions, while you do a task for me."

"Yes?"

"Your friends will sleep here while you are gone. When you return, you will sleep, then you will continue on your journey."

Talamaya nodded.

"A witch has stolen my favorite comb." The fairy ran her fingers through her hair. "My hair is so fine, only that comb can keep it from tangling. I want my comb back. But she won't give it to you for the asking. You will have to be cleverer than she is." The fairy leaned forward and whispered, "She is mean-hearted. If you are not careful, you'll be turned into a statue to join the others in her garden, which is already full of them. So beware. She acts sweetly on the surface, but she has a heart of stone beneath this."

Talamaya bowed her head to the fairy, then rose to her feet. "If it's in my power, I'll return with the comb. If I'm not able—"

"Your companions will be allowed to rest, as I have said, and be released to continue whatever way they wish in the morning."

The ladies and Gallant dismounted. Mexia gave Talamaya a hug. "May the gods be with you."

Gallant gave her an embrace and smiled at her when she raised her eyebrows. Then he grabbed his pants once he released her. "I promised to stay with you. If ye don't return in the morning, I will come and rescue ye, Princess Talamaya."

Kersta took Talamaya aside and embraced her, whispering into her ear at the same time, "The fairy wishes the comb, but it's not hers. The witch owns it. You must try to talk her out of it somehow."

The fairy said, "You must go on your way, princess. But leave your staff with one of your companions. You won't need it where you go. Your friends need their rest. Follow the trail of fairy dust. It will lead you to the witch's house on the knoll."

"Goodbye," Talamaya said to them. "I'll return soon, my friends."

She mounted her horse, her whole being filled with apprehension. How could she secure the comb without offending the witch? Had she led her companions astray by bringing them to the fairyland? What if the king and his and her men perished in the castle all over the want of a comb?

15

True to the fairy's word, when Talamaya reached the house of the witch, stone statues littered the yard of men, women, two dwarfs, and even two children. Talamaya dismounted from her horse and walked her through the statue garden. What if she could bring Mexia back here with her and set the people free?

That's what Talamaya wished to do more than anything in the world. But if they did so and the witch caught them, then what? All would be lost. Her knights, King Lazarion and his men, Mexia, and the peoples populating the whole continent could suffer at the hands of the maniacal wizard.

But wasn't setting them free, the right thing to do?

She turned her attention toward the one-story house. Despite the lateness of the hour, candles flickered in the two windows of the pink-stone home.

Even though there were no trees nearby, moss covered every square inch of the roof. No flowers, no shrubs, nothing softened the harshness of the stone statues. Talamaya shivered. She couldn't shake the desire to free the people.

Letting go of her horse's reins, she stepped onto the wooden porch and raised her hand to the door. Before she could knock, the door opened.

Inside a woman stood as beautiful as a Mesa elf, tall, slender, with golden curls resting all the way to her hips, ivory skin, and blue-eyed, but no pointed ears. Her gown shown as brightly as the golden rays of the sun. Talamaya closed her gaping mouth to hide her ignorance. She'd assumed the woman would be wickedly ugly and hideously mean. But the woman smiled sweetly and motioned for her to come in.

Talamaya closed the door behind her and crossed the stone floor.

"You are?"

"Princess Talamaya from Damar."

"Yes. You are."

"And you are?"

"Did the fairy not tell you? I am the mean-spirited witch." She smiled.

"Your name?"

"Margina."

"You know what I have come for then, if you know the fairy sent me here."

"To steal from me." Margina poured a blue substance into two goblets. "Share some minko tea with me."

"I would not steal from you." Talamaya took hold of the goblet. "I had fully intended to ask you for the comb, if you would graciously give it. If not, I would tell the fairy, you wouldn't give the comb to me."

Margina gave her a sly smile and waved at two stone seats. Once they sat, she pointed to a table. "You see on that table are forty-two combs. You may have any one of them."

"But the fairy wants one that is perfect for her hair."

"Since you have been so honest with me, something my other visitors were not, I'll give you any of the combs to take back to the fairy. But I must warn you, if you don't choose the correct one, she'll fly into a rage. No telling what she'll do. She can be very spiteful."

"I know the comb is not hers."

Margina smiled. "Do you now?"

"Yes, that's why I could not steal it. It isn't hers to have unless you wished to make a gift of it to her."

"Why are you really here?"

"To get the comb, so my companions and I could rest before we have to face the Cyclops."

"And why do you not return to Damar?"

"I must retrieve the scepter of Lanai."

"Ah, power and glory you seek."

"Only stability for the continent. There's a wizard, I believe, who's creating some kind of madness amongst the beasts who live in Inherian."

"Yes, he's coming to visit me right now."

Talamaya stood so quickly she spilled her tea on the floor. "Oh, my apologies, Margina." She dropped to her knees and cleaned the mess up with the underlining of her gown.

Margina smiled. "You're different than the others. No one has ever called me by name. No one has ever come here and told me the truth of why they come to visit me. All they have done is returned my generosity by trying to steal from me." She paused. "Would you visit me again?"

"If you'd like, but my quest is urgent. The wizard has imprisoned many, and I fear for their health."

The witch glanced back through her window. "You seek to free those who are imprisoned?"

"Yes. I even wish to free those who have been turned to stone."

The witch turned and smiled. "Would you visit me again?"

"Yes, but I must claim the scepter and free the men."

"All right. Promise me you'll return and drink tea with me again. If you can find a way to free the rabble from the stone, you may do so."

"How may I leave here to avoid crossing paths with the wizard?"

"You cannot." She motioned to a spinning wheel in the corner of the room. "Sit there and spin some yarn for me. While I visit with the wizard, you may get a good look at him. The next time you meet, you may not have a chance."

Talamaya hesitated.

Margina walked over and patted her shoulder. "You're my apprentice. Spin and I'll ready myself for the wizard."

Talamaya walked over to the spinning wheel, then sat on the wooden stool before it. Margina disappeared into a backroom.

Then Talamaya had an idea. Modi's tea had shown her the way before. Would it help her to select the right comb now? She tilted her flask to her lips and drank of the sweet tea. Then she attempted to figure out how to spin.

"All ready!" the witch sang out, walking back into the room.

Talamaya smiled to see the witch dressed in a somber black wool gown, her lovely blond curls turned to dingy gray. But her blue eyes still sparkled with the same kind of beauty.

Margina laughed. "You still see me as beautiful. I can see it in your eyes." She motioned to the spinning wheel. "Spin, my dear. He'll be here any moment."

"I don't know how to spin."

"Touch the wheel and the lambs' wool will spin into thread."

Talamaya did as she was told and at once the thick wool wound into threads.

"Good, you're an excellent pupil. A wonderful apprentice."

As soon as the words were out of her mouth, the door flew open. Talamaya's throat grew dry as her hands stilled on the wool in front of her. The wizard stood at least a foot taller than her brother and his coned hat added another foot to his height. With black penetrating eyes tinged red, darting from the witch to her, he strode into the house. His gray beard curled down to where she imagined his knees were under his black robes sprinkled with golden glitter.

"Is she here? The princess? Is she here?"

"As you can see, Grimoria, she is not. Would I have her hiding beneath a bed?" The witch poured two goblets of minko tea.

"The fairy said she sent her to your house."

"The girl obviously got lost. The way is dark this time of night. No stars even light the way. My house is far enough back off the road, she could have easily ridden right past. No doubt she's still riding, still seeking my place right now."

Grimoria glanced at Talamaya, her skin chilling as she turned her attention back to her spinning. "You have a new apprentice?"

"Yes."

"She has no wizardry powers that I can sense."

"No. She's willing to learn though. If she does not work out, she'll join the others." She motioned to her garden out front.

"I told you if the princess comes here, you must tell me at once."

"Of course."

"You'll not disobey me in this matter?"

"Why would I do that? I enjoy my place here outside the village of Miekal. The fairies and I have good sport with the humans and an occasional dwarf. What more could I ask for?"

"Remember my words. Should you hide the princess, or aid her in any way, you will suffer the consequences."

"My memory is adequate."

"Good." He looked back at Talamaya. "Have you asked her to select the comb to satisfy the fairy yet?"

"No."

He turned his attention to the witch. "Why not? You told me that's the test you use on all your new apprentices."

"I like this one. I didn't feel the need to ask her to choose the right one."

"You said that shows the individual may have some abilities that are trainable into mage's skills. That's what you said."

"I'll try her out later. For now, she's busy doing other chores for me."

"Make her do it, now. I wish to see if she has any wizardry skills."

Talamaya cringed. Except for learning how to make healing kits and take care of wounds, and learning all about the kinds of poisons and effects they had on humans, she didn't know one thing about magic. That was Mexia's area of expertise.

"Would you, dear?" The witch motioned to the table. Her eyes moistened with tears, adding concern to Talamaya's already heightened level of panic.

The witch touched the corner of her eye and when the wizard glanced at her, she quickly dropped her hand. Talamaya reasoned the witch tried to give her a clue. The comb would be blue like the witch's eyes.

Talamaya stepped over to the table. If she picked the wrong one would the witch turn her to stone, then once the wizard left, return her to her human form? That's all she could hope for.

The wizard chuckled. "She trembles she's so scared. She has no innate wizardry skills."

Talamaya observed the vast selection of combs, from gold to blue as the witch's eyes. But out of all the combs, twelve were blue.

The witch said, "What will you do with the princess when you catch her?"

Talamaya assumed the witch attempted to distract the

wizard while she moved around the table. Out of all the combs, one stood out perfectly, shimmering with sprinkles of fairy dust, like the fairy's blue skin, gown, wings, and hair. Could it be that obvious?

"I will deal with the princess when the time comes. But as for this girl, once you turn her into stone, I'll take her home with me and place her in my own garden."

So much for the witch rescuing her.

Talamaya reached for the most obvious comb and lifted it from the table.

The witch gasped.

The wizard snorted. "I'll follow the other road and see where the princess has gotten off to."

"Do. I have work to do with my new apprentice. Idle hands lead to devilish actions, you know."

The wizard waved his hand in front of his face and vanished.

"I wish I could do that," the witch said. She turned her attention to Talamaya. "How did you do that?"

"I picked out the one sprinkled with fairy dust. It seemed so obvious I was afraid it was a trick."

The witch stared at the comb. "It has no fairy dust on it. How do you see such a thing?"

"I don't know. It glitters and sparkles like no other. And it's the same color as the fairy, exactly, with the same kind of glitter."

The witch studied Talamaya, then looked back at the comb. "You have no wizardry skills that I can see. How did you know?"

"It is as I said."

The witch turned to the table. "Tell me then, which one is mine? I will give you no hints this time."

"If I select the wrong one?"

"There will be no consequences." She looked up at Talamaya. "Or rather...only one. If you cannot find the right comb, you will have to go back to the fairyland. Undoubtedly, the wizard will believe you are the princess as you travel back there. Otherwise, if you succeed with deciding the right comb, you'll stay here with me a while longer." She smiled. "The fairy is right. I have a mean streak. But so does she. Select the correct comb. Hurry."

"The children who are in your yard...had they tried to steal the comb also?"

"No, but their parents did. How could I do something as cruel as make them orphans? They joined them instead. Quit stalling and make the selection."

Talamaya studied the combs. This time she looked for the one that would match the characteristics of the witch. Nothing black, nothing blue, would do. The gold one seemed to nearly glow though. The witch was beautiful. The golden comb would match her beauty. With baited breath, Talamaya touched the golden comb. Instantly, she found herself in a small room furnished with a bed, table, and chair. One window opened out into a backyard where a cheetaur paced back and forth. Without her staff, there was no way Talamaya could cross the backyard.

She walked quietly over to the door and touched the knob. Twisting it, she found resistance. Locked. Placing her ear against the door, she heard the witch singing.

"I have an apprentice. I have an apprentice. Woe is the wizard who scoffs at me."

Did the witch think she could use Talamaya's so called wizardry skills to beat the wizard? The only explanation was Modi's tea had shown her the way.

Walking back across the floor, she flipped a corner of a rug up with the toe of her boot by accident. She knelt to pull it back in place, then saw the corner of a sheet of wood. After rolling the rug back, she smiled to see a trapdoor. Though if it only led to a crypt or dungeon or dank, dark, smelly cellar, she was doomed.

Pulling the door up with the utmost caution, she peered inside. Malachon's amulet glowed softly with light. The faint outline of steps disappeared into the abyss. Talamaya moved into the darkness and closed the trapdoor over her head.

With a cautious step, she ran her hands over a stone wall covered with wet moss, and reached a room. Could she maybe find a weapon to use on the cheetaur? Only her staff enhanced by Modi's touch would give her that advantage, she feared.

She tripped over a box, then peered into its contents, her eyes now adjusting to the low light. She recognized jars of ingredients for potions from the types Mexia used in her spells.

Talamaya continued her exploration stepping slowly into the darkness, the amulet at her throat giving off the same illumination as a candle's dim light.

"Psst," a voice whispered in one corner of the room. The sound was deep throated and low like that a dwarf would make.

She hurried across the floor. Her mouth dropped open, then she clamped it shut and furrowed her brow.

"Please, help me out of here."

She considered the lock on the metal cage that Tanner was imprisoned in. "I ought to let the witch eat you for supper, Tanner, if I didn't like your cousin, Gallant, so well that I couldn't do such a thing to you."

"She is evil, my lady. Help me out of here, and I will repay ye all I can."

She folded her arms. "You've already betrayed us once."

"I cannot any further. Please, I beg of ye. Get me out of here, and I'll get ye back to your friends."

"In the fairyland?"

"Yes, there's a secret passage to the dwarf mines down here. I stumbled upon it many years ago." He shook two of the rusty bars to his cage. "Get me out of here, before she discovers ye are missing."

"I cannot pick locks."

"The key is over there against that wall."

Talamaya hurried across the floor to where the dwarf had pointed. She tripped on another box, sending a smattering of goose bumps up her arms.

Finally, she reached the wall. Grabbing the key, she jerked it from the iron hook, then moved as quickly as she could back to the cage.

Once the rusted door squeaked open, Tanner ran out. Talamaya dashed after him, stopping suddenly when they came to a solid rock wall. He pressed a rock, making it depress. A door rumbled open. They ran into the passageway, and he closed the door again.

"Will she not follow us?"

He laughed. "Nay, she cannot leave her home. Did ye notice how beautiful she is? She uses a lot of her powers to remain that way. While she is at home, she is safe. If she leaves, she is as vulnerable to the wild beasts as we are."

They ran down one long tunnel, then turned right at a junction. "Where are we headed, Tanner?"

"If ye are here, ye have traveled through the fairyland. I imagine ye wish to return there for my cousin and your female friends."

"Yes. But where will you go?"

"Back to town. Tell Gallant—" He hesitated. "Well, tell him I will make it up to him one of these days."

"Why were you down here in the first place?"

"I hoped I could steal a potion to bring one of the stones back to life."

"A friend of yours?"

"Aye. The wizard said he would make the witch turn any one of her statues back into people if we would give ye up to him, should ye turn up. I didn't know my cousin traveled with ye. But when ye stole away in the night, I knew my only hope was to try and steal a potion from the witch and turn my friend back to flesh and blood."

"You could have asked us."

"What?"

"Mexia, one of my lady companions, can do what you seek."

He tugged at his beard and grumbled under his breath. "Aye. I have been foolish to trust the wizard when I should have trusted ye and my cousin."

"We'll try to help you as soon as we can."

"Tonight. It has to be tonight."

"Why tonight?"

"Once in a new moon the witch gets rid of all the statues so she can make room for new ones. A man comes and picks them up in his wagon, tonight, and takes them to a ship that is bound for Albion."

"Good, then that will even be better. We'll stop his wagon and free the people. It'll be easier if we don't have to do it in the witch's yard."

"We?"

"You'll help us."

"But—"

"If you wish to repay your debt to Gallant—"

"All right, all right. I don't know how he could have put up with ye humans since...where did he say ye rescued him?"

"Elan Pass."

"Aye, Elan Pass."

He trudged through the tunnel switching from one to another and eventually stopped in front of an iron door. He unlocked the door, then shoved it open with a rumble.

"I wonder if the wizard will have already passed by here," Talamaya whispered.

"Great. He is looking for ye already?"

AFTER HALF AN HOUR, they reached the perimeter of the fairy-land. "I will wait for ye here. Bring the others to this place as I don't want to have to do anything for the fairies."

"I'll return shortly."

Would he wait for her like he promised? Or would he tell the wizard where she was if he chanced to meet him on the road? Talamaya took a deep breath, trying to calm her disquiet as she walked alone to the area where the blue fairy waited.

The fairy popped up from her flower, startling her when Talamaya reached the location. The fairy folded her arms and tilted her chin up. "Have you the comb?"

Talamaya pulled it from the pocket of her cloak.

The fairy's eyes grew wide. "You stole it from the witch, and she didn't turn you to stone?"

"There was no need. I asked her for the comb and she gave it to me."

The fairy twisted her head to the side in disbelief. "Without using some kind of trickery?"

"She said I had to pick the right one from a whole selection of combs."

"Hmm. All right, then you may sleep in my field."

"I must take my friends from here to complete a task. Will we be free to return once we are done and sleep the rest of the night?"

"If you leave, you will have to do something more for me upon your return."

Talamaya was torn. She had to free the people from the stone, but she and her companions needed to sleep. What if the fairy wished another task of her that dealt with the witch? Talamaya probably would not get out of there again.

What if she just woke Mexia? The same problem would

occur. The fairy still could ask her to see the witch again, she was certain.

"Wake my friends, if you would. We'll go now."

"And return?"

"Maybe."

"I hope so. No one has ever brought me the right comb who managed to get free from the witch."

The fairy sprinkled dust on Talamaya's companions. Mexia yawned, Kersta rubbed her eyes, and Gallant grumbled.

Kersta spoke first as she sat upright. "You have returned. Did you get the comb?"

"Yes, we must go now."

"But we have not slept the entire night. In fact, I would venture to say, maybe only a couple of hours at the most."

"Yes, Mexia. I'm tired, too. Let us go, then we shall rest."

"Something is wrong?" Mexia asked as she rose to her feet and stretched her arms above her head.

"We must accomplish a task left undone."

"What now?"

The fairy interrupted. "You have done a task for me, Tala-maya, and though I would have allowed you to rest for the deed, you cannot. Therefore, I give you something else in return." She handed her a wand. "May it always light your way." Giggles amongst the fairies nestled in the flowers ensued. "Even during your darkest moments."

"I thank you for your generosity, fairy. I'm sure we can put it to good use."

"That you will, princess of Damar. That you will."

Talamaya motioned to the horses. "Bring your horses, ladies, Gallant. I have someone you'll wish to meet, Gallant, some distance beyond."

They glanced back at the fairy, who watched them, curiosity

evident on her small face, her eyes twinkling with mischief, her mouth curved up in amusement.

When they had moved away from the fairy flowers, Talamaya said, "Your cousin waits for us, or at least I hope so, nearby."

"I will wring his thick neck."

"We have a task to complete. He'll help us. And maybe, we can return to the goose-down mattresses we first lay upon tonight."

"What task must we perform tonight, my lady?" Kersta asked.

"First, we must stop a wagonload of statues from traveling to the seacoast. Then Mexia must free the people who are frozen in the stone."

"Oh, my lady."

"You can do it, Mexia. I have every faith in your abilities."

"Then we can go back to bed?" Kersta asked.

"If Tanner will allow us to return to his place, yes, but I must get Cristana first. I left her in the front garden of the witch's home before I went inside. When I was taken prisoner, I had to escape through underground mines underneath the house."

"Oh, my lady," Mexia gasped.

"Yes, well, in my wanderings, I found Tanner locked in a cage in a cellar."

"Hmpf, serves him right." Gallant swung his axe as if he was fighting his sworn enemy.

"Pssst, over here," Tanner whispered amongst a row of shrubs.

They hurried to join him.

Gallant said, "I could—"

"Before you get yourself tied in a knot, Gallant, I am here to make amends. The wizard passed this way a while back. And the empty wagon passed me going to the witch's house. It should return this way shortly."

"Good. Then we need to blockade the road to get him to stop."

"And then?" Kersta asked.

"Then Mexia will relieve the wagon master of his cargo."

16

After Mexia rolled some rocks into the road with her powers, the party of five stood behind them, waiting for the wagon to arrive. When the wheels rumbled along the road with its approach, the women readied their staffs while Gallant held up his war hammer.

Tanner grouched, "Am I the only one not ready for action?"

Talamaya motioned to the driver as he pulled his horses abruptly to a stop.

"What goes on here? I have no gold for the likes of you!"

"Your treasure is as precious as life itself," Talamaya said. "Step down from the wagon, and no harm shall befall you."

He jumped down, his eyes wary as he considered the weapons the ladies and one dwarf held. Their stern looks indicated they meant business, and Talamaya could see the man wasn't any kind of a warrior.

"They are just a bunch of stone statues," he said, his words harsh, but with a nervous edge to them as Tanner motioned for him to sit down at the side of the road, and Gallant hovered over him.

Mexia climbed into the wagon with Talamaya, while Kersta waited next to it.

"Oh," a woman cried out as Mexia freed her. "Oh, my children, my husband!"

"Shh," Talamaya cautioned her. "Lady Mexia will free everyone, but we must be quiet."

The woman fought tears and held onto her son's small stone hand as Mexia worked the reverse stone spell on her daughter.

"Momma!" she cried out when the girl was released and ran to her mother to give her a hug.

The boy was next, then the husband. "We cannot go through the fairyland," the woman said, "or we will face the same predicament as before."

Talamaya motioned to Tanner. "He'll take you to the mines when everyone is free."

"The mines?" the lady asked.

"They lead under the village of Miekal. One of the tunnels goes straight to my shop. From there you can return to your homes," Tanner said. He led them a short way off the road on the path to the mines.

Mexia released the next man.

Talamaya pointed the way for him to follow Tanner. She released three more men and a dwarf woman and man. Kersta led these along the same path Tanner took.

She broke the spell for the last three men, then Mexia rolled the boulders away to allow the wagon passage.

"Don't return here again." Talamaya jumped down from the wagon with Mexia. "If you do, Mexia will turn *you* to stone."

"Yes, yes, my lady." He hurried to climb onto his wagon, then headed back toward the seacoast.

Talamaya listened for a second as she thought she heard a horse's hooves clip-clopping on the road toward them. Fearing it was someone they would not wish to see on the road at this time of night, but hoping beyond hope it was just her horse that followed the others pulling the wagon, she whistled. To her utter delight, her horse came running.

Talamaya hugged Cristana's neck with tears in her eyes. Then they led the rest of the men to the caves.

Once the freed men, women, and children were safely inside with Tanner as their guide, Gallant pointed to a narrow passage through a mountain ridge nearby. "We can maneuver through there with our horses and around to the town from there, but it's a longer way around and not the most pleasant of journeys."

"But at the end of it we sleep." Kersta climbed into her saddle.

"If we make it," Gallant warned.

Everyone looked over to see Gallant's grave face, his brows knit deeply with concern, while his eyes nearly disappeared as narrow as his eyelids were drawn.

"What's in the pass, Gallant?" Talamaya asked, hopeful that the pass wouldn't be as dangerous as Elan turned out to be for her.

"Red devil wolves." He rubbed his leg where the injury had healed from the last fight he'd had with the wolves of Elan Pass.

"But you were alone last time." Talamaya hoped her words would reassure him.

"And there will be no blinding snow to make me lose my way."

"Yes, no snow enchantresses either."

They grew quiet as they entered the narrow pass, each with weapons readied for action as they listened to the wind howling through the passage.

The still dark mountains wore a red cast, dotted with firs and pines. Red needles shed during the spring, littered the path padding the horses' steps as they walked along the winding trail.

Cristana whinnied. "They are near," Talamaya warned as the

light from her fairy wand illuminated the pass with a shim-mering aura of magic.

"They are here!" Gallant shouted when a wolf lunged at his leg.

The red wolves, slightly smaller than their snow wolf cousins, had killer canine teeth just as deadly. The ladies struck the attacking wolves at random, killing them at once with a blow of their staffs. Then one howled the signal for retreat and the rest skulked off.

Talamaya looked back to see relief clear on Gallant's face this time. He managed a smile.

She smiled back.

They finished riding through the pass an hour later, much relieved.

Once they made it to the outskirts of town, Mexia said, "Princess!"

She looked over at her, barely able to keep her eyes awake even when Mexia said the word so sharply.

"You're falling asleep."

"Yes, if I don't get into a bed soon, I'll fall off my horse."

Gallant led them down several back alleys in case anyone followed their movements. Then finally they arrived at Tanner's stable.

Once inside, Gallant offered to take care of the horses, while the ladies slipped back into the house without objection.

As they approached Tanner's bedchambers, they heard the strangest noises. Talamaya reached for the doorknob to investigate.

"Oh, Tanner," they heard a woman say inside the room.

The ladies smiled to each other and continued to their room.

Without wasting another minute once they were inside, the ladies ditched their clothes and climbed into bed.

"Tomorrow, ladies, we'll try for the land of the Cyclops again."

"Yes, princess," the women replied.

Kersta asked, "What have you read about the creatures, my lady?"

Mexia turned on her side. "Yes, how are we to get by them?"

Talamaya didn't respond.

Kersta sighed. "She's asleep."

"Yes, we must sleep, too."

Talamaya closed her eyes. She had no idea what to expect from the Cyclops who threw boulders and trees at travelers who journeyed through their lands like a child threw sticks and stones at his enemy.

She wondered, too, what had become of Rupert. Had he made it through their lands, unscathed? Or would they find his body rotting amongst the boulders when they passed through that way in the morning? She sighed deeply. Somehow she had to get them through the lands safely.

A door slammed down the hall and Talamaya assumed it was Gallant retiring to his room for what remained of the night. When all was quiet again, she closed her eyes and tried to still her fertile mind. But in the dark, she saw Lazarion chained to a wall in some dank dungeon. His men all wore chains around their wrists and ankles, too, in a collection of cells against one wall. Across from them, the Damarian knights were chained.

There was no sign of Og though. Had he died along the way? Or had he escaped capture and still journeyed for the scepter?

If he claimed the scepter, she'd definitely move to the Maken Peninsula and live with the Amazon women. No way would she marry Og. Even, if he was king of Damar. The notion embittered her, making her queasy to her stomach.

She reached out her hand to touch Lazarion's cheek when he reappeared in her vision, the look of defeat etched in his features from his vacant stare, dark circles around his eyes, his hunched shoulders. She had to free him and all the rest of the men soon before they lost the will to live.

Shouldn't she be trying to free them first? What was the matter with her that she should only think of the scepter?

She rubbed her forehead, her mind muddled with lack of sleep and anxiety. *What is the right path, Modi?* What way should she go? But she hadn't even a clue as to where the men were imprisoned. And she knew where the scepter was. Yet, was she driven to get the magic rod first from a lust for power? Would she forget the men once she had the power in her grasp? Was she like Rupert, his only concern, retrieving the scepter?

A tear dribbled down her cheek. She had to save the men. If they died before she could reach them only because she had gone after the scepter first...

She sat up in bed. She had to find out where the wizard had hidden the men.

MUCH LATER THE next morning with a whisper of sunlight poking around the edges of a white linen curtain, Talamaya heard whispering. Her head throbbed and her skin burned. She opened her eyes to find Kersta, Mexia, and the female dwarf freed from stone, watching her.

"Oh, my lady." Kersta grasped her hand and squeezed it hard. "Mexia has used her healing powers on you all morning. And Tanner's friend, Leesa, brought you herbal tea from the soothsayer's cave that is located not far from here."

"We must see the soothsayer." Talamaya tried to rise. With the movement, she grew dizzy, her head swimming in a million different directions. Her eyes, hot and scratchy, blurred with an overwhelming tiredness.

"No, my lady." Mexia made her lay back down. "You must rest. Nania, the soothsayer from this region, wishes to see you, but not until you're well. Once the fever subsides, we'll take you there."

"We have to free the men."

Kersta smiled. "You cannot get your mind off the barbarian king. Even in your bewildered, feverish state, you couldn't help thinking about him."

"He and the other men are sick."

"Yes, princess, and your worrying about them last night, made you sick," Mexia scolded her. "We need you to lead us. We cannot do this without you, so you must get well. Then, we shall visit Nania."

"Nania." Talamaya stared at the ceiling. "A soothsayer?"

"Yes, she is sister to Modi," Kersta said.

"Modi."

"Yes." Mexia pulled the covers under Talamaya's chin. "Sleep, princess. When you're well, we will go."

"Sleep," she said and closed her eyes.

"Yes, princess, sleep," Mexia whispered and rested her hand on her shoulder. "We'll face many new dangers soon enough."

"How is she?" a familiar voice said from beyond the door. A voice that at once stirred Talamaya's blood. The same voice from the man who thanked them for saving his life on the plain, then abandoned them the next morning, leaving them to trek through the woods on foot.

"She won't be pleased to see you, Rupert. Go away and let her rest in peace," Kersta said.

"I vow to you—"

"If you don't wish Ren to split your skull you'll move away from the door at once," Gallant growled. "It's only because of the ladies' intervention that I have not already removed your worthless head from your body."

"Shh," Kersta said. "Go. Both of you. You're disturbing the princess's sleep."

Gallant grumbled all the way down the hall as both men's heavy footsteps retreated.

WHEN THE SUN was midway in the sky, Talamaya woke again. She opened her eyes and watched Kersta peeking out the window. Mexia patted her shoulder, and she turned to see her sitting beside the bed.

"Is she not awake, yet?" Gallant objected beyond the door.

Leesa said, "Gallant, if ye would be patient, the lady could get well. Ye know she cannot ride until she is cured."

"Aye." He stomped back down the hall.

"Has he been like this long?" Talamaya asked.

Mexia smiled as Kersta hurried over to the bed.

"You're awake," Kersta said. "How do you feel?"

"Don't rush her. She must have her full strength back before we leave here to do battle with the Cyclops."

Talamaya sat upright. "I'm fine."

Leesa stepped into the room and smiled. "Ye are awake. Are ye ready for some gryphon stew?"

The encounter on the plain left a bitter taste in Talamaya's mouth with the thought of eating the vicious creature. Yet not accepting the woman's hospitality...

"Boar stew? Perhaps, my lady?" Kersta offered.

Talamaya would never get used to Kersta reading her mind. "Yes, if it wouldn't put Leesa out too much. Otherwise—"

"Boar stew coming right up."

When the dwarf closed the door behind her, Kersta said, "She has been most concerned with your welfare, knowing without your help she would still be a statue somewhere in Albion by now."

"Mexia did all the work."

"Yes, and she has been most thankful to Mexia, too. Debt of gratitude to both you ladies. She'll take us to Nania's home as soon as you feel up to the journey."

Talamaya pulled her covers aside. "Help me to get dressed. I'm ready to ride."

"After you eat, my lady." Mexia recovered Talamaya with the coverlet. "We'll leave soon enough."

Talamaya stared at the quilt for a moment, then turned to the ladies. "Did I hear Rupert's voice last night? Or was I having a nightmare?"

"You heard him this morning," Kersta said. "He had trouble with the Cyclops when he tried to pass through their lands. He returned to town to see if he could get reinforcements to aid him."

"Us?"

"He knew no one else was foolish enough to try to cross the lands of the Cyclops."

Talamaya hmpfd her displeasure.

"Gallant has threatened him with bodily damage all morning. And Tanner, despite being the pacifist he is, joined in on the taunts. Even Leesa said for what he had done, she would never trust the knight again. She recommended Mexia turn him back into stone."

"And the knight's reaction?"

Kersta slid another pillow behind Talamaya's back. "He understands how angry we all are with him."

"We cannot stop him from going with us at the same time," Mexia said.

"No," Kersta added. "And he would be another to fight at our side."

"But can we trust him?" Talamaya asked. "He has taken our horses once. Would he do the same thing, later and leave us stranded again? The scepter lures him, I'm afraid, ladies. He cannot be trusted."

Kersta said, "Yes, but if we free his people, and Lazarion claims the scepter instead..."

Mexia shook her head at Kersta. "You're upsetting the princess. *She* will claim the scepter. Not Lazarion or anyone else."

"I'm fine," Talamaya said.

Gallant opened the door for Leesa. She carried a tray into the room, and he poked his head inside. "Is she well enough to travel?"

Talamaya smiled. "Good afternoon, Gallant. As soon as I've eaten, we'll see Nania."

"Good, I will ready the horses." He hurried back down the hallway.

Leesa set the tray across Talamaya's lap. "I would go with ye, but Tanner wishes to marry me. It's the best offer I have had in a year. Of course, he had asked me before I was turned to stone also."

"I'm happy for you," Talamaya said, "if that's what makes you happy." She savored the rich gravy flavored with pork, the meaty chunks tenderized to perfection. Every peapod tasted sweet and slightly crisp like she liked them. "This is the best stew I have ever eaten. I wish you would return with me to Damar and teach my cooks a thing or two about making boar stew right."

Leesa beamed and Talamaya realized then how much her words pleased the dwarf who attempted so hard to prove herself worthy to her.

"Yes." Talamaya scooped up another hearty portion. "I'll have to have another bowl before we leave."

"Aye, princess," Leesa said. "Three more should ye like."

Talamaya smiled. She figured the dwarf thought because she was so much taller, she would need to eat so much more. In truth, the dwarf bowls were smaller than what she was used to eating from. Another portion or two would be welcome.

Once she was done, she handed the bowl to Leesa who hurried to fetch more stew for her.

"About Rupert," Talamaya said as she ran her hands over the comforter, "we'll decide about him after we see Nania. I wish to know if she has any advice for us concerning him."

"And if not?" Mexia asked.

"I have it in mind that he shall aid us in freeing his king."

"Will you tell the king how his knight betrayed us?" Kersta asked.

"I fathom I won't have to."

Another hour passed as Talamaya finished her stew, dressed, and waited for the ladies to braid her hair.

Mexia smiled. "Princess, if you don't quit wiggling around, I'll never get your hair put up."

"I thought that it was just me who was being so inept," Kersta said. "But now that you mention it, the princess's head is like the owl, twisting around, listening, and watching for any signs of trouble."

"I'm impatient to get on the road, ladies. I feel I have further endangered the men with my delaying us so."

"You have been sick, my lady," Mexia said. "No one will fault you for something you couldn't help."

When they had clipped the rest of Talamaya's hair close to her head with gold hair clips, she glanced in the mirror and smiled. "Well." She touched the thick braids that twisted into rolls on her head. "I'll have to have you ladies fix my hair more often. It looks prettier than it has ever looked."

Mexia smiled. "Thank you, my lady."

Kersta snorted. "She only says so to get us to do her hair in the future. Her hair always looks beautiful."

Talamaya laughed. "Come, ladies, let us not dally any further. We must be off to see Nania."

They grabbed their staffs and headed out of the room. When they reached the landing, Gallant greeted them. "It is about time."

Leesa punched his shoulder. "Show respect. The lady has been ill. And ye and I both owe her a debt of gratitude."

"Aye." Gallant tugged at his beard. "Hurry up then, woman."

Talamaya raised her brows and smiled. Gallant would never change, yet, she wouldn't wish him any other way.

Tanner walked into the living area and handed Talamaya a ring. "I found it in the witch's cellar. I thought it might help me to escape, but I could never figure out what it did."

Talamaya twisted the ring around to examine it.

"I could have sold it for quite a price."

She looked down at Tanner.

"But I wanted to give it to ye. For rescuing me and for rescuing Leesa."

"And?" Leesa prompted.

Tanner shuffled his feet and cleared his throat. "For betraying your trust, princess."

"Thank you, Tanner." Talamaya handed the ring to Mexia. "Can you sense if it is magical?"

"It is, my lady. I can feel the magic tingling in my fingertips. But I cannot tell what power it possesses. The wearer may have increased strength or stamina, or special abilities. Or the wearer could be weakened if the witch intended for someone to steal it from her. It could even be a beacon, showing her where the wearer has taken it."

"I'll ask Nania if she knows anything about the ring."

Mexia handed it back to her, and she tucked it into her cloak pocket.

Talamaya looked around the room. "Where's Rupert?"

Gallant grunted. "He rode out while I saddled our horses. He said he would go ahead and clear the way."

"Or set a trap," Tanner mumbled.

They all looked at him. He looked down at the floor. "I told ye I was sorry for my actions."

"All right and we accept your apology," Talamaya said. "Come, we must be on our way."

She headed out of the house with everyone following close behind, like a mother goose led her goslings. "Is the way safe to Nania's?" she asked Leesa.

"Yes, my lady. It isn't far."

Once the party had mounted their horses, they waved goodbye to Tanner.

Cantering out of town, the horse's hooves clicked on the cobblestone road with melodic rhythm while the sweet fragrance of wild roses growing alongside it scented the air. Wisps of white clouds slipped across the blue sky making Talamaya sigh deeply.

Would the pleasantly serene day turn into a nightmare in a matter of hours, once they attempted their trek across the Cyclops' land?

17

Talamaya and her companions finally reached a bluff of rocks near where the path led through the pass where they had been attacked by red devil wolves the night before.

"Here," Leesa motioned. "She lives in this cave."

Gallant fingered his war hammer while Talamaya dismounted.

"Did you wish to speak to Nania about Ren?"

"Nay," he grumbled. "I don't believe in soothsayers."

"We will wait for ye here," Leesa said.

When the three women walked into the caves, Talamaya took a deep breath and studied the red crystals clustered like gem quality. She reached out and touched one. "Beautiful."

"Thank you," a voice whispered. "Come visit with me. I didn't think you would come to see me after all."

"Nania?"

"Yes, welcome. Come, see me."

"And my friends? Are they welcome, too?"

"You and they are one. Come, each of you, visit with me. Drink my wine."

Talamaya walked with her companions through a long tunnel until they came to a junction that split into eight paths. "Which way?" she asked.

There was no answer.

"Nania?"

She looked back at Mexia who shook her head. Kersta shrugged.

"Do you think it is a test?" Talamaya whispered to her friends.

"Yes," the cave whispered.

"I must follow the right path? Like Modi warned?"

Laughter bounced off the walls.

"Something else then? But what? Can you not give me a clue?"

"Follow your heart, dear princess."

"My heart?"

"What does your heart will you to do?"

"I must return the scepter to my father to keep the continent at peace."

Silence followed.

Kersta shook her head. "That isn't what you're thinking, princess. Your heart wars with your primary quest. You wish to seek freedom for the king and all the men the wizard has imprisoned. *That's* what your heart tells you to do."

"Yes, princess," the voice whispered. "Listen well to your friends. They will lead you to the right path."

Talamaya stepped farther into the junction. "But even so, I don't see which of the eight paths is the correct one to take."

"Take all of them. Or take none of them. Go back to the beginning if you must."

Talamaya walked into the tunnel to her right and listened. A lantern lighted the way some distance into the passage, but she could sense nothing that way. She walked to the next and found the same thing. Looking back at Mexia, she said, "Do you sense anything with your mage abilities?"

"No, my lady."

"What about you, Kersta? Do you read something in my mind that I'm denying myself?"

"No."

"I sense nothing." Talamaya walked toward the third passage in the circle of paths. Exasperated with herself for not being more aware of what she needed to do, she walked farther into the next tunnel. Shaking her head, she turned and walked out of it, then headed for the fourth passage.

"I need another clue. Maybe the fever dulled my senses." Then Talamaya had another thought. She pulled the cap off her pouch and sipped Modi's tea.

Laughter resounded.

Talamaya smiled. She wasn't sure the tea would help her see the way in Nania's cave, but the soothsayer seemed to be amused she'd use Modi's help to find out.

Walking back to the first passage, Talamaya paused. Again nothing touched her senses.

She continued to the second and third tunnels. Again nothing. Possibly Modi's tea wouldn't help her here. Then again, perhaps she hadn't made it to the right one yet. She tried the fourth tunnel, then whipped around to the fifth. Nothing. Three left. With her luck it was the eighth tunnel and if she'd started in that direction first...

The sixth held no clues, but the seventh, she wasn't sure. She motioned to her friends. Once they stood still, they listened.

"What do you hear, ladies?" Talamaya whispered.

"I'm not certain. What do you think you hear, my lady?"

"Breathing. Does it not sound like the rocks are breathing with some difficulty?"

Mexia nodded. "Yes."

"Shall we check out the last tunnel, before we go any farther in here?" Talamaya asked.

"To compare it with this one?" Mexia asked.

"Yes."

"But your heart wishes to explore this one, princess," Kersta warned.

Talamaya studied the tunnel. "Yes, but does my heart not also want to check out the last tunnel?"

"Not like it wants to check out this one, my lady. This one frightens you. It draws you and you fight it."

Talamaya touched the wall closest to her and withdrew her hand as if the rock had burned it.

"What is wrong?" Mexia asked, her eyes wide with anxiety.

"It felt as if the rock moved. Like a heart beat within it."

She hurried down the tunnel.

"Are you sure we should not try the last tunnel first, my lady?" Mexia said, as she and Kersta ran to catch up to her. "Kersta might be wrong."

"I'm not wrong," Kersta argued.

When the tunnel split into three paths, Talamaya hesitated. Then she pointed to the one to the right. "Do you hear the breathing from there?"

"Do you not want to check out the others?" Mexia cautioned.

Talamaya dashed into the tunnel with her friends running behind her. Then she stopped partway down the tunnel. Touching the rock, she whispered, "Lazarion." She could see him lift his head, half groggy with sleep. "Come, the men are inside these rocks somewhere. We must find the way in."

Mexia grabbed her wrist. "Your cloak, my lady." She pointed at her cloak and when Talamaya looked down, she saw a circular glow of gold.

"The witch's ring," Kersta whispered.

"But we didn't get to question Nania about it," Mexia said, when Talamaya pulled it from her pocket.

Without hesitation, Talamaya slipped it onto her finger. Instantly, she was teleported to the inside of a prison. Her heart thundered and her temple pounded with panic.

In the dimly lit room, a hand grabbed her skirt and tugged. She clasped her hand over her mouth to silence her cry.

"Oh, Hauk," she whispered and dropped to her knees before him.

"My lady," he said, his voice parched and barely audible.

"I must find a way to free you all."

"You must get away before they catch you." His eyes widened in fear suddenly, signaling danger.

The warning barely made it to Talamaya's mind when a hand touched her shoulder. She jumped to her feet and readied her staff.

Her mouth dropped open slightly as she saw the man standing before her. His pleasant features and impeccable clothes made him appear almost human. He must have worked with the wizard, which would make him a mage apprentice perhaps. How she wished Mexia was with her now.

"How did you get in here?" he asked, his voice soothing and reassuring.

She smiled.

His lips turned up. "I believe my master would like to see you."

"I am sure that he would. But I have other business to take care of, first."

Before the mage could react, she struck him with her staff across the chest. With one blow, he collapsed to the floor. She wasted no time in searching his velvet garments for signs of keys. Not finding any, she looked around the walls. None were hanging anywhere.

Then she saw Lazarion. Dashing across the floor, she reached her hand through the bars. "Sire, hold on. I'll free you once I have figured a way."

"Tala," he whispered, his eyes sparkling slightly with vague recognition.

"Yes, I'll free you and all the men. I promise, if it's within my power, or die trying."

She stood, then touched the lock, trying to determine if there was anyway to pick it. When the ring on her hand glowed with renewed gusto, she touched it to the lock. Instantly, it clicked open.

She gasped, then pulled the lock off and jerked the door open. Running into the king's cell, she struck at his chains with the staff. Like melted wax, the metal pulled apart.

She touched Lazarion's cheek. "Sire, you must help me. I'll free the men, but you must help me get them to their feet."

Then she thought of Modi's tea. It was thought to heal. Would it revive the parched men? She yanked off the cap to her pouch and held it to Lazarion's lips, then helped him to drink.

"Ah," he said, recovering. "Give it to my men."

"Drink more, while I free those in your cell. The tea replenishes itself. There's plenty for everyone here."

She dashed across the floor to where five of the king's men waited, their hands stretched, out, willing her to free them, too. With careful precision, she slashed at the manacles. And when she was done, she saw the king helping the first of his men to drink the tea.

Running across the prison, she returned to Hauk's cage and set the witch's ring against the lock. It opened, and she cast the lock to the floor. As quickly as she could, she released her own people, Hauk, Zornan, and Gynt. "Where is Og?" she asked the men as she moved to the other side of the cell and worked on the other knights' manacles.

"We lost him and five of his men in the dust of the plain, my lady."

"Killed?"

Hauk shook his head. "We couldn't say. The cheetaurs attacked and gryphon, too. As soon as we were able, we continued across the plain, trying to keep the rest of us alive. It was all we could do, beg your forgiveness, princess."

"There's nothing to forgive. It's enough that you are alive," she said, then hurried out of the cell. "Go to King Lazarion. Drink of the tea he has. It'll help to revive you."

Lazarion soon joined her. "The men are coming around. How did you get here?"

"A witch's ring helped me to get in. But I don't know how we'll get out of here."

He touched her shoulder as if in doing so it meant his freedom was near at hand. "Sire, perhaps we can overwhelm the apprentice mages with surprise."

"We have no weapons."

She pointed at the dead mage. "Maybe he has a dagger or something." She unbuckled the dagger at her waist, then handed the sheathed weapon to the king. "Here, take this for your protection."

Once she finished freeing the men, they gathered around her as if she had the answers to their dilemma. "I think with the aid of the witch's ring, we might be able to maneuver through the passage, but—"

Lazarion bowed to her. "Tell us what we must do." He readied her jewel-handled dagger as Hauk raised the dagger of the dead mage in the air in a salute to her leadership.

"All right, well, I'll lead, but don't fault me too greatly if I lead the wrong way." She glanced at the men, waiting for her to show them the way.

"Has everyone had plenty of Modi's tea?"

"Yes," several said while others nodded, the weariness and depravity they'd experienced still evident in their gaunt features. If she could get them out of the dungeons alive, her next priority was to have Leesa feed them her filling boar stew.

One of the men handed Talamaya the flask, and she strapped the pouch around her waist. Afterward, she headed toward a metal door. It opened with the touch of the witch's ring.

Before she could step into the hall, Lazarion and Hauk burst into the passage. "All is clear," the king whispered and motioned for them to follow.

They heard laughter behind closed doors to the right of them, and no sound from a room to the left. One of the men listened at the room filled with noise and whispered, "Sounds like the great hall back home. Perhaps they're sharing a meal."

Talamaya touched the door where there were no sounds and it opened. Peering into the room, she discovered it was a bedchamber. She stepped inside and found a staff and two swords in a wall closet.

She motioned to Gynt. "More weapons," she whispered. "Arm yourselves."

Six more rooms provided weapons for another eighteen men. But when they reached the next door, Talamaya paused. A glimmer of blue light trickled under the door.

No matter how quietly the men attempted to walk, with forty-five of them headed past the room, whoever was inside the chamber, would surely be alerted.

She motioned to a man outfitted with a crossbow and bolts. He joined her, and she touched her ring to the door.

"Hello?" a voice said inside the room when the door began to open.

She and the knight moved into the room at once, she ready to strike the mage with her staff, and the knight, with the bolt pointed at his heart.

The mage instantly raised his hands, and the knight released the bolt.

Collapsing to the floor, the mage had died instantly.

"Don't hesitate next time," Talamaya scolded. "A mage can destroy us with one spoken word. I would never have made it across the room in time to kill him with my staff before he spoke it."

"Yes, my lady."

Then she worried she was being too hard on the man and patted his arm. "One less to worry about, though, right?"

He smiled at her. "Yes, my lady."

They entered the hallway. Their expressions dark and angry, the men appeared ready to do battle, but at the same time, worry was etched in their wrinkled brows. Two of the men hurried into the room to retrieve the weapons, then when they rejoined the party, everyone moved forward again.

Talamaya nodded to Lazarion and his eyes sparkled with renewed hope. She sighed heavily, hoping to still her doubt. Would she lead all to their deaths? That's what made her head continue to pound with concern.

They headed down the hallway and again noticed a light underneath a door.

She motioned for the archer. This time he was prepared. When she opened the door, the mage's back was to them while he uttered some incantation over a bubbling pot. She nodded to the knight before the mage sensed their presence and whipped around. Although even so, the mage turned.

His eyes burned with anger, but the bolt struck his chest, and his eyelids closed, his hands clutching the offending weapon. He collapsed to the floor.

Immediately, another knight raided the mage's weapon's chest.

In the hallway, to the right of the passage, an open doorway led into an expansive room. Talamaya peered into it and stared at the light swirling in the center of the marble floor.

"It appears to be a portal."

"But where does it lead to?" Lazarion asked.

"Somewhere out of here, most likely. There may be no other way out, and if the men have to face the mages in combat all at once, several, if not all of our men, will surely die."

Lazarion shook his head. "We're trained to be warriors. But you, princess, shouldn't be here."

"We should chance the portal," she said, her words spoken in haste, before she changed her mind and said what she really thought of the king's words.

She looked over at the men who all nodded. None wished to return to the chains in the dungeon. If the portal meant a means of escape, they were willing to risk it.

Talamaya hurried across the floor. "All right, we all step into it at once as quickly as we're able."

She waited with four archers who guarded the portal in the event a mage happened to catch them trying to escape and attempted to sound an alarm. The rest of the men crowded together six at a time into the portal, then vanished from sight.

Lazarion touched her arm. "I cannot thank you enough, Talamaya, for helping us to escape. I have every intention of seeking your hand in marriage as soon as we return home."

She raised her brows at him. "But, sire, I have already said I don't wish to marry any. Besides, my father wouldn't permit me to marry anyone who isn't Damarian."

"You wouldn't wish any other than me." He lifted her fingers to his lips and pressed a gentle kiss on them. "You cannot deny the attraction between us."

She tried to hide a smile, which made him grin in response. Seeing him so happy, despite his wearied condition, she felt cheered. She glanced back at the portal. "It's time, sire."

"Come," she said to the men. "We'll go at the same time."

Lazarion grabbed her hand as they stepped into the portal. She figured he was determined not to lose her again, but instantly his fingers slipped away from hers, and her heart thundered with fright.

The men carrying the crossbows and the king disappeared, every last one of them.

But she stood alone in the swirling, shimmering, never-ending rainbow lights of the portal.

18

To Talamaya's alarm, voices approached from the wizard's hallway. *Mage's voices.* When they found her there, they would kill her for certain. Especially once they discovered the mischief she'd been up to. Dead mages and disappearing prisoners wouldn't settle well with them, she figured.

If she could blend with the wall of the portal chambers, she would have, but nothing could hide her now in the room devoid of even one stick of furniture.

Laughter fell on her ears, and she dashed off the portal stand. What had gone wrong? And where were the king and his men and the Damarian knights now? Why couldn't she follow them?

She glanced down at the witch's ring. With every intention of stepping back into the portal's colorful light and trying something new, she pulled off the ring. To her astonishment, she returned to the tunnel where she had first placed the ring on her finger. But Kersta and Mexia were nowhere in sight.

She touched the walls. The rocks no longer beat like a heart's steady thump, nor was there any sound of breathing stirring through them. The men were free, somewhere.

She dashed down the tunnel back to the junction.

And then at the passageway they had not explored, she heard Kersta exclaim, "I cannot believe there is *not* something we can do for her!"

A voice that sounded very much like Modi said, "Returned, she has, all on her own. She is very clever, you know."

Kersta and Mexia ran toward the entrance of the tunnel as Talamaya sprinted to join them.

"Oh, princess," Kersta said, nearly squeezing the breath from her chest, "you're safe."

Mexia embraced her warmly next. "Nania said you freed the men."

"I must speak with her." Talamaya grasped her friends' hands and pulled them with her toward the soothsayer's cave. When they finally reached the white crystal cave, Talamaya stared at the figure of Nania. "Modi?"

She smiled. "Nania, but yes, most who have seen the one think we are the other."

"Twins?"

She nodded.

"I have freed the men?"

"Yes. You took them through the portal, no?"

"Yes. But I could not go."

She smiled. "No. You wore the witch's ring. It is also a portal of sort. It clashed with the other. But when you removed it, you returned to the same place you had transported from."

"Yes." Talamaya slipped the ring in her pocket. "But what about the men? Where have they gone to?"

"They have been transported to the same place they had come from."

"The woods after the plain?"

"Yes."

"But they have no horses, no food."

The soothsayer motioned to seating. When the ladies sat down on the white marble benches, Nania passed a crystal goblet to Talamaya. "I would be remiss in not offering refreshments for my guests."

"Nania," Talamaya said, "they were starving."

She smiled. "Not any longer. You provided them with Modi's tea to strengthen them and counter the effect of dehydration. You gave them weapons to fight the beasts of the woods. With these, they will kill enough to provide them with food to fill their bellies. You gave them freedom, and the willingness to continue the quest."

Talamaya took a deep breath, then sipped the wine. "The quest to claim the scepter."

"There's only one you have to worry about in that regard."

"The wizard?"

The soothsayer nodded. "Of course, King Lazarion wants the scepter. It would give him the power to maintain the peace in the region. Just as any of the rulers, or even the knights who wish to rule, would hope to have the chance to claim it. But the king has another reason."

When the soothsayer didn't readily give the reason, Kersta asked, "It is?"

A smile couldn't have stretched any farther across Nania's face as she studied Talamaya. "Humans are a curious race. Even when they have strong feelings of attachment for another, they deny these feelings. Why?"

As hot as Talamaya's cheeks burned she knew she must have blushed to high heaven. Kersta laughed.

Mexia said, "What?"

"You fight the attraction, princess. Why?" Nania sipped her wine. "You cannot deny he feels the same way for you."

"The Damarian women have been kept in chains long enough," Talamaya said, before she took another sip of wine. "King Lazarion has said so himself. Marrying a man will put me back in chains, will it not?"

"It depends on the man, I would think."

"My father wouldn't allow me to marry someone who was not Damarian."

"And that would stop you?"

Talamaya looked down at her feet, then back at the sooth-sayer. Her heart struggled with her mind in turmoil.

"You wish the chains freed, yet you still agree to the bondage?"

"I've always sought my father's approval. Is that so wrong? He elevates my brother to the high council over me, because he's a man. I'm required to marry someone of similar rank... that's all that is expected of me." Even now Talamaya couldn't squelch the ill will she felt toward her brother for the slight, despite the fact the same rules had applied to women for nearly five hundred years.

"I want to retrieve the scepter for my father, to prove to him a woman is as capable as a man to reach the highest goals. I want my father to realize having a daughter is as important as having a son."

"And should you claim the scepter and return it home, then what? Do you think he'll allow you to serve on his high council?"

"But Aralias—"

"Ah, Aralias. She ruled when she returned home with the scepter. She changed the rules."

"But they were changed back upon her death."

"Yes, because of her two quarreling twin sons. But while she lived, the women had every right, like the men." Nania leaned back slightly on her seat. "What does your heart say, Talamaya?"

"I want the women to have the freedom the elf women of Mesa have."

"Ah, then make it so."

"How?"

She winked at her and laughed. "You know how to do it. Follow your heart, and the road will be clear."

Soothsayers. They were all alike. Full of riddles when what Talamaya needed were straight answers.

"You have your answers, princess." Nania smiled at her. "You will find the solution easy to handle when all is said and done."

She clapped her hands and as Modi had done to them before, the ladies found themselves at the entrance of the cave.

"I didn't have time to ask her about the Cyclops."

"Oh, my lady," Kersta said, giving her another embrace. "When you vanished right before my eyes, I nearly died."

"Me, too," Mexia said stroking Talamaya's arm. "Me, too."

"You thought *you* nearly died? Here I was standing in the prison, trying to figure out how to get the men out of their chains and back to health before I ended up in chains alongside them."

Gallant smiled as soon as he saw them, but his smile was instantly replaced by a scowl. "It is about time, woman. Leesa finally rode back home it took you so long."

"Where is Rupert, by the way?" Talamaya mounted her horse.

"He, well now that you mention it, I have seen no sign of him."

"Maybe it is for the best."

Talamaya looked back toward the forest that trimmed the village to the north. "Will they be all right?"

"Who?" Gallant asked.

"The king and his men and ours."

"She freed them, and they were sent back through the portal to the forest they were first taken from," Mexia said.

Gallant nearly smiled. "Good." Then he frowned again. "Do we await them?"

"No, we must get through the Cyclops' land before the light fades too far from the sky."

Talamaya led the party back to the road that approached the Cyclops' land in the east. She glanced at the road to the west, leading back through the fairyland and the witch's house on the knoll. "There's one place I wouldn't wish to return to anytime soon."

"Aye, ye have my very thoughts in mind, woman." Gallant nudged his horse to ride beside her. "So now what did the soothsayer say about the Cyclops?"

What indeed?

Ahead of them the path narrowed into a canyon. Red, gold, orange, and black earths wrapped around the face in bands of brilliant colors. The canyon walls stretched hundreds of feet high giving Talamaya a hemmed-in feeling. Her heart quickened its pace.

Kersta whispered, "Beyond the canyon is their land."

Then movement behind a stack of boulders made Talamaya raise her hand to stop her party.

In a cloud of red dust, Rupert rode toward them. "By the gods, I never thought you would get here. I have scouted out the area ahead. It's safe until we get to the edge of the canyon. As the land spreads out into a plain similar to the one where we were attacked by the cheetaurs, boulders are scattered, the size of Tanner's abode. And trees, some still sticking to the ground like they ought to be, and others littered about, dying from being uprooted by the one-eyed monsters, no doubt. To the south near where we must ride to the beach, an outcropping of rock houses a number of caves where the Cyclops live."

Concern about getting through the land and making it to the beach safely consumed Talamaya's thoughts as she squashed her anger at seeing the knight who'd stolen their horses and abandoned them. "But how do we get past them?"

"I thought you were going to ask the soothsayer the question."

"I didn't have the chance."

His brow furrowed. "Why not? I would have thought *that* the most important question to ask of Nania."

"She busied herself with other business. Namely, freeing King Lazarion and the rest of your men. And ours, too," Kersta said.

"They are freed?" Rupert not only looked shocked, but wary.

"Yes, and they on their way here."

Though with traveling on foot and needing food and rest, Talamaya doubted they would reach the land of the Cyclops for two more days.

"You freed the king?" Rupert asked, his voice incredulous again.

"Yes, and your brother, too, though we were in such a rush to find a way out of the dungeon..." Talamaya had not remembered to tell the king how Mexia freed Rupert from the stone, nor how he had stolen their horses and left them to fend for themselves on foot.

Rupert waited anxiously to hear what she had to say. She glanced at Mexia and realized then how important it was to her that the king and his men knew Rupert was all right.

Talamaya looked back toward the land of the Cyclops. "Well, you can be certain the king will wish a word with you about your unchivalrous actions."

Kersta gave Talamaya a knowing look, but didn't reveal the truth of the matter to Mexia that the princess had failed to tell the king anything about him.

Rupert shifted in his saddle, then glanced back the way they had come.

"Shall we proceed, ladies, gentlemen? I wish to reach the shores of Neferon by nightfall," Talamaya said.

"And then?" Kersta asked.

"We'll need a boat to transport us to the Island of Lanai after that."

The journey took an hour even without any obstacles in their path to slow them down. When they arrived at the end of the canyon, a vast plain stretched before them. Only as Rupert had said, large oaks provided ample shade in circular patterns across the boulder-strewn land.

"I have read they're afraid of the canyon and never venture through it. I wonder why that is," Talamaya said as they sat quietly observing a rise in the land along one edge.

"Over there are the caves where they live," Rupert offered. "Beyond that is the beach of Neferon. As to your question, it's said they're afraid of the canyon."

"Why?"

"Someone said they think it's haunted. Maybe because when a strong wind blows through it, the wind howls."

"You don't have a howling spell of some sort you can cast, do you, Mexia?"

Mexia ran her horse's reins through her fingers. "My lady, I have already done one foul deed with turning a knight into stone."

"And then undoing the spell and saving several others who were locked in the same kind of spell. If I had your kind of abilities, I would conjure up anything I could, to help us."

Kersta nodded. "Oh, yes, Mexia. If you can do anything possibly to aid us, do. I beg of you."

Mexia frowned, seemingly deep in concentration. "I cannot recall one spell that makes a spooky sound, princess."

"It does not have to be that. Just anything. Something that would aid us."

"I worked hard on a love spell once."

Gallant groaned. "And if you make one of the Cyclops fall in love with one of us, then what?"

"I only mentioned that it's a spell I have practiced."

Talamaya eyed her suspiciously. "Who did you practice this on?"

"One of my maids, my lady. A knight who loved her dearly, and she feared giving her heart to him. I helped her."

"Oh," Talamaya said, relief hung on her word.

Kersta smiled.

Talamaya took a breath, thankful Mexia's spell casting practice hadn't caused the alliance between her brother Grisom and Saqualian. Something else had made that happen, and she was certain the interest had not arisen naturally of its own accord. When she returned home, she had every intention of determining the truth of the matter.

"Think, Mexia. What else have you practiced that has worked well?"

"A memory spell. I was trying to study for a potion test, and I kept mixing up the quantities for the ingredients. It isn't open book, you know. And several of the healing potions are extremely complicated. So I used a memory spell and remembered every one of them."

"And that would help us here, how?" Gallant asked, waving his hand at the land.

Mexia shrugged.

"Can anyone else think of anything?" Talamaya asked, looking for advice from her companions.

"Only to move into the shadows of the trees one at a time," Rupert said. "I'll go first, if you wish."

Talamaya looked at her friends. They all agreed. "Okay, go,

Sir Rupert. Another will follow you once you have made it to the second tree."

"My lady." He bowed his head, then he kicked his horse and cantered to the first tree, two hundred yards away.

He paused there, watching for signs of the Cyclops and seeing the way was clear, he rode safely to the next tree. Pausing in the shadows, he motioned to Talamaya.

She turned to her companions. "Who wishes to go next?"

Gallant said, "I would not want us men at the other side while the women were left behind."

"I'll go next then," Kersta said, her voice unsteady.

"The gods be with you, Kersta," Talamaya said.

"And with you, princess, Mexia, Gallant." Kersta rode to the first tree and once she was safely underneath its branches, Rupert moved to the shelter of the third oak. Kersta glanced back, and Talamaya motioned to her to continue forward.

Talamaya turned back to Mexia. "You go now, Mexia."

"I'm still trying to think of a spell, my lady, pardon my delay."

"Gallant, go ahead then."

Talamaya feared Mexia wouldn't make it if she fell behind.

Rupert was near the end of the plain where a short ride would take him to the beaches where the Cyclops purportedly never ventured.

Kersta and Gallant had moved far enough forward for another to take her place at the first tree in their path.

Then they heard the roar, deafening and terrifying all at once. The ground shook with the Cyclops's steps. Three of them stomped out of their caves.

"Come, Mexia," Talamaya yelled. "We must ride like the wind."

"But I have it, my lady. Why did I not think of it before?"

"Hurry!" Talamaya kicked her horse to a gallop and waved

for Kersta to follow Rupert to the beach where he'd already made a quick escape.

Kersta shook her head and waited. The Cyclops seeing only Mexia and Talamaya riding across the plain toward the first tree, headed for them, like mean kids who intended to stomp butterflies, attempting to evade annihilation.

"Mexia!" Kersta screamed.

Talamaya looked back and to her horror, Mexia sat on her horse in place, wiggling her fingers in the air and mouthing an incantation.

One of the Cyclops headed for Kersta as she rode toward it screaming, "Come get me, you one-eyed monster! Ha!"

Gallant shouted, "Blasted, woman!" He rode toward Talamaya, trying to distract the other Cyclops as it stomped toward her.

Only inches from Mexia the third stopped in place frozen into the most hideously, ugly statue Talamaya had ever seen.

Talamaya rode toward Kersta and Gallant, criss-crossing between the Cyclops, keeping them distracted while Mexia worked her magic on another of them.

"My horse is tiring!" Kersta yelled.

"Ride to the beach!" Talamaya shouted to her.

When Kersta rode off, Talamaya glanced back to see the second Cyclops statue already in place, and Mexia working quickly to conjure up the spell for the third.

The Cyclops yanked a tree out of the ground and as he raised it in the air, Mexia completed the spell.

Immediately, the Cyclops turned to stone.

"Thank the gods, Mexia, you're a spell caster," Talamaya said, "and if your father doesn't pay for your way to get special schooling from the wizard in Langdon, I will."

Mexia beamed at her, and they cantered across the plain, with Gallant pulling in beside Talamaya.

"Why did you not think of that before?" he grouched. "Before we rode into danger?"

"I had to get closer, for one thing."

"We had to distract them anyway, Gallant. She wouldn't have been able to have done it on her own," Talamaya said. "Where did Rupert go?"

Gallant pointed his war hammer ahead of them. "As soon as the Cyclops roared, he took off for the beach."

Talamaya shook her head. "He is never to be trusted."

19

W hen Talamaya and her companions reached the golden beach, they could see the island vaguely several miles out surrounded by a green mist. The air, laden with the smell of fish, salty seawater, and rotting seaweed, seemed heavier, more difficult to breathe in, wetter, like the air of Elan Pass, but much warmer.

"Where's the mermaid you and Malachon spoke of?" Mexia asked.

"She must be farther down the beach. There are no boats here either. We must find one that will take us across the water. Is there anything on Malachon's map that indicates a place where we might get a boat?"

Kersta hurriedly pulled her map from her cloak pocket. "Sorry, my lady. In my worry about the Cyclops, I never looked beyond their land on the map."

"No rush. We have to wait until it gets dark. Malachon warned us the mermaid would be dangerous during the daylight hours."

"To the right, my lady. There's a fishing village by the name of Seaphoma."

"I wonder if Rupert has already been there," Talamaya said.

"If Malachon is right, he'll not get far if he leaves for Lanai at this time of day." Kersta folded her map away.

They walked their horses in the direction of the village, each watching for signs of it.

"Does your father know you can cast the stone spell?" Kersta asked Mexia.

"No. And I'm sure he'll frown on it."

"You saved our lives back there," Kersta said.

"Oh." Mexia smiled. "Yes, I guess I did."

"Certainly you did," Talamaya agreed. "Now if you could conjure up a boat..."

The ladies laughed.

Gallant pointed at the hoof prints in the sand. "Another horse has recently trod this way."

"Rupert," Talamaya said, her voice tight with anger concerning the knight's action at leaving them behind.

Mexia scowled. "Aye. Even now the breeze sweeps the sand back and forth, burying his tracks. The traveler had to have come this way recently. My guess would be it was Rupert."

When the small dwellings of the village came into view, Talamaya took a deep breath. "I imagine the fishermen fish at night to avoid the mermaids in this region. If so, there may be no boats available to us to use for the journey to the island of Lanai."

"Unless we pay enough for passage." Mexia touched the amulet at her throat.

"I won't give up Ren."

Talamaya smiled. "Nor would we wish you to, Gallant. Nor will we give up our staffs."

"Look!" Kersta pointed to the cresting waves.

"Is that the mermaid? The one you saw in your vision?" Mexia asked. Then she gasped. "She's bare breasted."

"Yes, ladies. She's the one."

The mermaid smashed her dinner on the rocks, then bit into the still shell-bound creature, her red curls draping over her shoulders.

Talamaya shuddered. "No way will we take a boat out until after she's well fed."

They continued along the beach and rode to the first of the dwellings. Decorated in driftwood, its thatched roof looked like it had weathered one too many storms in recent days.

"Hey!" a man shouted in greeting, waving his hand as he squinted his eyes at the travelers. He wore only a pair of breeches and boots to the women's surprise. His leathery tanned skin indicated he spent much of his time in the salt air and sun. He combed his fingers through a matted black beard, then his eyes widened. All at once, he dashed back inside his house.

"This isn't good, princess," Kersta whispered. "The man has it in mind that the three of us women are looking for husbands."

"Where would they ever get such a notion as that?"

"From a knight who passed through here less than an hour ago."

"Rupert."

"Yes."

"How bad is it?"

"Bad, my lady. They have lost several women due to an illness and have been without them for nearly a year. Most women don't like the idea of coming here at all. They lose their men to the sea. The violent storms have killed many in the past. But the men love fishing above all else. They often seek women from the farm villages who tire of the hard life there."

"And I thought life as a Damarian woman without much say was bad," Talamaya mused.

"Yes, well many lots in life aren't perfect, by any means, my lady."

They headed for the first of the wharves where men gathered together, mending their heavy-duty fishing nets. When they saw the travelers, they jumped up. The interest they showed in the women, made Talamaya stiffen her back with renewed determination to fulfill her quest and not be sidetracked.

"You be the ones the knight spoke of?" one of the men asked, hurrying forward to greet them.

Talamaya motioned to a boat. "We wish to pay for passage to Lanai."

"You may have a trip there free anytime, my lady." He smiled and smoothed down his brown beard. Fish scales still laced through the curly hairs. She assumed he had cleaned fish earlier in the day, though from their unkempt appearances she reconsidered that they may not have bathed for days.

She fought the urge to wrinkle her nose at the smell of the men, fish and body odor combined. He stepped closer. She shook her head. "The knight, if it was the one who traveled with us, tells you men lies. We come to..."

She hesitated. Would the man understand how important claiming the scepter was to the whole of the peoples on the continent of Inherian? Probably not. The simple fisherman only cared about the weather and the fish they'd catch that day. And a wife to mend his socks and keep him warm on a cold winter's night.

She shuddered at the notion. To smell like fish and the salty air always.

He offered to help her down. She hesitated. "We have been told a great cave lies on the island of Lanai. We are explorers and wish to see what treasure it holds."

The man laughed and his friends added to the chorus. "Ladies, such as yourselves, would not wish to venture into *that* cave. No one whoever goes in, comes out alive."

"Sir Malachon from Damar, did."

The men exchanged glances. "Yes, well, he was the only one, and he was witless after the experience, too."

"Yes and crazy, too," another of the men added, nodding vigorously. He ran his hand over Kersta's horse and smiled up at her.

The first of the men who had spied them, bolted out of his house with a pearl necklace dangling in his clenched fist. "A gift, my lady, from the sea!"

The man's hair was now drawn back in a knot, and his beard was neatly braided. He wore a clean, soft shirt and breeches of brown suede, apparently to impress one of the potential brides-to-be. "Come, I'll show you my house."

"We only wish to take a boat to the island."

"They wish to explore the cave," the one man said, then laughed. The others echoed his laughter.

Gallant grumbled under his breath.

"What say you, dwarf?" one of the men said, eyeing him with suspicion.

"The women only need to be transported to the island, man. Cannot ye get that through your thick head? They are not looking for husbands."

"They appear to be the right age," one of the men said, scratching his beard. "A woman like that should be married."

"Ye would have the king of Damar on your backs if you married any of these women."

"Oh?"

"The one is King Sal's daughter."

The men all laughed.

The fisherman who had spoken first about Malachon said to his companions, "They're already a bit daft. We'll prepare a feast." He turned to Talamaya. "Here, we allow the women to decide a husband. If you should not be able to make a choice, we'll draw sticks."

Talamaya shook her head. "*After* we visit the cave. We'll do nothing else before this."

"They cannot visit the cave," the fisherman touching Kersta's horse said. "They wouldn't survive there, and we wouldn't have wives."

"You wouldn't wish to stop us from our quest," Talamaya said. "Mexia is a powerful mage. If I ordered her to, she could turn every one of you to stone. We only wish to take a boat to the island. When we return, we shall discuss this matter of marriage."

The men glanced at Mexia as she raised her staff to indicate she was the one Talamaya spoke of.

"Beg your pardon, my lady, if I don't believe you," the cleanly clothed fisherman said.

"I doubt you'd wish to see her turn one of you into stone to prove herself."

One of the men pulled a fish from a bucket. "How about this?"

"Set it on the ground if you don't wish to be turned to stone also."

He did so and Mexia wiggled her fingers and spoke the incantation. Everyone watched the wriggling fish as it flopped around on the wharf. When it didn't change, the fisherman laughed.

"Good trick." The fisherman turned to his companions. "Daft, I tell you." Then he motioned to the women. "Come down from your horses, ladies, and sup with us."

"Why did it not work, Mexia?"

"I don't know, my lady. I have the spell down completely. Unless...unless there's something else blocking my magic in this cove."

"What could that be?"

They glanced around at the backdrop to the village. Blue cliffs rested along the northern edge of the beach. Five shaded regions colored some of the stone black in parts below the jagged peaks. Mexia pointed to the black areas. "Caves."

Turning to the fishermen, she asked, "What dwells in those caves?"

"Dragons."

"Ah. Perhaps that's it, princess. Maybe the magic of the dragons impedes my own use of spells. If I were more powerful, they would not."

"If the men won't take us by boat to the island, perhaps a dragon will fly us over," Talamaya said.

"We leave them alone, and they leave us alone," the man in the clean garments said. He motioned to a pile of fish. "We give them what we cannot eat or sell of the day's catch. They wouldn't like it if you bothered them in their lair."

"What happened to Rupert? The knight who came through here?" Talamaya asked.

"He bought passage on a boat. Insisted he go across to the island. Foolhardy, we told him it was. But he would not listen."

Talamaya studied the cliffs. "I have read if you do a good deed for a dragon, he'll do one in return for you. Come, ladies, Gallant. Let us meet one up close."

She kicked her horse and sent the sand flying as she galloped toward the cliffs. Her companions followed her as the men yelled, "You'll get yourselves killed! And then where will we be?"

Kersta hollered after her, "My lady, are you sure that this is the right path?"

"I have read that dragons are good, unless turned to evil by an extremely powerful wizard."

"Like the one who you must fight later, my lady?"

"If the dragons have not destroyed the village yet, I would say they're still pure of heart. I'd like to meet with these. I've heard if you're gentle with them, and do something they bid, the rewards you'll reap can be more than any gold heaped at your feet."

"Meaning?"

"We might get a ride to the island without having to become brides to any of those smelly fishermen."

Gallant chuckled. "I was beginning to think it was me who smelled so badly."

Mexia shook her head as they reached the cliffs. "I don't know about this, princess."

They stared up at the seemingly insurmountable climb.

"You can wait here for me. I'll be right back." Talamaya slipped off her horse.

Gallant hopped down from his, but she motioned for him to stay. "I need you to stay with the ladies and the horses to protect them. I'm afraid our staffs no longer have their magical powers either."

"I'll go with you," Mexia said. "I would rather face the dragons, than marry one of those fishermen."

"I second that." Kersta dismounted.

"Well, what about me, woman?"

"Will you stay with the horses, Gallant? Keep our staffs and our other things safe? We cannot maneuver up the cliffs with them."

She glanced back at the fishing village. "At least they're not pursuing this further."

"I don't believe they have given up hope, my lady," Kersta said. "I could read several of the men's minds, and they were plotting ways of keeping us here. For the moment, they figured they would let us be as they don't believe we'll get very far up the cliffs. But when we return, they will marry us, as they intended."

"We'll deal with that, when we have to." Talamaya grabbed a handhold and stuck her foot onto a step-like rock, then began to climb up.

"Are you certain this is the right thing to do?" Mexia asked, as she waited for Kersta to follow Talamaya up the cliff.

"You don't need to follow me, ladies, truly. I'll be down when I'm finished up here."

"Her heart is in it," Kersta said.

"Mine is not. Does that not count for something?" Mexia asked.

Talamaya chuckled. "You can stay with Gallant." She gripped another rock and pulled herself higher. "This is really not too bad for climbing. Plenty of finger and foot holds, so far."

She continued to move up slowly, making sure she had proper footing before she reached higher for the next handhold.

"I hope these dragons of yours will give us a ride back down, my lady. I fear by the time we reach the top it will be getting dark."

"Hmm, I hadn't considered that. But the men won't take us out on a boat. Of course, if this doesn't work, perhaps we could steal a boat tonight and make our way across to the island."

"That does not sound like the way of righteousness, my lady."

"I'm trying to think of a way to get across to the island, without swimming there."

"With the mermaids? No, thank you." Kersta paused to get her breath. "Are we not there yet, princess?"

"A ways to go, Kersta. Don't look down."

"I hadn't intended to."

When the light began to fade from the sky, the flapping of wings and stirring of air made Talamaya realize a dragon had left his lair. She turned to see the magnificent beast, its blue-silver scales sparkling in the fading light as it made its way to the sea. With every stroke of its powerful wings, the air rippled and sent a breeze stirring.

"I hope," Kersta said, "this doesn't mean we'll reach the caves and the dragons will all be down below."

"Then we shall await their return. Think of it as an adventure."

"Meeting a handsome new knight is an adventure," Kersta said.

"Learning a new spell is an adventure," Mexia added.

"Climbing hundreds of feet up a cliff face to empty dragon caves is not," Kersta continued.

"I agree with Kersta," Mexia said.

Talamaya chuckled. "Gallant is rubbing off on the two of you ladies."

A second dragon flew out of a nearby cave.

"I wonder how many there are up here," Kersta said.

"Hurry, ladies. I'm nearly to the top."

The ladies grew quiet as they followed Talamaya the rest of the way up to the ledge. She reached her hand to Kersta. "See, it wasn't that difficult. The footing was similar to stairs, nearly."

"It's the going down that looks to be most frightening," Kersta replied.

They pulled Mexia to her feet next. "I sure hope you're right about this, princess."

They turned their attention to the wide ledge that wound its way along the cliff, making an easy path to three of the caves. Other openings were higher in the rock above.

Talamaya led them into the nearest one. She pulled the fairy's wand from her belt and lighted their way.

"Whew," Mexia said. "I was afraid the magic of the wand would not work either."

"Maybe it is because fairies are innately magical. You have a knack for magic, but it's not an inborn trait. Perhaps that's why the fish wouldn't turn to stone." Talamaya paused. "Hello?" she called out. Her word echoed back to them.

"Must you make it so obvious we're here?" Kersta asked.

"I would rather they know we're here than startle them with our sudden appearance."

"The cave is empty," Kersta said, as they searched the cavernous room. Blue crystals sparkled over all the walls and dried grass covered the floor. "Dragon carpeting."

"Come, let us check the next one."

"What if all the dragons have left the caves by now?" Mexia asked.

"Then we'll wait for their return."

"And Gallant?"

"I'll call down to him and tell him where we'll be in case he couldn't figure that out."

When they arrived at the opening of the next cave, Talamaya peeked her head around the massive stone, hiding the contents from sight. A dragon. Talamaya's heart began thumping hard. "Hello?" she said to the dragon, resting on a pile of hay, its blue wings folded against its body.

The dragon lifted its head and grunted. "Human."

"May we speak with you?"

The almond-shaped, blue-green eyes of the dragon studied her, then she turned to look behind Talamaya. "Who is we?"

"I'm Princess Talamaya." She motioned to Kersta and Mexia to join her. They both shook their heads. "Well, hiding beyond the outside of your cave is Lady Kersta and Mexia. We are from Damar."

"You have traveled far."

"Yes."

"You seek the scepter?" The dragon moved slightly and groaned.

"Yes. How did you know?"

"Most strangers who come to this land seek the scepter."

The dragon's eyes focused on Malachon's amulet glowing at Talamaya's throat. "What happened to the knight who wore that amulet?"

"His mind was injured...I believe in the Cave of Sorrows. But I helped him to recover some of his memories, and he seemed much better. He wished to aid me on my quest, and I hope to help him further upon my return."

"He was a good human."

"Yes. He was always kind-hearted."

The dragon shook its head. "Why would a female of your kind seek the scepter?"

"My brother was poisoned. Otherwise, my father had intended for him to come here instead of me."

"That's not the answer I seek."

"Pardon?"

The dragon snorted. "Your father would send another man in your brother's place, would he not?"

"I have come because Aralias came before me."

"Aralias."

"Yes. She claimed the scepter and ruled over Damar."

"She fought Grimoria."

"You know of the wizard?" Talamaya grew closer as Kersta and Mexia stepped into the cave.

"Yes."

"What do you know of the wizard?"

"Aralias and her companions turned him to stone." The dragon stared at the floor for a moment, then looked back at Talamaya. "Yes, five-hundred years ago this year. She had just come of age. Have you?"

"Yes."

"Her brother had died from a jousting tourney when the wizard began to cause problems in Inherian. The wizard came from Langdon. A rogue wizard, they called him. He turned the beasts against the civilized races, then he made man turn against man. Aralias was the only one who had the desire to bring peace to the region. Everyone else wished the power of the scepter to rule over the continent, as an emperor rules over a mighty empire."

"Even the Amazon women of the Maken Peninsula?"

"Yes, even they were infected with the curse of wishing the power beyond any reason." The dragon shifted again. "The wizard waits for you and your friends. He doesn't intend to lose this time."

"Will you help us?"

"Why?"

"You're good of heart, dragon. Are you not? You help those who do right."

"It's not my war."

"Yet, if the wizard succeeds, would he not attempt to control you, too? Controlling only the peoples and beasts of Inherian would not satisfy him long. Would he not wish to control all that are magical, harness your powers to suit his dark purposes also?"

20

The dragon lifted its head in the cavern, then groaned again, closing its eyes.

"What ails you?" Talamaya asked.

"*You*, human. You're making my head hurt."

Talamaya considered offering Modi's tea to the dragon, then figured it was a foolish thought.

"Aralias made the same argument once—that the wizard would eventually attempt to turn the dragons into his minions."

Talamaya sighed. "I guess I'm a lot like her."

"You are. Which is dangerous for you."

"Why?"

"The wizard will have learned from his mistake the first time. He'll not fall for the same maneuver twice."

"But I don't know what Aralias did to stop him exactly the first time."

"Yet, have you not followed her same path? She came here seeking help, too."

"Oh."

"Some humans believe in reincarnation."

"Not the Damar."

"Did you speak with the fairies?"

"Yes."

"Did they think you were Aralias?"

"Very much like her."

"I say the same." The dragon shifted its weight again and grunted.

"Are you injured?" Talamaya asked, reaching down to touch the dragon's leg.

"No."

"Then what's wrong?"

"I have that uncomfortable condition called motherhood. I don't believe I have ever been so full of eggs in my whole dragonling-bearing time."

A female dragon. Talamaya would never have guessed. "Are you due soon?"

"Any minute."

"Oh. I'm sorry to have disturbed you so."

"My mate left to bring me food. He complained I grouched too much. Let him carry a belly full of eggs the next time."

The ladies chuckled.

Talamaya said, "You don't know how many human women feel the same way during childbearing. Is there anything we could do to help you?"

"Within the Cave of Sorrows, there is a pile of treasure. Amongst the gold and gems rests a magical item. It belongs to the dragonkind. When you have finished your quest, bring it to me. Malachon promised to, but he never returned."

"Yes, well, I'm certain his mind was shattered by something in the cave." She touched the scales of the dragon, warm and pearl-like. "What will I be looking for?"

"You won't miss it once you see it. I can sense its presence in the caves. We dragons cannot visit such an evil place. And no one who has ventured there has lived long enough to return the item here to us."

"Not even Aralias?"

"Alas, even she was so overwhelmed by conquering the wizard and claiming the scepter, she forgot to return here with the item."

"Do you know what caused the knight's madness?"

"I don't know what awaits you there."

"We haven't been able to secure passage to the island yet. We had hoped to pay for a boat to transport us there, but the men of the village won't aid us."

"Why?"

Talamaya looked at her friends who waited for her to explain their predicament. "Well, the fishermen had lost their wives to some kind of sickness. They want the three of us to become wives for some of the men."

"Wives?"

"Mates."

"Ah. And you are unhappy with this arrangement?"

"She cares for the...King Lazarion," Kersta said, smiling.

"Ah. You could swim, could you not?"

"Too far, and the mermaids would present a problem, I'm afraid."

"You could fly."

"You would take us?"

The dragon groaned. "You humans are known to jest."

"I'm sorry. I forgot how close you are to having your offspring."

"My mate will take you."

A flapping of wings and the wind stirred inside the cave as a dragon filled the entrance suddenly. "Your mate will do what? And who are these humans who disturb your rest?"

"Aralias of Damar," the dragon said.

"Talamaya," Talamaya corrected.

He grunted. "She is the one. What has taken her so long? Everyone has been on edge that she had not arrived long before this."

"I don't know what all the fuss is about." The dragon licked her foot as if she was taking care of a wound.

"You're the only one who's unconcerned about Grimoria returning to power."

"I have other concerns that plague me at the moment, dear heart." She flapped her wings in annoyance, making the ladies step back to avoid getting slapped. "However, she and her companions are having difficulty getting across the water."

"I'll take them. Did you tell her we need the dragon magic from the Cave of Sorrows?"

"Of course."

He took a deep breath and turned his attention to Talamaya. "When do you wish to go?"

"Now if we could. We must get our staffs and our companion awaits us at the bottom of the cliff."

"The dwarf?"

Talamaya nodded.

"He's halfway up them if not farther by now."

Talamaya smiled. "He must have worried about us."

"Have you figured out how to kill the wizard this time and for good?" the male dragon asked.

"I don't know what Aralias even did the last time."

The male dragon covered his head with his wing, then folded it back against his body.

"Turned the wizard to stone," the female said.

"Yes, but how did she manage it? Did she have wizardry skills? And if so, how could she have done so against someone so powerful?"

"Her companions helped her."

Talamaya glanced at Mexia, then turned back to the dragons. "But he'll be expecting it."

"Most assuredly. Let us hope you figure it out when you get there."

The male grunted. "She made the mistake of only freezing him in stone that lasted for five hundred years."

"That's why she has returned. To finish the deed," the female said as she rolled over on her side, then closed her eyes.

"If you say so, dear."

Talamaya and her companions exchanged glances.

"Will you take us now?"

"Here ye are!" Gallant said, stomping into the cave. "I thought ye needed rescuing."

"Hmpf, from you maybe, dwarf," the male dragon said.

"Take them to the island, dear heart. The time has come, and I don't need all of this company."

"As you wish." He stepped onto the ledge. "Climb on and hold tightly."

"We need our staffs," Talamaya said.

"And my war hammer."

"I'll take you to your horses first at the bottom of the cliffs."

After they all climbed onto his back, everyone clung onto him the best they could. He chuckled.

"What's wrong, dragon?" Talamaya asked.

"One of you is tickling me."

He flew down to the bottom of the cliff, then waited while the party retrieved their weapons. Within minutes, they had remounted the dragon, and he flew low at first, then high over the top of the village. The sun had dropped low in the sky turning the blue to brilliant orange.

"Look!" Kersta shouted, pointing to the beach. "King Lazarion and the rest of the men."

"Tala!" he yelled, galloping toward the village with the others racing to catch up.

She waved at him as the dragon swooped over the sea. "Good, they're not far behind. I'm certain the fishermen will take them over in the boats when they wouldn't us."

"Look!" Mexia called out. "The mermaid." She gasped.

"And a boat wrecked on the rocks," Kersta said.

"Fly lower," Mexia urged the dragon.

"The mermaid has taken a victim," the dragon said. "Are you sure you wish to see it?"

"I must know if it is Rupert," Mexia said.

The dragon drew closer. Everyone looked down to see the knight lying still in the mermaid's arms as she rocked back and forth on the coral and smiled.

"Is he alive?" Mexia asked.

"Nay," Gallant answered. He pointed with his war hammer. "The other side of his head has leaked all the blood out."

Mexia turned away. "Then I won't need to turn him to stone."

Talamaya reached forward to touch her arm. "I knew he couldn't make it across the sea when it was still light out. Had he stayed with us, he would have been all right." She couldn't help feeling sick to her stomach at the sight of the dead knight, her stomach rolling with nausea. But she knew, too, his heart had been corrupted by the need for power no matter who he hurt in the process.

"He would have attempted to claim the scepter and had he that would surely have been a travesty." Mexia shuddered. "Though I didn't wish to see him die in that way."

"Many have died on this journey already, but I fear many more will, too, if we don't stop the wizard," Talamaya agreed.

"The men are already launching the boats into the water," Kersta said.

"Good, I'll feel better knowing they'll be close behind us, should we need them."

"So what shall we do with the wizard, my lady?" Kersta asked.

"I haven't a clue. I keep hoping something will show us the way."

The dragon flew into a bank of green mist where the air was fragrant from the multitude of pink and orange flowers blanketing the earth. "The Cave of Sorrows is near. I'll leave you here as the sphinx who guards the cave and I don't get along. When you have our magical treasure, I'll come back for you."

"A sphinx?" Mexia asked.

"Yes. She has the head of a woman, the body of a lion and the wings of a gryphon. And if you don't answer her riddle correctly, she'll strangle the life out of you."

"What riddle is that, dragon?"

"She changes it at will. Very few can guess the answers of her riddles."

"Will she ask it of each of us?"

"She'll ask one for a party such as yours. You can decide amongst yourselves what the correct answer to the riddle is. But if you guess wrong, she'll draw the breath from your bodies and cast them aside."

"Thank you, dragon. If I am able, I'll retrieve your magical item from the cave."

He bowed his head. "You'll find great reward in your actions. Straight ahead stands the cave."

Then he turned and flew off, leaving the party standing in a field of flowers, a slight breeze stirring the fragrance in mischievous twists and twirls. The sun disappeared behind the world and now only the fairy's wand lighted their way with a golden glow.

"Are we ready?" Talamaya asked her companions.

"Do ye sense how quiet it is? Like Wildwood Forest when the dark elves appeared? I would think there would be seabirds along the shore, at least."

"Nothing is written about this island, except that the Cave of Sorrows possesses the scepter and treasures are piled in hoards in the cave. But from what I understand, except for Aralias, no one has ever made it out of there alive."

"And poor Malachon," Kersta added.

"What about her companions?" Mexia asked.

"Nothing was written about them."

Talamaya motioned to her friends. "We must do this. Any who wish to stay behind, may wait for the king and the rest of the men."

"I won't be left behind," Kersta said.

"Me neither, woman." The dwarf motioned with his war hammer in the direction of the cave.

"I have come this far, I won't let you down, princess," Mexia said.

"All right, here we go. No going back now." Talamaya walked forward, the green mist opening a few feet in front of them as if the fairy wand parted it just for them.

Then they spied the sphinx, resting on her haunches like a great lion, her wings flat against her body, her eyes closed.

"She's asleep," Kersta whispered.

A smile twitched on the sphinx's lips.

"Not really," Talamaya whispered back.

"I don't like this, my lady," Mexia said.

"He awaits you," the sphinx said, her eyes widening. "Or so I believe. You're the first women to come here since the time Aralias and her companions visited. I suspect you're the ones he waits for."

Talamaya placed her staff on the ground. "Why would the wizard not take the scepter for his very own?"

"He cannot. The scepter can only be removed from the Cave of Sorrows by one who's pure of heart. Once it's beyond the confines of the cave, it belongs to whoever can hang onto it long enough."

"I thought it had magical powers."

"Ah, yes, for some. Are you a descendent of Aralias?"

"Yes."

"Then maybe you can wield its power. Are you ready for the riddle?"

"Did the other women get out of the cave all right with Aralias?"

"I wouldn't know. I keep unworthy travelers from entering the cave."

"You mean those who cannot decipher your riddles."

"That is what I said. I pay no attention to who leaves the cave." She narrowed her eyes. "Do you wish to enter, or not?"

"Yes. Ask your riddle." Talamaya took a deep breath, trying to calm her nerves.

"I'll give you an easy one because the wizard said he would do battle with me, if I didn't."

"I thought you would be more powerful than he."

"We would not know, unless we tested your notion, now would we? The riddle..."

Everyone tensed to hear the riddle, and then the sphinx began.

"I, a traveler to many worlds, beaten and pummeled near death, have seen many battles, am slashed and take the brunt of the brutality of men, unable to defend myself. There are no salves to cover my wounds that grow and deepen with every fight."

Kersta whispered to the party, "A shield, I believe."

"Aye, though I never use such a thing, it sounds as good an answer as any other," Gallant said.

Mexia nodded.

Once Talamaya had everyone's agreement, she turned to the sphinx. "A shield is wounded in battle, cannot fight back, and there are no healing potions available to cure its wounds."

The sphinx's lips turned up slightly. "Yes, you're clever. But since there are four of you, I'll ask another question. One will be allowed to journey into the cave, however, no matter how you answer the next riddle."

"The dragon said you would ask the party only one question."

"The dragon doesn't say what I shall do," the sphinx huffed with contempt. "The next riddle." She crossed one of her paws over the other. "A thing hangs by a man's thigh, hidden by a tunic. It is firm and strong. After the man hitches his clothing upward, he grasps the head of the object, and he pokes it into the hole it has often filled before. Joyous, the man reaps reward."

The ladies' cheeks grew red and Talamaya's warmed. They pondered the riddle for a moment, then turned to see Gallant smiling. "Aye, I know the answer to that one." He pulled his cloak aside and underneath his tunic, a key hung to a chain at his waist. "A key."

"Is that the consensus?" the sphinx asked.

Everyone agreed.

"One more may enter the cave." She licked her paw, then looked at Talamaya. "Any that you choose, as before. I will give another riddle.

"My house is full of noise, but I remain quiet. My house will exist long after I'm gone. At times I rest, while my dwelling still runs. I lodge within it as long as I live. Should we two be separated, my death is sure, but my house will continue on as before."

Talamaya took a deep breath. "If he's separated from his dwelling he'll die. Everything needs air to live."

"What about a fish?" Mexia asked.

Kersta nodded. "Aye, a fish. It is not loud."

"And the water, its dwelling continues to move, even if the fish rests." Talamaya waited for everyone's agreement. When she received it, she said, "You are the fish and your dwelling, water."

"One more shall find her way into the cave. Your last riddle. When I was very small you paid me no mind, insignificant as I am. But as I grew, I hardened. You sought me then, and with a rock, you shattered my armor. I die at your hand, once hoping to be the beginning of a great and mighty thing that would outlive you by mayhap hundreds of years."

Talamaya turned to her companions. "What about the nut of a tree? When it's small, no one wishes it as it would be too bitter to eat. It has a hard armor-like shell. If it is planted, it becomes a tree that lives much longer than man."

"Aye, that it is," Gallant said folding his arms.

"Yes, princess," Kersta said.

Mexia nodded.

Talamaya took a deep breath. "A nut from a tree."

The sphinx tilted her head to the side like the fairy had done when Talamaya had amused her. "You're very clever, human. The wizard will find you difficult to beat once again, I venture."

She motioned toward the cave. "Go, enter at your own risk. Your task with me was easier than anything in there will be."

"What made the knight, Malachon, go mad, can you tell me, sphinx?"

"He was good hearted. He might have claimed the scepter if the cave had not shattered his mind so."

"What did it?"

"Only those who seek the truth, will know. I have never been inside. I only keep those who are not worthy of entering from going in there. That is all."

The sphinx turned away from the party and closed her eyes,

but added an additional thought. "You have seen the mermaid of the sea, human?"

"Yes?"

"Her home keeps her safe."

"Yes, sphinx?"

"For many it can be a watery grave."

"So we should ride with the dragon when we return to the mainland?"

The sphinx smiled.

Talamaya motioned to her companions. "We're bound to find out, soon enough."

Walking into the dark cave, Talamaya noticed the air grew cooler, moister, and was scented with the same fragrance of flowers. Both the fairy light and Malachon's amulet illuminated the cave in a wash of gold light, highlighting the moistened moss and clusters of purple gems. Tendrils of purple flowers with green leaves striated with purple veins clung to the walls in spots further softening the appearance of the angular, sharp, colorless, crystal shards poking out of the walls.

Water dripped into pools at various spots in the cave, making a kerplunk periodically. Somewhere deep in the bowls of the cave system, a stream flowed underground. The sound of the water gurgling in dips and dives over the uneven rock soothed Talamaya's frayed nerves.

She pointed to three passages along the wall. "Shall we go to the right one first?"

"What does your heart desire to do, princess?" Kersta asked.

"Not that again," Mexia said.

"Nania said for her to follow her heart."

"I wish to go to the right. I find comfort in going in that direction."

"Then we go to the right." Gallant stifled a sneeze. "Though I don't see how ye would find peace in such a place as this. Even the odor of the flowers makes me want to sneeze."

When they reached the passageway, Malachon's amulet turned from a gold glow to blue.

Kersta touched it. "What does it mean?"

"I don't know. Let us continue."

They walked to the end of the tunnel where it opened into a cave filled with treasure. Gold coins, gems of every color of the mines of Inherian, golden goblets, jewel-handled daggers and swords, filled the room all along its perimeter from floor to ceiling.

Talamaya glanced at her companions, all whose eyes sparkled with wonder as their mouths hung slightly agape. "We must find the dragon's magical item. But nothing else, must we take."

"How will we know what it is?" Mexia dug her hands into the pile of coins nearest her and began to shift through its contents.

"The dragon said only that we would know it when we saw it."

"Why could they have not been more help than that?" Gallant grumbled.

"Perhaps," Talamaya answered, "they didn't know what we would call the item."

"This could take days." Kersta considered the jewels on a goblet. "Would it maybe have the inlaid figure of a dragon?"

"I don't know, Kersta. Sort through the coins quickly. I'm certain it could not be something like that. It might be an amulet. We never did ask anyone where Malachon got his."

"How is it to protect you or aid you in the cave, my lady?" Mexia pulled a cloak out of the pile of treasure she worked. "This is odd. It is so plain when everything else is so rich and beautiful."

"It would not be something a dragon would have that was magical," Talamaya replied.

Mexia tossed the cloak aside.

"Wait," Kersta said. "There is something to what Mexia says. Why would such a plain thing be in all this treasure unless it was not worth something?"

Kersta draped it over her shoulders and vanished.

21

"Kersta!" Mexia and Talamaya cried out. They ran to where she had stood and bumped into her.

She pulled off the cloak and laughed. "It's an invisibility cloak. Did anyone say we weren't permitted to use anything we found in the cave to aid us?"

"No," Talamaya said. "In fact no one said we couldn't take anything from the cave either. But Modi said we had to do what was right."

"And Nania said you had to follow your heart. What does your heart say about us using something that may aid us to defeat the wizard?"

"Wear it, Kersta." Talamaya turned her attention back to her pile of treasure. "Maybe we can find more amongst the other mountains of treasure. Hurry, I'm afraid we're running out of time."

"Have you felt anything bad in this cave, princess?" Mexia asked.

"No, it's like this is a safe refuge for any who come here. How do you feel about it?"

"I sense there's great magic here, but none that would

harm us."

"Good. Maybe we can find some more magical items that will aid us against the wizard."

Gallant yanked out a war hammer.

Mexia smiled. "It's the most beautiful war hammer I have ever seen. Not that I have seen many, mind you."

"Aye, but it isn't half as endearing to me as Ren." He dropped the hammer on the pile and continued to plow through it with his short arms digging as quickly as he was able.

Talamaya dug at her treasure with renewed gusto like a dog sent the dirt flying out of a hole as she pushed deeper into the pile of coins, tossing them behind her.

Coins tumbling to the floor from all the treasure piles made a tinkling sound with an occasional clunk or clatter when a goblet or sword were tossed aside.

"What about this?" Gallant asked.

Everyone stopped working.

He held up a helm, plain, dented, with two curved horns on top and a narrow slit only for the eyes.

"Maybe it would scare the wizard to death," Kersta offered.

"Do ye not think it odd it is so plain, woman?" he growled at her.

"Put it on, Gallant," Talamaya proposed. "I have heard of a helm that protects the wearer from mind spells. Can you cast a spell that would make Gallant do something, Mexia? Something not harmful, of course, in case the helm doesn't work."

Mexia smiled. "I can do what the fairies do. Make him dance."

Gallant put the helm on, then folded his arms.

"Are you game, Gallant?"

His brows furrowed, he gave his head a nod. "Aye."

"Go ahead, Mexia."

Mexia cast the spell. Nothing happened. She shrugged.

"Maybe my spell didn't work."

"Or maybe the helm did." Talamaya sighed deeply. "If you make him dance, can you get him to stop afterward?"

"Yes. I can make him twirl in place twice."

"Will you try it, Gallant?"

"Aye." He took off the helmet and watched Mexia, his eyes narrowed in distrust.

She wiggled her fingers and cast the spell. He twirled in place twice and Kersta laughed. He cast a disgruntled look at her, then shoved the helm on his head. "I have my protection."

The party of four resumed their search.

After several more minutes, Mexia shouted, "Oh, oh, oh, look!" She pulled a leather belt out of her pile.

"That is the ugliest, most stained, piece of worn out leather I have ever seen," Kersta said.

"Yes, is it not beautiful? Someone must have treasured it faithfully." Mexia slipped it around her waist. "Nothing happens."

"Hmm...still, if it is like the other items of clothing, then it must provide some kind of magical protection," Talamaya said. "Wear it, Mexia. Only time will tell."

Talamaya continued to search her pile as everyone returned to their work. Then her fingers hit a glass-like object. She dug to pull it out from under the hundreds of coins that still buried it. As she pulled it free, Malachon's amulet glowed brightly reflecting off the pewter-framed mirror. At the top of the oval frame, a silver chain hung from the center.

"A mirror?" Kersta asked, joining Talamaya to examine it more closely.

Talamaya stared into the mirror, expecting to see her reflection. Instead, she saw the female dragon struggling to lay her eggs. "It's the dragon's magical item. It just has to be."

"But it's not something that is ugly that you can wear for

protection against the wizard, my lady."

"We could search here through the night and may never find anything else." Talamaya pulled the chain over her head. "Once we are done here, I'll return this to the dragons. But for now, we must find the scepter. And face the wizard, I'm afraid."

Kersta pulled the cape back on and yanked the hood over her head. Instantly, she vanished. "I'll walk ahead of everyone, my lady, if that pleases you."

"All right, Kersta. I hope the wizard cannot see through the cloak."

They headed out of the cave and into the passageway again. Talamaya squeezed Mexia's hand. She gave her a tentative smile.

When they were back at the first cave, Talamaya considered the next two tunnels. "I believe the scepter is in the second tunnel."

"But?" Kersta asked.

"Something waits for us in the third."

"The wizard?"

"I don't know."

"Then should we not get the scepter first?"

"Yes, I feel it with my heart, we must get it first. After that, we'll have to face the wizard."

"Have you figured out what to do then, my lady?" Kersta asked.

"No." She headed straight for the second passageway. "As I'm sure Aralias didn't know when she took on this quest in the beginning."

Talamaya's heart couldn't have beat any faster than it did now as she hurried through the tunnel. Her only hope was she could get the scepter and leave again, without her companions being injured—or worse, dying—in the process.

When they walked into the room, there was no need for fairy light. Lanterns illuminated the entire cave in a brilliant white light nearly blinding them. Then to everyone's mixed relief and concern, the light dimmed. At the back of the room stood a golden chest on a raised pedestal and four braziers stood burning in each corner of the room.

"Is it in there?" Mexia asked.

"Yes," a woman's voice answered. Everyone turned. Standing against one of the walls the spirit of a woman dressed in luminescent white gowns waited. Her hair, as white as the fresh fallen snow of Elan Pass, gathered about her shoulders in curls. She smiled at each as she considered the companions.

"I am Aralias. You and your friends have come, Talamaya, in answer to my prayer. I cannot rest until you have killed him for good. Put an end to this monster right, the way I should have done." Her brown eyes rested on the mirror. "I should have returned the magic to the dragons."

Talamaya dropped to her knees quickly, showing her utmost respect. "I promise to, Queen Aralias."

"Rise, dear child. You have a long ways to go to right the wrongs."

"What am I to do with the scepter, my lady?"

"Do what your heart compels you to do."

"I want my father to respect me...well, respect all women in Damar."

"And?"

"But, I'm not certain I wish to rule her in my father's place."

"It isn't in your heart to do so, Talamaya. We are different, in that respect. For me, I had no choice. My father and brother had died. I had to rule, and I wished to do so. It's not the same for you. You must do what your heart tells you to. You'll see the way when this is all done."

"How will I kill the wizard? I have no magic skills, my lady."

"Your heart will show you the way. Hurry, claim the scepter. He comes."

Aralias faded into the stone.

Talamaya dashed for the golden box.

With a jerk, she yanked the lid open. Inside, fifteen scepters rested against black velvet. "Which one is it? Which one, Aralias?"

"Someone's coming." Gallant readied his war hammer.

Mexia stepped against one of the walls away from the entrance, while Gallant hurried over to the other side.

"Tala!"

"Oh, Lazarion," Talamaya cried out. She glanced up at him briefly as he strode down the passage toward the cave entrance.

"My men and yours are still trying to answer riddles the sphinx poses to them. I was lucky and answered hers right off." He considered the golden chest. "The scepter?"

"I cannot tell which it is. There are too many."

"Use your heart," Kersta said.

They looked at the place where she stood, but saw no sign of her, hidden as she was in her invisibility cloak.

"Kersta has died?" Lazarion asked, his words showing concern.

"No, she's invisible." Talamaya assumed he thought Kersta's spirit haunted the cave. She ran her fingers over the scepters. When Malachon's amulet glowed and the right scepter turned warm to her touch, she lifted it in her hand.

Instantly, a blue tunnel of light swirled near her. She backed away from the gold box, remembering the words of the sphinx. The wizard could not kill her here. He had to wait until she took the scepter outside the Cave of Sorrows.

Mexia wiggled her fingers at the portal, whispering an incantation under her breath.

The wizard suddenly appeared. Immediately, he waved his hands at Mexia and silenced her words, paralyzing her at once.

He cast a spell on Gallant when he rushed forth with his war hammer. But the wizard's words had no effect. The wizard's mouth dropped open. Quickly, he vanished as Gallant clobbered the rock with his hammer where the wizard had only been seconds before.

"Troll dung. I hate wizards like him."

Talamaya ran for Lazarion before the wizard reappeared, knowing he couldn't strike her with anything deadly if he needed her to take the scepter beyond the cave walls. But he was sure to try for the king next.

Lazarion grabbed her and tried to pull her out of the way as the wizard reappeared and cast a spell at him.

"No," she screamed, and moved her body in front of his again.

"Curses, Aralias!" the wizard said when the spell reflected off the dragons' mirror hanging at her neck and struck him in the next instant.

"Mexia!" Talamaya shouted and ran to her, then shook her. With the spell caster paralyzed, Mexia was freed from his spell, but she stood dazed for a second. "Use your stone spell, Mexia. Hurry."

She began her incantation again.

Lazarion struck his broad sword at the wizard at the same time as Gallant hit the sorcerer, neither having any effect. Kersta tried next with her staff. Nothing happened.

"Everyone step back," Talamaya said as Mexia nodded.

She finished the spell and the wizard turned to stone.

"But it's not enough," Talamaya said. "We have to do something more. Something that will keep him from coming back." She considered the sphinx's words. *For many the sea was a watery grave.*

"Perhaps the wizard, once he frees himself from the stone, cannot make it to the surface of the water if we dump him into the sea to a watery grave."

"We will try it," Lazarion said.

"Let me see if I can move him with a spell of levitation," Mexia said. She wiggled her fingers and moved the statue off the floor a few inches, then dropped him. "Well, it may take a while, but I think I can get him to the entrance of the cave. Then no one has to die at the claws of the sphinx."

"I will tell the men we are coming," Gallant offered, then ran down the passageway.

Kersta embraced Talamaya to her surprise, not expecting the unseen figure to hug her like that.

"Kersta, you gave me a fright."

"I'm sorry, my lady. I forgot."

She removed her cloak.

Lazarion took a breath. "I thought you had become a ghost."

Talamaya stepped aside as Mexia moved the statue toward the passageway. Lazarion grabbed Talamaya's hand and held it tight as if he didn't wish to lose her again. "What happened when you sent us to the Forest of Grundgen, Talamaya?"

"I couldn't follow you, sire. The mage apprentices were nearing the portal chambers, and you and our men had vanished through the light. I was not sure what to do. In a panic, I pulled off the witch's ring and poof, I returned to Nania's tunnel. We came here as quickly as we could to get the scepter."

He squeezed her hand. "I can see that we will have many discussions about what will be done in the future, my love."

"And you, sire, will be most willing to let me have my way." She smiled at him as he gave her a small smile.

"I can see that you will be a most demanding wench."

"Does that bother you?"

"I believe it shall add some spark to my otherwise dreary reign."

"I haven't said I will marry you. You seem to take that for granted."

His smile remained as he hurried with her through the tunnel as if what he had decided was a foregone conclusion.

When they entered the main cavern, Talamaya glanced back at the tunnel leading to the unexplored cave. Sheer terror tore at her, mixed with an overwhelming desire to see what awaited her in the last cave.

"I must go through the other tunnel," she whispered as if whoever waited for her there might hear she intended to meet him soon, and she didn't wish him to know it.

Kersta shook her head. "We have the wizard imprisoned in stone, my lady. And you have the scepter. We have done all we can here."

"I must. I'm drawn there. Are you not the one who reminds me often enough that I must follow my heart?"

"But, my lady, you seem terrified and since we have met nothing evil here, except the wizard, I believe Malachon must have visited the room and that's where his mind was—"

Talamaya shook her head. "Not another word, Lady Kersta."

Kersta glanced at the king, then looked back at Talamaya and bowed her head in defeat.

"Go. Follow Mexia and Gallant outside. I'll be along in a few minutes, once I'm truly done here."

"Yes, Princess Talamaya."

Kersta waited, though, not moving from her spot.

"What are you bound to do?" Lazarion asked Talamaya.

"What needs to be done. You don't need to come with me."

He readied his sword. "I believe maybe your lady is right, and you shouldn't visit the cave, princess."

"Nania told me I must always follow my heart."

"Then this is good." He smiled at her as she frowned at him. "Between you and me, is it not?"

"I haven't agreed to anything between you and me, sire."

"I will have a word with Nania, to convince you otherwise, if need be. But for now, I won't let you go into this cave alone."

She held her staff diagonally across her body. "Good, let us discover what harmed one of Damar's most noble knights."

When they reached the end of the third tunnel, they found the air as frosty cold as Elan Pass. Unremarkable, the cave's gray walls revealed nothing, but in the center of the cave, a pool of water stood.

Talamaya crossed the floor to the pool as Lazarion attempted to stop her.

"Perhaps, your lady was right and this isn't such a good idea, Tala."

"I have to discover what shattered the knight's mind, sire. I must. Then I can save him."

Without further hesitation, she looked into the pool. Immediately, Malachon's amulet began to glow, reflecting off the still water.

Talamaya's head spun briefly and when she blinked her eyes, her surroundings had changed. Instead of the pool, a floor of uneven rock filled the cave and along the walls, five tunnels exited.

"Lazarion," she whispered. No sign of him, or anyone else existed in the damp cave that sent a shiver of cold up her spine.

Lanterns illuminated the cave with dim light, and she counted five tunnels. She barely took a breath. She had no weapons, no staff, no fairy wand, no scepter even. How had she come here, leaving everything and everyone else behind?

A high-pitched roar behind her made her whirl around to face the menace.

Standing ten feet away, Grimoria smiled at her and stroked his long gray beard. How could he be here when Mexia had imprisoned him in the stone?

"Aralias," he said. "You may have defeated me temporarily

again, but this time I'll keep you here with me...and if we cannot work out a mutually satisfactory agreement, you'll remain here forever."

Talamaya tried to reach Kersta. "*If you can read my mind, Kersta, have the men dump the wizard statue into the sea. Don't wait for me. Kersta, drown the wizard, and hurry. We must destroy him, before he can destroy me.*"

"What made you come here this time?" he asked. "You avoided this cave...well, you avoided all but the cave that held the scepter the last time. What made you think to come here?"

Talamaya touched her throat and felt the dragons' mirror still there. Would it help her, or not? And around her neck, Malachon's amulet still rested. Maybe that would aid her.

"What made Sir Malachon, knight of Damar, go mad?"

He motioned to the tunnels around the room. "You'll take one of them and find out for yourself. You still have not answered my question."

"I came here seeking to help the knight. But believe I need to destroy you...further."

He lifted his gray brows in amusement. "Your companions cannot help you here. In the meantime, your people suffer greatly at the hands of one who is most desirous to punish them."

"Who?"

He smiled. "It need not concern you. As to another matter, the witch made the mistake of aiding you. She paid with her life."

"You killed her?"

He smiled. A scream from deep inside one of the tunnels made Talamaya glance back in that direction.

"It waits for you, dear Aralias. When we have finished our little talk, you'll go see what it wants."

"Why did you kill the witch?"

He grunted. "I told her not to aid you. So what did she do? She disobeyed me. I should have known you were not her apprentice, but she'd had three before you, very similar in appearance. I thought she feared me enough to do my bidding without deceiving me. I suppose your selecting the right comb had something to do with it. She must have had the notion you had some magical abilities and could defeat me." He paused and twisted his mouth in annoyance.

"But it was her giving you the ring to my castle that aggravated me the most. Of course, she denied knowing anything about it. In fact, she said she'd lost it somewhere. But one of my mages described you to me perfectly before you vanished in the portal chambers using the ring. The witch had to die for her transgressions. I expected you to return to her house. But there was never any sign of you. Where did you go?"

"I wished a word with Nania."

His eyes darkened. Then he waved his finger at her. "Then there was this business with the Cyclops."

"You made the gryphon attack us on the Plain of the Ancients, too?"

"Mindless creatures. Easy to control."

"Did you make the dark elves move to Wildwood Forest from Albion?"

"A rather nice touch, I thought. They planned some new maneuvers for your return trip to Damar, but alas, now, only your friends shall benefit from their tactics."

"Kersta, if you're near enough to read my thoughts, bury the statue of the wizard at sea."

"Any other questions before I go?"

Talamaya's mind raced. She had to keep him talking, answering questions to give Kersta and the others time to drown the wizard. Whatever she had to face in the tunnel could probably shatter her own mind like it had Malachon's. Further, if she made it out alive, she had to have all the answers to their questions. This was the only chance, she believed, she'd ever have in getting them.

"Why did you do all of this? Was it just for the power?"

"I loved you. I have told you so before. There's nothing worse than being rejected by the one you love, Aralias. Nothing."

"I'm not Aralias. I'm Princess Talamaya."

He smiled. "You are one and the same. I would know you anywhere, anytime. Shall you meet my friends now?"

"Since I'll never leave here, I have to know, who has poisoned my brother, and what is the cure?"

"Had you kept your promises, dear Aralias, you would know the answer to that."

There were many promises she hadn't kept. Which one did he refer to?

A scream shattered the silence in another tunnel.

"They're restless."

"What promise have I not kept?"

"I must go now. I'll see you soon though. You have locked me down here for another five hundred years. Just think how much we can truly get to know one another. Maybe in time, if you're worthy of me, I'll release you from your prison when I'm released, but only if you join me. I'll rule of course, while you satisfy all of my other whims." He twisted a strand of his beard in his fingers. "For now, however, run along and meet my friends. They won't hurt you unless you're idle for very long. And perhaps, they'll make you desire my protection. I can give it to you, if you ask for it. We can have a most enjoyable time down here away from the rest of the world, if you allow yourself the pleasure."

He waved his fingers in front of his face and vanished. His voice lingered afterward, "Just call my name, my love, and I'll come to protect you."

22

A cackling laughter echoed through a tunnel as whatever made the grating noise neared the cave. Talamaya waited, not sure that running through any of the tunnels was her best choice of action. But it was the appearance of a two-headed cheetaur, its perfectly patterned body of spots blending into its sleek fur that decided the matter for her.

Both heads bared their long-jagged teeth at her, wrinkling their noses at the same time. Then a low-throaty growl escaped their lips, precursor to the lunge. She ran down the nearest tunnel, her skin clammy with perspiration, her head pounding with indecision. Which way? Which way did she need to go?

She needed enough time for her companions to kill the wizard, but then a horrible thought plagued her. Even if they dumped his statue into the sea, he might not be killed instantly, rather, only when he turned into human form in five hundred years. All those years she would have to outwit and outrun the evils that lurked in the caves? She'd lose her mind...just like Malachon had done. Was that how he was set free?

Her stomach turned to ice as she came to a crossroads in the tunnel. Go straight? Turn to the right? Or turn left?

She ran straight ahead.

Maybe, if she lost her mind fast enough, she could leave. And maybe one of her companions would help her to relive the horrors and free her mind again.

But Malachon wasn't quite free yet. And perhaps if she experienced the hell he had, she couldn't be freed ever either.

The racing of footsteps behind her made her dash down another tunnel, and to her horror, it dead-ended. She ran back to the junction and darted down a different path. A maze. That's where she'd ended up. A gray-walled maze where every passage looked identical to every other.

The dripping of water caught her ear. She ran into a smaller cave this time. In the center stood a pool of water like the one she'd looked into in the beginning and ended up in this wicked place.

Would peering into it, move her to another cave? Another set of tunnels? More horrors?

She looked into the water, not able to contain her longing for escape and anything she could do to bolster it. In astonishment, she stared back at herself, only this version held the scepter, in one hand and the staff in the other. King Lazarion spoke to her, shouted at her, called to her, and hugged her to his chest.

Tears filled her eyes. He couldn't know where she'd gone to. Her body still stood in the original cave beside the pool, while her mind was lost deep inside the nightmare created by the wizard in the bowels of the cavern.

"Sire," she whispered, tears collecting in her eyes. She touched the water, reaching out, wishing more than anything else in the world but to touch him. The water rippled as her hand moved into it.

Suddenly, Kersta appeared as she pulled the invisibility cloak from her shoulders. She pointed at the water.

Did they see her? Could they see her in the water reaching out to them?

Kersta spoke hastily to the king, and he shook his head. She continued to talk, her lips moving quickly as she mouthed the words. Her hands waved frantically in the air as he stared at her. Then a scream grew close to the cave Talamaya now stood in. She ran to the entrance.

The cheetaur looked down one tunnel, sniffed the air, and then turned in her direction. She couldn't face it in the cave. It had no other exit. Yet, she hated to leave the only image she had of the outside world.

When the cheetaur turned to see her, she ran down the tunnel away from it, then dashed into another. How long could she continue to run from the cheetaur?

She darted down another passageway, then stopped as it ended in another solid stone wall. Again, the cheetaur growled. She whipped around to face it, except this time she had nowhere to go.

It lunged, its teeth bared, its four paws airborne, and she closed her eyes.

Heat surrounded her, instantly drying and warming the cold, moist air. She opened her eyes. Before her, a pile of ashes was all that remained of the two-headed cat.

She studied each of the three walls that hemmed her in. What had incinerated the cat?

Puzzling over the matter, she headed back down the passageway, determined to return to the pool of water. But after many false starts, her mind fuzzed with exasperation. Then she heard another low growl. Turning, she caught a glimpse of another cheetaur. This time, she stood her ground. Her energy spent, she couldn't run forever.

It stalked her, creeping, crouching, and then lunged.

The dagger-like claws of the cheetaur extended. She fought the urge to close her eyes. Then as before, a red-orange flame burst forth—straight from her body. Heating the passageway, warming and drying the air, the fire turned the cat into ashes.

She looked down at the mirror. No, not from her body, but from the reflection in the mirror. In the glass, the male dragon sat on his eggs and nodded to her. The dragon had killed the cat with his breath. Their magic might keep her alive after all.

Again, she attempted to find the passageway back to the pool of water. Instead, she found the way into the main cave where the five tunnels began.

Grimoria appeared in a swirling blue light several feet away, startling her. "Have you been having fun, my dear?" He yawned. "You have not called for me yet, as I thought you would. You're stronger-willed than any woman I have ever known. No matter. We have many years to break you down so that you're a more compliant mate. But if you should decide to join me, my chambers are much more hospitable than..." A look of pain crossed his face. "What have you done?"

"What?"

"You, you..."

Sweat poured down his skin and he took a step toward her. No, not sweat. Seawater?

"What have you done?" he moaned, grabbing his face.

His gray beard disappeared into a torrent of water. He narrowed his eyes at her. "My apprentices will take my place. They will...ahhh," he cried out in agony.

His body dissolved into water and before it could reach the toes of her boots, she collapsed.

"Kiss her, my liege. Kiss her and bring her back to us," Kersta yelled.

What a ridiculous thing to say. Kiss who? Why was Kersta

yelling so? Talamaya's eyes refused to open. Would she see a cheetaur at her throat?

Warm lips touched hers, and she succumbed to the touch.

"Talamaya," was mouthed against her mouth as Lazarion pressured her deeper.

She kissed him back, her hands grasping at his arms greedily, and the tears of joy flooding down her cheeks. In a blur, Lazarion's face appeared close to hers as she chanced to open her eyes. He wasn't a dream. He was real, flesh and blood. She sobbed as he held her tightly, squeezing the breath from her chest. "Never let me go," she whispered. "Never let me go."

"Oh, my lady," Kersta said. "You're back. Oh, princess! You're all right, are you not? Your mind is still intact?"

"It's my heart I have to worry about," Talamaya said under her breath as Lazarion lifted her from the floor.

"Your heart is quite intact, Talamaya," the king said, holding her close. "It's my heart that nearly stopped to think I'd come so close to losing you."

She nestled her head against his chest and listened to his heart thumping at an increased beat as he walked her out of the tunnel. Smiling, she took a deep breath. "Your heart sounds just fine to me, sire."

"You know there will be war between our kingdoms if your father does not permit me to court you."

She chuckled when he carried her outside of the cave. "But I have the scepter now."

"Yes, not your father."

"But I had intended to give it to my father."

"Nothing will stand in my way, my lady."

"What happened to you?" Kersta asked.

"Did you read my mind? I so wanted you to, but I was afraid you were too far away from me to hear."

"Yes, my lady. I read your mind. Drown the wizard, you

repeated with much urgency. If I had not joined the king in the cave with the pool, I probably would not have heard you. Since you bade me leave the caves, I could not follow you or be reprimanded. At least not unless I was invisible." She shook the cloak. "I wore it and joined you and the king in the cave. We tried to break the spell the water held over you but could not. I feared whatever you saw would break your mind, like Malachon's mind was shattered."

"Did you see what I saw?"

"Yes, my lady. Everything. The wizard's words as he spoke them once your mind interpreted them. The cheetaurs and the fright they gave you. The reflecting pool where you attempted to reach us. I knew you touched the water from where you were imprisoned. I wanted you to know that King Lazarion had ordered the men to take the statue out to sea. Anything, to ease your worry. But alas, I cannot transfer my thoughts to yours. Mexia went with the men to ensure the wizard didn't somehow come back to life miraculously. She was not sure her powers were as great as Aralias or her companions' abilities were. What if he was only turned to stone for hours, not years?"

"But he was tossed in the sea?"

"The boat has not returned yet. What happened to you, my lady? How did you break free of the pool?"

"The wizard dissolved before my eyes. Did you not see this?"

"Oh. I was not sure. I saw a waterfall briefly, then you collapsed."

"Then you urged the king to…"

Kersta smiled. "A knight's kiss revived me once when I had a bad fall from a horse. Why not the king's kiss?"

"You could have tried to give me some of Modi's tea."

Lazarion chuckled. "The tea would not have had half the effect I had on your quick recovery."

"You may set me down, now, sire. I can walk."

"Are you sure? The color has not fully returned to those lovely cheeks of yours."

"Yes, I'm sure."

He set her down on her feet, but she gripped his arm when her legs grew wobbly. She realized then, she hadn't quite overcome the terror of the cave. "We must be sure the wizard is truly dead." She looked over at the sphinx, whose eyes remained closed, but smiled in response to Talamaya's words. "He is dead?" she asked the sphinx.

The sphinx yawned. "He is dead, but another will take his place someday."

That wasn't what she wished to hear. She touched the mirror at her neck. She had to return the magical item to the dragons as she promised.

"I must return something to the dragons." She had barely finished speaking when the male dragon appeared out of the mists.

"You have it."

"Yes, and it is what helped us to imprison the wizard this time and saved my life when I faced his 'friends' in the maze."

"You are the only one who remembered us. It was only appropriate that we help you in return."

She took the chain from her neck and put it over the dragon's head when he lowered it for her.

"You'll always be welcome here, princess."

"Thank you for all your help. I hope your mate is well."

"She's tired, but much relieved to be unburdened with the duty of carrying her brood any longer. I must return to sit on the eggs while she feeds."

"Tell her I wish her well."

"Do you wish to return to the mainland now?"

"We have some unfinished business here. We'll take one of the ships home."

He bowed, then turned and flew into the mist.

Taking her hand, Lazarion led her to the shore where the boat sailed into the cove.

"We saw what was left of Rupert on the rocks. I take it Mexia freed him from the stone after all."

"Yes, sire. She did. He was grateful that she had saved his life."

"And?"

"There's nothing more to say," Talamaya said to the king, not wishing to speak of the knight's deceitfulness. He was dead, after all. What difference did it make to anyone now?

"He abandoned you."

She looked up at him. His eyes studied her response carefully.

"I know he wouldn't have been trusted alone with the three of you women. He would have thought none capable of retrieving the scepter, and with me out of the way, he would have claimed my throne."

"Yes, sire." She glanced at Kersta and saw her holding both Talamaya's staff and the scepter.

Kersta smiled. "You didn't have enough hands to hold everything."

Talamaya laughed as Lazarion's hand tightened on hers as if he feared she'd let loose of him to retrieve her weapon and scepter.

Mexia waved at Talamaya and Kersta, then she was helped out of the boat. Running across the beach, she beamed. "We threw him into the water."

"Yes, and now he's dead."

A young man who looked very much like Rupert, stood near her. Wasn't he Rupert's brother? The one who said he'd kill the wizard who'd turned Rupert to stone?

"We must leave for Damar at once." Talamaya pulled Lazarion toward the boat.

Gallant waved his war hammer from the bow at her. She nodded in greeting.

"I take it that Rupert's brother is no longer angry with Mexia," she said to Lazarion as Mexia lingered farther back from them, now walking beside the man.

"Our people have seen how important having wizardry skills can be when fighting others who have magic. Bernard, like all the rest of us, have learned the lesson well."

They boarded the boat and as it rocked, Lazarion took her arm to give her stability.

As soon as everyone had climbed aboard, the captain of the ship headed to the shore of the mainland.

The breeze caught Talamaya's hair, pulling strands loose from her braids. Lazarion touched one and pulled it behind her ear.

She knew what he had in mind. Another kiss. And she couldn't allow it. Not in front of his men. Not before she had permission to court him.

She looked at Kersta whose eyebrows and lips raised. *What does your heart say?* she could almost hear Kersta ask.

Her heart told her to allow him to kiss her. But though he seemed to want to do so, he waited. Did she need to give him permission? She pulled him to the bow of the boat and with the wind filling the sails, she watched the foam of the water breaking against the ship. The full moon shown overhead while stars sprinkled the black velvet night with thousands of white lights. The salt spray licked their faces. She couldn't think of a more romantic spot to kiss a king.

She turned her face up to see what Lazarion was looking at and smiled to find him watching her actions with intrigue. She reached up and touched his lips with her finger. "Perhaps I can convince my father you should be allowed to court me."

"Oh?"

She touched his broad firm chest with her fingertips. As soon as she did, his hands grasped her arms. He pulled her in close, pressing his lips against hers with a passion she'd never expected. And she melted, all the tension she'd experienced in the cave, vanishing all at once. When he let her up for air, she grabbed the railing.

He smiled broadly and wrapped his arm around her waist and pulled her close again as they watched the ship rise and fall in the crest of the waves. "Do you still feel we are barbarians?"

"Most assuredly," she said, her whole body still tingling from his kiss.

He chuckled under his breath, the sound seductive and deep, making her think of Kersta's words. He wished to be with her, naked.

He leaned over and kissed her forehead. "You are like the minko flower, my lady, delicate, fragrant, as soft to the touch as its velvet petals are to the skin. Yet if the flower is trampled by a hundred horses, it is resilient, springing back to life at once. You're as durable, despite appearing so fragile."

"Fragile?" She would never have described herself in such a way.

His arm embraced her tighter. "I have offended you."

"I don't see myself as fragile."

Again, he chuckled.

When they reached the shores, the fishermen waiting for them there, eyed the women with interest still.

Gallant grabbed Kersta's arm when she was set ashore. "She is already spoken for."

"A dwarf cannot have a human female for a wife. Tell him, King Lazarion," one of the fishermen said. "We have taken care of your horses, the ladies', and the dwarf's." He waved at the animals waiting on the shore. "As you have asked us to. But the ladies are ours to keep."

"What is this all about?" Lazarion asked Gallant.

"Rupert told these men that the women wished husbands amongst them. They won't listen to reason."

"Oh." The king smiled and helped Talamaya onto her horse. "This one is mine."

Gynt, Hauk, and Zornan quickly shoved Gallant aside as they offered to help Kersta to her horse, the three men bickering over her to Talamaya's amusement.

Mexia headed for her horse, but when one of the fishermen tried to stop her, Bernard stepped into his path, his sword raised in warning. "The sorceress is with me."

Smiling, Mexia mounted her horse.

With everyone readied for the travel, both Damarian knights and those of Lazarion's rule, rode together while Talamaya, her companions, and the king led the way.

When they reached the land of the Cyclops, where the gigantic statues decorated the area, Lazarion turned to Talamaya. "I cannot believe you came through here without waiting for our help."

Despite being exasperated that he still felt the men had to protect them, she couched her feelings. "The trek was not easy." *Men.* She shook her head inadvertently.

But then the scepter began to vibrate.

"Use it to take you home now that you're beyond the dragon's magic," Aralias's voice said to her. *"Speak the words, Talamaya. Save your people as the wizard has poisoned them."*

"The wizard? He is dead."

"The wizard, Saqualian, the wizard Grimoria's daughter. Hurry before the people of Damar are no more," Aralias said.

"*Saqualian wanted to marry my brother to be queen of Damar. Why would she want to kill our people?*"

"*Revenge for her father's death.*"

Talamaya took a ragged breath. "*What will cure our people?*"

"*The cure was provided to you when you first underwent your journey.*"

"*Modi's tea.*" Talamaya silently spoke the words that ran through her mind. "*Ras caladonian sirat morsover balok riven.*"

In a blink of an eye all who were with her on the beach now stood before her castle gates, while a violent storm raged about them. Thunder vibrated the ground as sheets of lightning illuminated the black clouds. A pounding rain poured down on the already weary group.

"Halt, who goes there?" a knight asked, his hooded cloak covering his armor and face as he greeted them from underneath the guard's shelter.

"Princess Talamaya and her companions."

"My lady," the knight quickly bowed. "Thank the gods you have returned. Have you got it?"

"Sir Malachon?" Talamaya recognized his voice finally, but not his features hidden in the dark.

"Yes, my lady. Sometime ago, the cloud lifted from my mind."

She smiled. "Good. Please let us in so we may see to the sick."

"The sick."

"Yes, you're not afflicted, are you?" She assumed he wouldn't be since Modi gave him the tea to drink.

"No, but many are."

"We'll cure them."

He opened the gate and she and the men rode into the outer courtyard. A man hurried out to greet them, cloaked the same as the knight, trying to stay dry in the inhospitable weather. "The knight at the gate should have turned you away, travelers. We're sick here. You must leave at once."

She dismounted and motioned for the others to do the same. "I'm Princess Talamaya, and we bring the cure."

"Princess," he said and quickly bowed.

"Tell me what goes on now in the house of Sal."

While the horses were led into the stables, the weary group of men and women followed the man into the castle. He led them down the hall, their boots slapping against the floor like soldiers on parade, marching out of step.

"There has been a great plague."

"The king? What news is there of my father?"

The man shook his head.

She grabbed his arm and halted his step as everyone behind her stopped. "What of my father?"

"He died yesterday, Princess Talamaya, forgive my saying so."

Talamaya couldn't have been struck harder than if she'd been hit by Kersta's staff when she wasn't paying attention. Her stomach grew queasy and her legs felt like the bone had turned to gruel. To have fought so long and hard to bring the scepter home, only to find her father dead...

Mexia grabbed her arm and Lazarion helped her stay on her feet. "My lady," Mexia whispered, "more than anything now, our people need your strength."

Talamaya swallowed the tears that choked her throat. "And Grisom?"

"He's still hanging by a single thread of life."

"My mother?" Talamaya said, hurrying toward her parents' chambers.

"The same."

She turned to Kersta. "Take Mexia and your drinking pouches and fill vases with Modi's tea. The men will take the tea to everyone who's still alive in Damar and give it to them." Her gaze shifted to the man before her. "Are you not affected?"

"I just came back from a trading expedition."

She pulled her flask off and handed it to the man. "Drink then. This will protect you, should you come in contact with the poison."

When the ladies hesitated to leave her, Talamaya frowned. "What is the matter, ladies?"

"What about Saqualian?"

"As soon as you are finished, meet me at Grisom's chambers."

The ladies hurried off with the men, all but Lazarion who stayed close to Talamaya as their escort handed her flask back to her.

They continued to the king's chambers. "Who has been in charge then?" Talamaya asked.

"Og."

She stopped. "He has made it back here?"

"Yes, he said he could not reach the scepter. He came back late last night with only five of his men."

When they reached the chambers, Talamaya bade the men wait outside, despite Lazarion's concern for her. She hurried into her mother's room where a lady who looked nearly as sick as her mother, her skin pale, her unkempt hair dangling in gray curls over her shoulders, sat beside the queen's bed.

"Oh, my lady," the woman said, weeping and tried to kneel.

Talamaya crossed the floor to the bed and lifted the lady to her chair. "Please, drink this tea. It is the cure." After the lady took a couple of swallows, Talamaya turned to the bed. "My lady mother, you cannot die on me." Tears moistened her cheeks to her annoyance. She lifted her mother's head and poured the sweet tea down her mother's throat, making her gag slightly. Her eyes fluttered open.

Before she could croak out a word, Talamaya said, "Mother, I must see to Grisom, but I will return to you soon."

"Your father has died," her mother said, her words heavy with grief.

Talamaya wiped the tears away and kissed her mother's cheek. "Yes, my lady mother. I have been told. I must try to make everyone well. Then I will see you in a while. Rest and get well." She offered some more tea to her mother, then kissed her cheek again.

At the entrance to the room, she grabbed Lazarion's arm and hurried down the hall to her brother's chambers. "I must locate Saqualian next." She turned to the man who now dogged their steps. "Where is Og?"

"In the throne room. He has been quite angry the king sent you to fetch the scepter. He wished more than anything to have you as a bride, you know, my lady. He feared you would never make it back alive."

When she reached her brother's room, the scepter glowed. She pulled it from her belt. "Saqualian," she said under her breath, her blood heating with anger.

Talamaya stormed into the room as the king yanked his sword from its sheath. "Get away from my brother, you...you wizard!"

The woman's narrowed eyes couldn't grow any smaller as she opened her mouth to speak, undoubtedly to cast some kind of a curse. Immediately, Talamaya held up the scepter, and instinctively felt its power.

Saqualian's eyes grew big, and she gasped, then grabbed the scepter.

A flash of light blinded Talamaya as heat from the scepter forced perspiration to freckle her brow. The energy from the staff flooded every inch of her body as several yelled in distress, evidently worried about her.

"I am Grimoria's daughter," Saqualian hissed, "and you shall pay for imprisoning my father the first time."

Talamaya managed to croak out, "He's dead now and no longer will harm any."

"You will die!" the wizard shrieked.

"Talamaya!" Lazarion shouted.

The brilliant ice white light blinded her, and all she could make out was the blurry form of the wizard who still gripped the scepter in her greedy hands. But Talamaya wouldn't release the staff no matter what, though her blood heated from the power of the scepter.

"Use the ancient words, Talamaya," Aralias said. *"Send her to her father's grave."*

Struggling with the wizard, Talamaya pulled the tip of the scepter toward her forehead. When she was able, she touched the rod to her skin and started the incantation. *"Malan tession ror callow rarrelent mass done!"*

The wizard shrieked again, the light grew brighter until Talamaya could barely stand it as her head pounded with pain. Then the wizard's force on the scepter faded and she disappeared.

"She escaped," Lazarion said, dashing forth, searching for any signs of her, underneath the bed, behind the curtains, in the wardrobe.

"She is dead," Aralias said.

Talamaya stared at the ghostly figure of Aralias who seemed to smile back at her from across the room. *"You have done what I failed to do, vanquished the wizard and now his daughter forever. Keep the peace, dear Talamaya, as I once did. The scepter will ensure that the balance is maintained between the peoples of Inherian, as long as you use it for good--to keep the peace."*

"Talamaya," Lazarion said, touching her arm. "Talamaya."

She stared at him, finally seeing him as the brilliant light faded from her vision, and Aralias vanished from sight. She took a deep breath and took hold of his free hand as he held his sword still in the other. "She's gone," she said in almost a whisper.

"Vanquished?"

"Dead." She glanced at her brother, lying still so pale in bed.

Kersta had already given him tea, and Grisom opened his eyes and motioned to Talamaya. "I knew you would come see me."

She hurried to join him and knelt beside the bed. "Grisom, I have the scepter." She showed the golden rod to him, sparkling in the lantern light. "War has been averted. The wizard, Grimoria, and his daughter are dead."

Grisom tried to sit up and Lazarion and Talamaya helped him, propping pillows behind his back.

"How? You stole it from Og?" Grisom furrowed his brow at her as he examined the scepter in his hands.

"Goddess no. I claimed it. Kersta, Mexia, and I retrieved it from the Cave of Sorrows."

Her brother was still sick, Talamaya reminded herself, though she couldn't help the anger she felt at hearing his words.

Grisom twisted the scepter in his hands. "Og said he came back with the scepter. He didn't show it to me, that I recall. I've been too sick. But you couldn't have claimed it. You're just a girl."

She raised her brows, stiffened her back, and folded her arms. Now she was pissed. "I'm a woman, for your information, not just a girl. As you're a man now, and not just a boy. And I did too retrieve the scepter."

Grisom's gaze shifted to Lazarion as he sheathed his sword. "Who is he?"

"King Lazarion."

Her brother's eyes grew big, and he tried to climb out of bed. "We have lost."

She made him lie back down. "We're not at war."

"Arrest this man at once! He's not Damarian!" Og said to his men as they stormed into the room.

Talamaya whipped around and readied her staff and stepped in front of Lazarion. "He's a guest under my protection. Step away from him if you know what's good for you."

"You cannot be serious. The man has raided our borders," Og said.

"Og, have your men stand down or I'll knock them down."

His lips twitched in a smile. "I'm in charge now."

"I have the scepter," Grisom said. "I rule now."

Talamaya twisted around and relieved her brother of the rod. She tucked it into her belt, and turned in time to catch one of Og's knight's thrusting his sword at Lazarion. Her staff connected with the sharp metal before Lazarion had time to pull his sword from its sheath.

The knight's steel shattered, and he jumped back. He cried out and grabbed his arm as if he was in pain.

The others stepped back.

"Seems you have learned a few tricks on your journey to claim the scepter," Og said, bowing his head slightly in reverence to her.

Movement at the door made Talamaya look in that direction. Gynt helped her mother into the room, her face still pale and her movements slowed.

"Queen Isa wishes a word with her son and daughter," Gynt said.

"My lady mother." Talamaya curtsied as the men hurried to show their respect.

Gynt helped the queen sit in a chair by Grisom's bed. She held her son's hand and smiled. "I'm pleased to see you're getting better."

"I'll be on my feet and ruling by morning, my mother."

"What do you say, Talamaya?" her mother asked.

Talamaya hesitated to answer. Nania's words whispered in her ear, *"When all is said and done, you'll know what to do."*

Aralias's words came back to her also. *"You are not me."*

And Modi's words of wisdom—*"Take the path that is right."*

Talamaya knelt at her mother's feet. "I have learned much in the past few days. For one, I don't wish to rule Damar, not now. But if I did, would the women not benefit? Yet if my heart doesn't wish me to rule, would our people suffer?"

"You cannot reign, Talamaya," Grisom said. "We have always had a male ruler."

"The history books must be rewritten. If I don't lead our people, will this happen?" She patted her brother's hand. "Aralias ruled as queen, dear brother. And she did a wonderful job. I believe we need a queen also, to set things right for the women in Damar."

"You wish to lead our people then, Talamaya?" her mother asked.

"I wish *you* to reign, my lady mother. I must travel to Langdon with Mexia. She has training to conduct there. And after I return, I wish to learn more about King Lazarion's people." She reached her hand back to Lazarion.

He crossed the floor and interlocked his fingers with hers.

"What about the scepter?" Grisom sputtered. "You're giving it to Mother?"

"No, Grisom. I'll keep it safe." Talamaya patted it, resting at her waist.

Her mother looked up at Lazarion. "What do you say about all of this, sire?"

He smiled. "I most humbly ask to court your daughter, my lady." He bowed his head.

"And you, my daughter? What say you?"

Talamaya rose to her feet. "I believe there's much we can

learn about our neighbors. Possibly in the future, we may even have an alliance between our peoples."

"Near future," Lazarion said.

"Through marriage?" Grisom said through clenched teeth. "You mean to marry him?"

"Grisom, you said already you didn't think I should marry Og."

Og stormed out of the room with his men racing after him.

Grisom tried to get out of bed. "I meant someone like Sir Gynt, or—"

"What do you think, my lady mother?" Talamaya asked.

"Knowing you, Talamaya, I'd say your mind is already made up."

Lazarion squeezed Talamaya's hand. She looked up to see his smile stretching to the moon.

Facing her mother, she nodded. "You always did know me, my mother, even when I didn't know myself."

Mexia and Kersta burst into the room with Gallant pounding the floor behind them. Mexia blurted out, "What have we missed? Something about going to Albion and kingly alliances?"

Talamaya looked at Kersta. She shrugged. "Sorry, I could not contain my enthusiasm when I heard the news."

The queen smiled. "You can read minds, Lady Kersta?"

"She can read minds?" Lazarion and Gynt both asked, their voices mixed with surprise and concern all at once.

Talamaya smiled at Lazarion. "Come, walk with me through the gardens before we retire for the night, sire. Is there anything you wish to speak with me about?"

He hurried her out of the room. Rubbing his whiskered chin, he said, "I didn't know Lady Kersta read minds."

"Does this concern you?"

He studied her carefully. "I guess I'll have to watch what I think about when I'm in the lady's presence from now on."

"You don't have to, sire. I find your thoughts most...revealing."

He chuckled as the tips of his ears turned red. "I don't wish to delay our...alliance."

She laughed. "I don't wish to be rushed into anything. What if I find your women are treated much the same as we are here?"

"You wouldn't find that."

"What would I find?"

"A very willing, compassionate, and understanding husband." He leaned down to kiss her mouth.

Pressuring her to succumb to his longing, she kissed him back with just as much enthusiasm, licking, tasting, and nipping his mouth, hungering for even more. She took a breath, trying to slow her rapidly beating heart. Fire coursed through her as his heated body touched hers. No doubt when she returned from Albion, she wouldn't delay the inevitable.

"I believe you've proved your point." She smiled up at him.

He cleared his throat. "You mean you wish to marry me, and soon, I hope?"

She nodded and he wrapped his arm around her waist as he walked her into the gardens.

"You do realize what some will say?" he asked.

"What is that, Lazarion?"

"I married you to obtain the scepter."

She chuckled. "They'll say worse about me."

"Oh? What is that?"

"They'll say I married the barbarian king."

Lazarion's laughter carried across the courtyard, filling Talamaya with cheer and the first real hope she'd had for a better life since she'd turned of age.

Now the chance for a new future for the continued peace for those living in Inherian existed. Hope was renewed for an everlasting alliance between Lazarion's people and those of the

Damar. And her mother's rule would enable women to have a status equal to their male counterparts in Damar.

Talamaya snuggled her head against Lazarion's chest. Best of all, she had a mate to share her dreams with.

After she helped escort Mexia to the wizards' school at Albion and investigated what the people were like there. For the first time in her life, she was free of the Damarian rules that bound her, and she had no intention of casting aside her freedom anytime soon.

To Albion, she vowed, and a new adventure.

ABOUT THE AUTHOR

Bestselling and award-winning author **Terry Spear** has written over fifty paranormal romance novels and four medieval Highland historical romances. Her first werewolf romance, *Heart of the Wolf,* was named a 2008 *Publishers Weekly*'s Best Book of the Year, and her subsequent titles have garnered high praise and hit the *USA Today* bestseller list. A retired officer of the U.S. Army Reserves, Terry lives in Crawford, Texas, where she is working on her next werewolf romance and continuing her new series about shapeshifting jaguars and also writes new YA books. For more information, please visit www.terryspear.com, or follow her on Twitter, @TerrySpear. She is also on Facebook at http://www.facebook.com/terry.spear. And on Wordpress at:
Terry Spear's Shifters
http://terryspear.wordpress.com/

UNTITLED

Excerpt from THE MAGE OF MONROVIA, BOOK 2

The Mage of Monrovia

Terry Spear

The humid air hung heavy with the odor of freshly caught fish as Lady Mexia and her companions, crossed the main square of the port city of Langdon. Just a brief walk away stood Mexia's destination, Langdon Castle, the wizard's school of higher learning, and the surprise that awaited them that even her companion, Princess Talamaya, with her ability of second sight, had not foreseen. Or so Mexia thought.

The princess and Lady Kersta of the Kingdom of Damar, and their dwarf friend, Gallant of the village of Kern strode with her, just as determined to see her attend the school as Mexia was. Dread bunched into knots in Mexia's stomach as the twelve white towers surrounding the castle, came into view.

On top of several of the spires, owls of various kinds, slender bodies with long close-set ear tufts; rounder, larger shaped bodies with large farther set ear tufts; heavily fringed facial disk owls, with no visible ear tufts...and more, posed as if waiting to have their portrait painted on the spot.

Mexia studied the birds, most watching the party with intrigue, and she wondered if they were the mage apprentices' familiars, out for a breath of fresh air or exercise. None of her wizard family had ever had familiars before, and she wondered then, would they help or hinder a mage's work?

Kersta's pixie face illuminated with a sunshiny smile. Though nearly everyone from Damar had brown hair and eyes, hers was darker than Talamaya's. Kertsa's curls, nearly black, dangled free from her braids secured against her head from the sea breeze's constant tugging. She patted Mexia's shoulder. "I can see the apprehension in your thoughts. But your father gave you all the knowledge he had of wizard ways, and I'm sure you'll do fine."

Princess Talamaya patted the golden rod secured at her waist. "And the spells and trials you overcame with us as you helped us to claim the Scepter of Lanai should give you an edge." Her heart-shaped face tilted upward slightly with triumph as her lips curved up with reassurance.

"Hmpf," Gallant grunted yanking at his partially braided brown beard that reached all the way to his belt. "Schools of learning like this are for those who never truly venture into the world and experience it for themselves. Ye are better off without them."

Mexia observed the rainbow of lights swirling before closed iron gates. "I wish to be a High Wizard, someday." She stretched her hand toward the portal. "I have not learned how to close or open a portal for one. Not even my father knows how to do such a thing." She turned to the princess. "And though we destroyed the blood-thirsty wizard, Grimoria, the mage apprentice who stole his book of spells is certain to strike out against us one of these days, once he feels he's powerful enough. With the training I receive here, hopefully I will be better prepared to defeat him, too."

"Of course," the princess said. "I worry you have such high hopes for the school but may be disappointed."

Mexia frowned at her. "You have seen a vision about this, my lady?"

"I am sorry, Mexia, that I have said nothing about this before, but yes. I see the four of us trekking through a forest filled with dangers." She waved her hand at the town. "There are no dangers here, no woods inside the city of Langdon. So why do I see this if you are busily studying in these hallowed halls?"

She took a deep breath, exasperated that the princess would withhold the information from her. Did the princess think Mexia would falter to attain her quest over such a vision? "I am determined to do this."

The princess smiled. "And we are just as bound to see you succeed. Our home of Damar will benefit from everything you're able to learn here. Shall we enter?"

Mexia nodded. "I sense the gates are locked. If we step into the portal at the same time, we should be transported into the castle, I suspect."

"Or the woods where the beasts lay in wait for us?" Gallant grumbled.

"You can wait for us here," Kersta responded.

"Aye, and where will ye be if ye need my protection?"

Kersta chuckled. Mexia shook her head, amused. The two of them would never quit squabbling.

The four stepped into the portal. Instantly, they were transported into a massive hall where youthful mages, their faces sporting a trickle of whiskers, or none at all, stared at the party briefly as they hurried on their way. Marble floors inlaid with wizardry symbols met her eye. The room seemed larger for the twenty-foot ceiling that rose above them painted in images of wizards mastering various skills: levitation, casting lightning spells, taming dragons.

Then three of the students, who appeared older than most already having reached the height of men, and each wearing the start of a beard, watched the newcomers with interest. There was some discussion between them as the princess whispered, "I see no sorceresses."

Kersta nodded. "The notion has crossed the mage apprentices' minds...why are three women and a dwarf standing in their school with magically-enhanced weapons at their beck and call?"

"I have no magic," Gallant argued patting his war hammer secured in his belt at his waist.

"They are eyeing the Scepter of Lanai. Do they know about it?" the princess asked.

Mexia nodded. "Yes, my lady. They would be able to sense every item we carry that has some magical powers."

"One of the men is approaching," Kersta whispered.

Out of the three, he was the shortest and least appealing. Mexia turned her attention to the other two, the one who was speaking, and the other who remained silent but studied her with intrigue.

Kersta whispered, "The one you find most appealing, Mexia, is the most dangerous. Use caution."

Mexia turned to her. "I am not interested in any here. I am only concerned with further schooling."

She focused on the mage who drew close to her. His hair, beard, and beady eyes were colored a monotonous coal black as he stood before her. His attention darted nervously from one of the companions to the other, then back to her.

"What do you wish here?" he asked, directing his question to her, his words meant to intimidate, but his voice slightly high-pitched, making him appear more anxious than anything.

"I wish to see the High Wizard. I came here to take the test of admission."

He snorted and folded his arms. "Women do not attend Langdon Castle. Learn your witchery skills at home, little girl."

Mexia's blood boiled, but she curbed her anger and smiled sweetly instead. "Perhaps you are mistaken."

"I told ye, woman," Gallant said, "ye are too good for the likes of this place. This young upstart paid his way to get in here and has not half the wizardry skills of ye, I tell ye."

The mage quickly shifted his gaze toward the dwarf and glared at him.

The princess motioned her hand at Gallant to silence their companion. He grunted in response.

Kersta tapped her staff on the marble floor. "You wonder about the Scepter of Lanai."

The mage eyed her suspiciously.

"Lady Mexia," she said pointing at her, "turned the wizard, Grimoria, to stone to help the princess retrieve it."

The mage shook his head. "You lie. There was no way a female mage ever did something like that. Furthermore, women will never train here!" Without another word, he vanished.

Ignoring his vile comments, Mexia sighed. "That's what I want to learn to do. Vanish like that."

The second mage apprentice approached her, his hair and beard a lighter brown color like the princess's, and his eyes a hazel tone, but there was no smile on this one's stern lips either. "You were told to leave this place, were you not?"

"I wish to speak to the High Wizard about attending school."

"And were you not told witches do not go here?"

"I'm a mage apprentice, taught by my own father, a wizard in his own right."

The mage's thick brown brows rose slightly in amazement. "He was schooled here?"

"No, he learned on his own."

"A country wizard?" He laughed.

Mexia gripped her staff, annoyed beyond reason to be treated in such a manner by a fellow mage, then noticed both her lady companions did the same with their own. She loosened her hold on her staff. Fighting with a mage apprentice would not help her to enter the school, she suspected. Keeping one's temper was the basis for all wizardry training, after all.

"I have every intention of attending school to further my training."

He clicked his fingers, and the other mage joined him. "Tell the witch, she is not welcome here."

"She wishes?"

"To see the High Wizard so she may be enrolled in classes here."

The man stroked his blond beard as his blue eyes remained fixed on Mexia. His disarming gaze spellbound her as she considered his sturdy jaw, softened by the beard, while his wavy hair flowed past his shoulders in strands of sun-drenched golden strands. "Then she shall see him."

"What? If you bring her before the High Wizard, he will have a fit!" the other mage exclaimed.

"Your name?" he asked Mexia, ignoring his friend.

"Lady Mexia of Damar."

His eyes widened, their rich blue color darkening to stormy midnight. "You helped..." He paused as he turned to consider her companions. "Princess Talamaya." He bowed. "Lady Kersta, and the dwarf, Gallant. You defeated Grimoria." He looked at the scepter. "I thought that was the Scepter of Lanai."

Mexia folded her arms. "Yes, but one of Grimoria's mage apprentices has stolen his book of spells, and now threatens to take his place."

"See what happens when a witch does a job more suited for a mage?" the other apprentice said.

"There are none in Inherian but my father and me to fight this rogue wizard. I must further my training to ensure the safety of our realm."

"She has a noble cause, do you not think, Ros?"

"It will matter not to the High Wizard. No women are allowed, no matter what the reason, Derek."

"Your friends will have to wait for you here," Derek said to Mexia. "And you will be required to leave your staff behind. No weapons are allowed in the High Mage's chambers."

She handed her staff to Kersta.

"Good luck," the princess said and gave her a warm embrace. Kersta followed suit.

Gallant grumbled something inaudible.

Derek said, "Do you need help to get to his office?"

Despite hating to admit she could not go there on her own without needing his aid, she said, "Yes."

He smiled the most heart-warming smile. Kersta scowled at him. Mexia knew Kersta was reading his mind and his actions didn't reflect what he had on his mind, at least that's what she assumed.

He reached out his hand to Mexia. She hesitated. He raised his brows. "Are you coming?"

She placed her hand in his, and he drew her close. Despite his touch warming her entire body with intrigue, she heeded Kersta's words. The mage apprentice was a danger to her, and she had to keep her distance.

Instantly, they arrived at an office where shelves filled with books lined three of the walls. A massive oak desk filled a quarter of the floor space in the room.

"Master Harazod?"

The wizard appeared. His white silky beard reached down to the toes of his shoes that curled up to the strands. He narrowed his eyes at Derek, ignoring Mexia completely, annoying her at once. "The news of our uninvited guests has filled the halls. I cannot believe you, of all my star pupils, had the audacity to bring one up here to see me."

"This one is Lady Mexia, my lord, of Damar."

The wizard stared at Mexia for a moment, then tugged at his beard. "Grimoria," he said under his breath.

"Yes, my lord. She is the one who turned him to stone...well and drowned him." Derek's voice was laced with enthusiasm.

Harazod waved for Derek's silence.

"What do you want here?" Harazod asked Mexia.

"To attend school, my lord." Despite wanting to stick her chin up in the air and fold her arms in defiance, she curbed her feelings. Attending the school was more important than giving in to malicious slights. "I wish to learn all that I can so that I may one day serve as the High Wizard of Damar. But before this, I must prepare to meet Grimoria's mage apprentice, who is as evil as his master. He stole his spell book and threatens revenge against my kingdom."

"Women do not attend school here."

"But I've studied for the entrance exams required to attend here. And your school policy states that a mage may attend who has used his magic to save others' lives, without even taking the exams. I have saved many lives through the use of my spells on several separate occasions."

"*His* magic, not hers." The wizard furrowed his brow, then his face brightened. "Obtain a letter of recommendation from the mage of Monrovia, the High Wizard, Parenkin. If he gives his recommendation, you may attend as the only woman ever to do so."

Mexia smiled. "Thank you, my lord, for giving me this chance to attend your grand school." She caught Derek's eye. She couldn't tell what he was thinking from the scowl on his face. Was he mad that Harazod would even consider allowing her to enter the school? Or was there something else brewing underneath that wrinkled brow?

"I will return you to your companions. Wait there while I

have a word with Derek. Then he will join you and send you on your way."

Before she could open her mouth to utter a word, he nodded his head at her. In the next instant, she stood beside her friends as soon as she blinked her eyes.

"What did he say?" the princess asked.

Kersta handed Mexia's staff back to her. "She has to get a recommendation from the High Wizard, Parenkin."

"Do not tell me," Gallant said, "he is in the Darkland Forest that we must now trudge through."

"He resides on the highest peak of Mount Monrovia," Derek said, startling them as he appeared next to Mexia. His arm brushed hers while his breath touched her cheek as he spoke. "You will need a map." His close proximity heated her whole being once again and a flush of heat rose to her cheeks.

He handed her a piece of leather parchment where rivers and towns, mountains and forests, were drawn in a crude manner. "Truthfully, it grieves me to see the first sorceress I have ever met who has already done so much for the cause of magic by ridding us of the rogue wizard, Grimoria, made to do such a quest. Personally, I would have welcomed you to the school for all you have already accomplished. But unfortunately, I am only a fourth-year student, soon to get my wizardry status, mind you. I still must follow the rules."

"And?"

"All I can do is warn you. The path you take to Monrovia is fraught with danger. You'd best give up this quest and return to Damar before you or any of your companions can get hurt."

Kersta said, "And?"

He shrugged. "That's all I can say."

Mexia could see the intense look on Kersta's face as she studied Derek closely with narrowed eyes, meaning only one thing, she attempted to find out the truth to the matter by reading his mind further.

He held his tongue.

Kersta smiled. "We will speak of this further, Mexia, once we leave here."

Mexia ran her finger over the map, then looked up at Derek. "Which way is the best for us to go?"

"None. The continent of Albion is an inhospitable place, except for the city of Langdon, and two cities you may pass on the way, should you be lucky enough to reach them. Dark elves inhabit the forests. The mountain cheetaur and white devil wolves guard the pass of Monrovia. Trolls have become a plague along the river of Nenda. Trekking across the bridges often leads to a much-shortened life span."

"And those who can aid us?" the princess asked.

"None can aid you."

"Why?" Mexia asked.

"I do not know what the people are like on the continent of Inherian. But here, you will not find any who will help you. Everyone goes about their own business. No one cares about anyone else's."

"Thank you, Derek." Mexia tucked the map into her cloak pocket. "We will see you upon our return, I suspect."

She stepped into the portal along with her companions and before they were whisked away, caught his eye one more time. What was there about the man that sent every bit of her body into a tingling mass of nerves? Was it the same as the princess felt about her betrothed?

When they reached the outside of the castle gates, Mexia stood in a daze still, not being able to get her mind off the mage apprentice.

Kersta broke into her thoughts. "Are you sure you want to do this, Mexia? I feel he was hiding something from me. I believe he sensed I could read his mind and didn't wish to reveal anything he ought not to."

"Like?"

"I'm not certain, Mexia. I believe he feels you cannot make it to the mountains of Monrovia, first off. But, there is something more. Something that he was thinking that I couldn't quite reach."

"What?"

"I sensed he is torn between the admiration he feels for you, well and something more, and wanting to keep the status quo. They're attempting to keep you out of the school, and if you're trying to get in gets you killed, it proves their case. You didn't belong."

"I do not wish for any of you to come with me," Mexia said, "if the way is as dangerous as he says. But I must go to Monrovia. If the rogue mage apprentice attacks us at home, and I am not prepared, all of us are as much in danger."

"I agree," the princess said. "I have every intention of helping you, dear Mexia. I am ready to go to Monrovia."

"Aye," Gallant said. "I wish to see my wife in the city of Barston. I've heard tell it is located in the valley outside of the Darkland Forest. I am game."

"And me," Kersta said. "I would not let you go alone." She turned to Gallant. "I thought your wife left you for another man."

"Aye. I wish to see her is all, woman."

She smiled. "And yet you say you do not love her."

"How can I love a woman like that? I just want to see her is all."

"Then we head to Barston first?" Mexia asked, interrupting the conversation before it got out of hand.

"I say we get an early morning start," the princess said. "What with our trip across the sea, it is already late afternoon.

We should eat, sleep, and first thing in the morning, be on our way."

Mexia studied the map of Langdon City. "There is a tavern located on the other side of the castle. I wonder if they will let women stay there."

"We will have to check it out, eh?" Kersta said as she headed in the direction of the tavern.

Twenty minutes later, they reached the two-story stone building, the sign freshly painted swung slightly in the breeze.

"This is it," Kersta said. "The Dragon's Keep."

Mexia pushed the door open, and instantly, the room filled with boisterous conversation died to a perceptible hush. A barmaid sashayed over to the party of four. Her red curls partly squashed on top of her head, the rest dangling to her shoulders, looked to have been given nary a thought. Her faded blue gown revealed her breasts in ample proportion. She patted Gallant on the head as his eyes remained focused on the low cut of her gown. She waved at an empty round table. "Ye wish meal and some ale?"

"A meal, yes," the princess said. "We bring our own drink with us."

Mexia touched her flask at her waist. The gift from the soothsayer, Modi, a healing tea that replenished itself in their flasks, was all that they drank on their travels.

The woman eyed them with suspicion, then nodded. "Very well. Have a seat and I'll bring out your meal."

She hurried off as the ladies and Gallant sat down on the wooden chairs. Gallant grunted as he peered at the women, nose level to the table. "Ye think they'd be a bit more considerate and make taller chairs for dwarfs."

Kersta smiled. "Maybe they have a pillow for you to sit on."

He shoved his bedroll underneath him. Now he sat higher

and smiled back at her. "Sometimes, ye have clever ideas. Sometimes."

Mexia looked around the room at the men gathered at several of the tables, all bearded, mostly unbathed, appearing to be rogues...all of them. "Seems the place is lacking in women here, too."

"Aye, they be pirates over there," Gallant said, motioning to a table in the far corner of the room. "We should stay clear of the likes of them. No one would be interested in a dwarf, but if they knew Princess Talamaya was King Lazarion's betrothed, or that the two of ye ladies come from the noble families of Damar... well, ransoms for your safe return would be on their minds."

"Then we must not mention this to anyone," Kersta said, casting a dirty look at Gallant. "Anywhere."

"Aye, but all they have to do is see the way ye are dressed. It doesn't take a High Wizard to be able to sense ye ladies are of nobility, and your kin would have means."

"How do you know they are pirates and not just seamen?" Mexia asked. "It is a seaport after all and to me, they look just like the sailors on the ship we were transported here on. Same knee-high boots, knee-length breeches, blousy shirts with the full sleeves ruffled at the wrists and beaded, braided, dirty matted hair."

"It is the beady eyes that give them away."

Mexia smiled as she considered Gallant's tiny black eyes. "Were you once a pirate, too?"

He growled at her. "Woman, are ye trying to be as dense as that one?" He pointed to Kersta. "Look at the scabbards they carry."

The women cast casual glances at the four men, chugging their ale, deep in conversation some of the time, staring at the women most of the time.

"Scabbards," the princess said.

"Aye. The Black Hawk ship I heard tell frequents this port. The captain is Prince Eric, the Mad, they say. He leaves the town well enough alone. The wizards wouldn't permit his pirating here. That's why the place is safe for travelers."

"But?" Kersta asked.

"If we leave the town, and they should wish to pursue us, well, ye ladies, the wizards would have no say in it."

"They would not wish to travel through the Darkland Forest, would they?" Mexia asked.

"They are cutthroats themselves. A few dark elves would not discourage them, I assume, if they figured the three of ye would be worth the trouble."

Mexia sipped from her flask, then turned to Kersta. "Can you read their minds?"

"Too much distraction in here with so many people. But they definitely are interested in us. They're just wondering how strong the dwarf is."

Talamaya ran her hand over her staff. "They will find trouble if they think the three of us women incapable of a good fight."

Mexia nodded. Glancing over to the other corner of the poorly lighted tavern, she noticed a cloaked figure sitting in the shadows, his hood pulled over his head, hiding his face. Did he watch them, too? Every male in the room, from the pirates at the one table to the men who looked like some kind of soldiers of fortune at another, observed them.

"What do you think about the men sitting at those three tables?" Mexia asked Kersta.

"The soldiers?" Kersta said.

"Yes."

Kersta considered them for a moment. "Not sure. They seem to be lower-ranking foot soldiers wearing the poorer padded leather armor rather than chainmail. None have helms. I don't see any with broadswords. All carry short swords."

"And no leader?" Mexia asked.

"Doesn't appear to be any."

Mexia took a deep breath. "Deserters, do you think?"

"They might be."

"What about the man in the corner of the room? The one hidden beneath a hooded cloak?"

Kersta concentrated. "He's angry. But I cannot tell what about. He feels the whole world owes him, and he'll rip it apart until he gets what belongs to him."

"Something was stolen from him?" Mexia asked.

"I don't know. Like the pirates, he wonders who we are and how much we are worth."

"Maybe this was not such a good place to come."

The barmaid balanced two trays as she hurried across the floor, then slammed them down on the tables.

Gallant scowled at her. "The lady said we did not wish to drink anything."

"The gentleman in the corner of the room over there," the maid said pointing with her elbow to the cloaked man, "wished to buy you each a drink."

The princess nodded. "You may tell him we thank him for his generosity."

When the maid left them alone, Kersta said, "But we will not drink this ale, will we, princess?"

"We drink Modi's tea. Nothing else."

Gallant dug into his wild boar steak with enthusiasm as the ladies buttered the hot pieces of bread they tore off the loaf in front of them. The door to the tavern opened, and a breeze of warm air filtered in.

They turned to see Derek and his two mage friends enter the room, their velvet cloaks, brocade gowns, and neat appearances giving them away as mage apprentices from the wizardry school.

The maid hurried to see to their needs. They motioned to an empty table, two tables away from Mexia's.

Kersta cut up a slice of boar. "Kind of unusual, I would think."

"What's that, Kersta?" the princess asked.

"I would have thought they would have to eat at the school."

"Derek said he was a fourth-year student. Maybe he and his friends have more freedom."

Kersta nodded. "And yet, there are no others here."

"What do you see, Kersta?" Mexia asked.

"They are purposefully blocking my reading of their minds. Which makes me think they do not usually come here."

Mexia studied Derek. His angular jaw was softened by his curly blond beard and his blond hair was neatly tied back in a knot behind his head now. But it was his eyes that drew her in.

Kersta touched her hand. "He is dangerous, Mexia. He's more powerful than you. I fear he's casting some kind of spell over you."

"Aye, my wife did the same thing to me." Gallant ripped off a piece of bread.

The princess studied Derck and frowned. "He is the one I saw in my vision, wearing regal blue velvet robes. He appears to have some kind of royal lineage by the way he dresses. And as Kersta says, he has some kind of power over you, Mexia."

Mexia shook her head as her gaze remained focused on Derek's eyes. Her lips turned up slightly, making him smile back.

Gallant cleared his throat. "Maybe ye have it wrong. She seems to have all the power over him."

Kersta grabbed her staff as one of the soldiers stood and sauntered over to the mage apprentices' table. "There's going to be trouble now."

"What's wrong?" Mexia grabbed her staff and scooted her chair away from the table.

Kersta shook her head as she considered the confrontation between the men. "The soldier doesn't like mages, and he intends to throw them out of the tavern."

Mexia laughed, setting her staff back down. "Oh, that's all. I thought something awful was going to happen. The mages can handle one drunken soldier."

Kersta raised her brows. "Then the soldiers intend to bed us for the night."

FOREWORD

Scepter of Salvation

Princess Talamaya turned eighteen in the human kingdom of Damar, just like her twin brother. Only when she comes of age, she must wed the king's choice. When her brother comes of age, he's allowed to sit on the council. But everything changes when a wizard pits beast and man against each other in Inherian—all because of the loss of the Scepter of Salvation and she must return it to their kingdom.

Princess Talamaya and her friends, Lady Kersta and Lady Mexia, must retrieve the Scepter of Salvation when her brother is poisoned. Visions plague Talamaya of a world beyond her own, of a destiny she has to fulfill. But the barbarian king is also after the scepter, and the black-hearted wizard who is trying to gain control will do anything to keep them from retrieving it.

She must free a knight from his madness.

Help a female dwarf escape from the dwarven mines.

Aid an Amazon fighting the Dark Elves.

Rescue even the barbarian king.

Save a crusty old dwarf from the wolves of Elan Pass.

And outwit the dark wizard once more.

Above all else, she must always take the path of right-eousness.

Which is much easier said than done.